Soljer Soljer

Colonel Mahip Chadha

Third Gorkha Rifles

authorHOUSE®

AuthorHouse™
1663 Liberty Drive
Bloomington, IN 47403
www.authorhouse.com
Phone: 1-800-839-8640

Published by AuthorHouse 12/15/2011

ISBN: 978-1-4670-6739-3 (sc)
ISBN: 978-1-4670-6738-6 (hc)
ISBN: 978-1-4670-6737-9 (e)

Library of Congress Control Number: 2011919244

This book is printed on acid-free paper.

FOR KIRAN

Wife friend and companion for 42 long years

Life in an Infantry Battalion of the Indian Army

ACKNOWLEDGEMENTS

I dedicate this book to The Second Battalion The Third Gorkha Rifles-*The Second Third* and to the Third Battalion-*The Thud Thud*! The former is responsible for grooming me and imbibing in me an honourable code of conduct– a set mode in which I tried to live my life in the Army and as a pensioner. *Thud Thud* taught me to value the deep affection for the organisation, and the mandatory concern and affection between the officers, which needs to be cultivated; without which life in a battalion becomes unbearable. I can never forget the men of both battalions in which I served; for they taught me to serve without complaint and imbibed in me a subtle sense of humour which only a Gorkha Johnny can interpret.

It also bound me to Nepal our neighbouring country which we still have not learnt to respect.

I would also thank Paramjeet Bhutani, a friend of many years- ever since I was a young 2/Lieutenant in Bareilly, for reading my manuscript and correcting many grammatical and spelling mistakes that I had overlooked. When I asked her about the book, she said that she could not put down the book till she had read it from cover to cover in three days!

Such comments definitely boost the morale of budding writers like myself!

Generals Gambhir Singh Negi who wrote the review for the back cover of the book, and Amar Aul of *Thud Thud*, deserve a BIG Thanks, for encouraging me in my writing while General Mohan Bhandari of *The Garhwal Rifles* supported me whole heartedly in my new venture and also wrote the Foreword for the book. He is a stalwart who strongly believes that the association between the Second battalion and The Garhwal Rifles needs to be strengthened; because the Second Third is the parent unit from which the illustrious Garhwal Rifles were raised. The soldiers of the Regiment wear identical stripes as the Third Gorkha Rifles

I would also like to thank Rod Goodwine of Author House, USA, for being very patient with me—for I was and probably still am, an ignoramus in the field of publishing! The heartening note is that I am learning—as King Bruce and the spider will testify!

Thank you all!

Colonel Mahip Chadha
Third Gorkha Rifles
New Delhi

A Tribute To a Gorkha

Maj Gen W Ross Stewart

When God first chose a Gorkha
As a vassal of his own
He Took a Chunk of Cheerfulness
And Laid on Flesh and Bone
A Face! Well Some Deny It
But A Soul No One Could
For Anyone Who Has Seen It
Wishes His Was Half As Good

Faith! There Is Little Small About Him
Save The Question Of His Size
From The Mountains Which Beget Him
To The Laughter In His Eyes
His Sports, His Love, His Courage
Preserve The Sterling Ring
Of The Simple Minded Hill man
With Manners Of A King

He Has Given Of His Thousands
And He hasn't Yet
There's Never Been a Murmur
Of What He Himself Will Get

CONTENTS

FOREWORD

The threat of war in the world has not receded. Leaders and astute statesmen will guide the destiny of their nation states when they have the backing of a crisp and effective battle tested force behind them—one which evokes awe in the minds of the enemy. Therefore, it is the soldier who can be a potent aggressor or a noble defender of the faith We must not squander the potential might of our soldiers in peace and render them impotent in war. A little respect for these centurions is definitely due from citizens from all walks of life, because these men have trained to give their lives today; so that their countrymen could enjoy a better tomorrow!

The Indian Army was raised from the fledgling embryo created by the British East India Company, nearly 270 years ago. This small force was essentially created to suppress the local inhabitants. Notwithstanding this lacuna, sections of the populace, the so called martial races; joined it and took up the profession of arms as a matter of honour, employment family tradition and pride.

It was never a mercenary army.

The British fostered a regimental spirit that bound the officer and men in a common spirit of camaraderie and espirit-de-corps. This emotional equation was battle tested over the years and gave birth to the regimental ethos where officers and men sacrificed their lives to uphold the dignity, integrity and honour of their Flag. It is the British who raised regiments based on ethnicity.

This became the soldier's code of honour.

The ethos of the present day Indian Army and its concept of nationalism was a result of national integration which free India developed after amalgamation of all 'native' armies and princely states. The Indian Army is the largest volunteer Army of the world. During the Second World War, Indian soldiers were a critical instrument in winning the War. The Indian Army is the totally apolitical Army in the Third World, and has been instrumental in binding the secular thread of a great nation that is India. The ethnicity of the infantry battalions, the bonhomie they feel for each other in the fields of professional competitions, sports and on the battle field has no parallel anywhere in the world! Truly, the Indian Army is nationalistic in letter and spirit and this espirit de corps; has been battle tested time and again till it has become a benchmark.

All this has been possible because of the great camaraderie between the officers and the men and their total devotion to the nation. This gallant combination has always been the battle winning factor and has been instrumental in sustaining India's faith in democracy, pride, integrity, stability and development of communal harmony. Not a day passes without breaking news of some deed of valour; performed by our men ably led by their Officers with impeccable credentials. While India is well on her way to become a developed nation there is a definite lack of awareness in the citizens about matters military or the invaluable contribution of the Armed Forces to the country; both in times of war and in peace. Our Officers have responded well beyond the call of duty whenever they have been detailed for tasks within India or abroad. Glitter during ceremonials and as part of daily routine in the Officer's Messes or during official functions with the men, contains a decorum which is impeccable and impresses the youth to an extent that they are willing to make the Army a career.

The Indian Army can claim with pride that it has stood true to its salt; whether its troops are serving in minus sixty degree Celsius in the Siachen Glacier; in the sweltering heat of Rajasthan or fighting in the humid and dense forests of the North East or the high altitude regions of our sacred frontiers. Folk songs of bravery, chivalry and sacrifices of our officers and men reverberate all over India.

Having hung up my spurs after serving the Army for almost 40 years, Colonel Mahip Chadha has singled me out for a great honour—to write a few words for the foreword of his book *Soljer Soljer*!

Colonel Chadha, whom I have known intimately, since we were in the National Defence Academy; is a superb writer and has an inimitable style of conveying his thoughts and views in an uncanny manner; that simply mesmerize you when you begin to read his books.

Mahip, was commissioned into the Second Third; the VC *Paltan- our Regimental Mother Ship*. Mahip, I commend you– my friend for this excellent piece of work. Maybe in you we have discovered the story teller– one who can make our citizens understand *what we do*; *how we do and finally why we do*– so that our countrymen can go about business as usual! I exhort all especially the younger generation of India- our hope and our future to read this book and take inspiration from it.

With regards and wishing your book God Speed!

Lt Gen Mohan Bhandari PVSM, AVSM*, DLitt. FIMA
The Garhwal Rifles

PREFACE

Six Third Gorkha Rifles or 6/3 GR, does not exist in the Indian Army. It is a figment of my imagination.

For a story teller it is not too difficult to create a battalion out of nowhere—allocate some officers and place close to eight hundred men in it and what is more—provide it the necessary arms, ammunition, vehicles and stores to make it a composite whole!

All that is required is to breathe life into it.

Which i did!

A large number of the Gorkha regiments had adopted towns which they treated as homes for the regiment and its battalions as their permanent peace stations, because they had assets at these places-some had also nostalgia for their place of birth. Almora was the small town in the Kumaon Hills where the British defeated the Gurkhas found them excellent fighters and decided to enlist them into the British Army in India. The First Battalion of the Third Gorkha Rifles made a home for itself at Almora, which had a climate favourable to the men provided adequate area for training and was appropriate for a battalion. This included the lines for the men called the Alexandra Lines after Queen Alexandra; their Patron, after whom the regiment was called QAO Third Gurkha Rifles.

The Second Battalion could not be raised at Almora and was raised eventually at Lansdowne in the Garhwal Hills because there was an outbreak of cholera in Almora. This location was finally handed over to the newly raised Garhwal Rifles, originally a part of the Second Battalion. The Third Gorkha Rifles moved to Dehradun, which became the home for all the Gurkha Battalions, except those which went over to the British Army, and the First and Fourth Gorkha Rifles whose Centre, 14GTC, was established at Sabathu, in Himachal Pradesh. Collectively these regiments were addressed as the Gurkha Brigade. So the bulk of the Gurkha regiments found a home at Dehradun. Each regiment had only five battalions and in some regiments there were six, it became necessary to group two regiments together to make one Training Centre for them. We therefore had 39GTC, 58 GTC, 14 GTC and the 11GRRC.GTC stands for Gorkha Training Centre.

This is the story of an infantry battalion which is just like any other battalion of the Indian Army, except that some customs and traditions changed in tune with the history or the ethnicity of its troops. The amazing fact is that the troops and their mannerism have a profound impact on the officers who are affected deep down in their souls irrespective of their own ethnicity.

The sense of humour, laughter, methodology in dealing with routine and disciplinary matters are seriously affected by the close contact with the troops of their regiment and even in later life these infantry officers have a great affinity with their regiments and especially the battalions in which they were either commissioned or commanded. This is essentially due to close bonding that officers develop with their men, their language, religious beliefs, eating habits and of course the feeling of camaraderie which takes root in their souls. The desire– nay the obsession, is that they should know their men and their men's habitat as well as their men- for only then does the soldier respect you from the depth of his soul!

In Sikh and Sikh Light Infantry battalions, or in the JAT units the officers use profanity, honed into artistic levels to get their message across- very much like General Patton advocated. In contrast, officers in a Gurkha battalion or an Assam unit seldom take recourse to abusive language.

In a Gurkha battalion rarely is a kancha, or *little brother*, punished by that famous book called the MIML or the Manual Of Military Law, because Gurkha officers fumble while referring to it —but ask any officer of the Madras Regiment or the Sikh Light Infantry and he would be able to quote verbatim because they use it so often! It is also because the troops require the book to be thrown at them or not, depending on the volatility of their temperament, education or their docile nature or otherwise! The Quarter Guard cells in some regiments have to be booked in advance or are allotted by the Adjutant whereas they are undersubscribed in many others! In the Indian Army, pure battalions– ones with ethnic soldiers of a certain region are easily motivated and are easily corrected by invoking the name of the regiment or by referring to their religion or ethnicity, where as a different motivation has to be applied in battalions with mixed troops.

Battalions also remember and regard their officers cherishing them as though they were icons from whom so much had to be gleaned and some of these officers could recall historical facts with relative ease. The younger officers therefore gathered around these story tellers and learnt a trick or two about the finer points which made their battalion tick. Many a misadventure of senior and junior officers revealed during these sessions added to the mirth. Some battalions even had Scrap Books to record these misendeavours for posterity.

The battalion was therefore a mother who faithfully retained memories of her sons alive and dead in her regimental history and welcomed them during Dushera, Battle Honour Day or on the Raising Day, so that each of these stalwarts had time to meet his colleagues, for the ladies to exchange news of their offspring, indulge in match making and catching up on the news about others; who could not make it for the function. It is a touching scene at such gatherings when these old fogies meet each other and retain their levels of seniority despite their ranks or age!

The only example of such comradiere is with the Armoured regiments and the Engineer regiments who have a lineage and history dating back to the days of the Laat Sahib!- --His Lordship! Certainly, the feeling of belonging swept across to the Artillery and the Air Defence Artillery which adopted the system of officers becoming part of the regiment they are commissioned in.

I have created these chapters to indicate to the natives-sic-citizens of our country that this is their Army and they should try and understand the travails and hardships which soldiers undergo while in uniform and out of it. Not many know that the Army trains for war when units come for their peace tenures. True there are parties and celebrations but each of these is done for a reason, and in keeping with the traditions of the battalion and not merely for the heck of it. Parties cost money—and soldiers do not have surpluses!

Life in the Infantry is purely composed of sweat and blood. There is little time for rest and relaxation– some training, sports or regimental event keeps one on his toes—but it is a clean life and the ladies are pampered so much that many officers have been known to say with a sigh—better to be an Army wife in the next birth. Where else would a General get up from his chair when a young officer's wife walks into the room!

Yet, when a couple of Generals are implicated in a scandal, the country, oohs and aahs about the tarnished image of the services.

Yet not once has the image of our Babus-our glorified bureaucracy, been taken to task for the gross injustice they have meted to the national image and the Army in particular. A basically raw politician can never hope to master the intricacies of strategy and weaponry in the short span of his tenure as Defence Minister or Defence Secretary and allow regular and speedy modernisation of the services, unless he is a brilliant retired Services Officer or has other suitable credentials.

Why would the pay scales of the services be decided by these- Holier than Thou, Baboons– sorry spelling error—Babus who do not think it fit to include a representative from each service! And woe is me that not one of the Chiefs put his foot down to such gross injustice to their command, or put in their resignations! It is veritably a carrot and stick story—but tell me would the God in the Heavens, give lesser marks to a general, admiral or an air marshall, if he did not become an Ambassador or a Governor?

I think not, because to become the Chief of a service is the greatest honour one can achieve in a lifetime!

A very appropriate illustration from history speaks volumes in this context, unless the humble Indian soldier continues to serve; with the faith that his General will take care of this end.

Kautilya to Chandragupta his King--

My Lord, that the day when the Mauryan soldier has to demand his dues or, worse, plead for them, will be a sad day and will point to multiple and multi-level failures in the governance machinery in Magadha. The day will neither have arrived suddenly, overnight nor in vain. It will also bode ill for Magadha. For then, on that day, you, My Lord, will have lost all moral sanction to be King! It will also mark the beginning of the end of the Mauryan Empire!!"

Across the border, we have a potent enemy not only in rhetoric, but one who takes delight in cross border forays to create an unhealthy environment in our country where the Muslim population lives in comparative peace and harmony. Even though we are not formally at war, - a state of war continues through wolves in sheep clothing—it is no laughing matter for those who live constantly under the shadow of the gun.

I chose to write because our citizens have very little knowledge of our soldiers and our Services—there are so many stories to tell!

Jai Hind!

With humility

Colonel (Retired) Mahip Chadha

Third Gorkha Rifles

Almora Ahoy

We had never heard of Almora, except that it was the birthplace of the First Battalion, raised at this little town; after a pitched battle; from the remnants of the Gorkha soldiers who had fought the British, A quaint little ramshackle and rusty town which appeared to have been part of a time warp. The British had decended from Katarmal—that helmet type feature with an outcrop of pines on it; which made it look like a Johnny's haircut and had then climbed to Sitoli Ridge outside town. They had regrouped and attacked the Gorkha garrison there.

Between Katarmal and Almora flowed the Kosi river which grew into a torrent in the monsoon.

We were from the Sixth battalion of The Third Gurkha Rifles, the youngest sister in the regiment—*the Kanchi*..

To reach Almora one had to travel by train to Kathgodam or Haldwani and drive up to Bhowali at the foothills of Nainital and then move via Garam Pani to Almora. Garam Pani was where a diversion forked out like the tongue of a snake, towards Ranikhet.So we had a set of four places to visit all within thirty kilometres from Almora. The Jewel in the Crown was Nainital of course, but it was getting very over crowded. Each of these quaint little towns had their own peculiarities—Almora was the most densely populated, Ranikhet was serene and beautiful, Kausani was picturesque and allowed a beautiful glimpse of the snow clad mountains.

Nainital was just Nainital—a beautiful gem, where Sherwood reigned supreme!

It was an unusual name, for a town, but we knew that it nestled up in the Kumaon Hills; had gradually developed into a horse shoe shaped town, because it was built on a very large curve hugging the hills on the road leading to Bhowali and Kathgodam. There were no large buildings or monuments—The Ambassador Hotel, owned by Sardar Ram Singh, was quite a landmark adjacent to the KMOU bus terminal. The owner and his family were quite heartbroken by a tragedy in their family and were in the process of winding up their assets in Almora. They also owned a shop in the upper bazaar—Malli Bazaar, which they had bequeathed to their loyal servant who had served them well over the years.

A very renowned shop which sold a special sweet called *baal mithai* was opposite– it was too sweet for our liking– looked as though someone had cut long cubical pieces of brown chocolate and rolled them onto homeopathic pills! The locals called it *baal*—that's it and everyone understood.

There was an antique petrol pump next door and it was indeed a lucky day if one wanted petrol and found some. The road led to a slope which pointed towards the Kosi River and simultaneously from the dilapidated garage, at the fork, a road branched upwards to the old Church on the hill, which featured a very steep climb indeed! There was a school– Adam's School, if I recollect correctly and Jitu Pant's house.

If one looked up towards the left, while coming from the Ambassador Hotel towards the Post Office, one could see a maze of steps and a fortress like construction on which was perched the upper township and one could descend to the main motor road from the many steps leading downwards almost upto the movie hall below the road where the Joshi family lived.

Short of the fork, a lane, cobbled beautifully– branched off leaving the temple to the left and moved away towards the Courts and further to the Alexandra Lines, the barracks of the First Battalion, built by them as well; to billet the new converts to the British Army in India—so we were literally speaking, in a groove of history. This lane became deserted as it grew dark and on a cold night we could literally feel myriad of eyes watching our progress towards our unit lines—and if perchance someone met you the next day, a summary of your sojourn would be presented to you correct in every detail to the extent of where you had probably taken a leak. The houses on both sides of the market were built with their length along the road almost like a broadside view of the British wooden warships—with the only difference that the portholes for the guns were replaced by windows, These windows were shut early in the evening and yet prying eyes kept a track of whatever happened probably through the many peepholes or cracks in the windows. full of secrets—methinks!

It was a very secretive town– somewhat like Peyton Place and similarly full of scandals too.

One could discern a number of places where you could be mugged but as a rule the town folk were a gentle and peaceful lot and steered clear of us!

Near the Alexandra Lines, was an old cinema, about to crumble into dust, but the owners did not seem to notice or really mind, as long some cash flow carried on---there was one more cinema on the main road a little ahead of LR Shah—the old style shop whose owners spoke in whispers as though their clientele was still from the British regiment stationed up there. The shop boasted fine stuff preferred by the officer class of yesteryears and it therefore went out of business soon after independence. Crested stationery once in fashion those days—was still available, fine cutlery was also out of vogue but the owner still kept some from the old days.

I still have a tiepin and a pair of scissors from that quaint shop and I had bought some tinned food as well..

But LR SHAH remained a landmark—a reference point if you please.

Further down—a road branched away uphill to the infantry battalion from the Third or the Ninth Gorkha Rifles which was always posted there, and the little cantonment of Almora, which boasted of a broken down church, a small but beautiful MES Inspection Bunglow, a cottage perched on top of a knoll where Tagore once stayed and then the beautiful Officer's Mess, the property of the First Battalion of the Third Gurkhas, since their raising in Almora. Later the battalion was persuaded to sell off all the property they owned to the Military Estates organization by the Army Commander.

The Mess was attractive and had a regal bearing– as if it had been transported from England by the English Officers who were probably homesick. It was situated in a hollow and it could be seen as you descended from the gate. An old and beautiful building flanked by the bandstand on one side and the cookhouse on the other. The careless outcrop of trees around the Mess gave the impression of having grown on their own; but I think the trees blowing in the wind and probably planted by an officer of the First Battalion– a landscapist perhaps; gave an incredibly pleasing look. There was a lingering impression, as though someone had tried to capture the scenery around an English country side.

Another sign of home sickness I presumed.

A track ran down from the old church and met the main road to Almora from where one could take a shortcut to the firing ranges or *chandmari* as they are called in Hindi! Sometimes one came across some ragged but beautiful children with blue eyes– third generation probably, the result of seed sown in the wind by some desperate English officer during a brief fling with a local mistress!

There was a leprosy hospital tucked away inside that area.

What was special about Almora?

At that time, it boasted of an adherence to rituals and devotion to Hinduism in the extreme—anyone who broke the many taboos was forced to leave the faith of his forefathers and decide between conversion to Christianity or to Islam. It was these taboos which slowly increased the population of these two faiths, which welcomed them with open arms into their fold!Hill folk are usually loathe to offend their gods and goddesses, and are in perpetual awe and fear from the forces of darkness and of the invisible hordes of ghosts who inhabit their countryside!

The area was owned lock stock and barrel by the wealthy Joshis, Tewaris, Bhats, Pants and other Brahmins, who had probably fled from Maharashtra during the Mughal wars and sought sanctuary in the rich and beautiful Kumaon hills, and after a few generations become sons of the soil! This is heresay from the locals– we had not had time to dig up proof– just as it was said that the Bengali rich migrated to Mandi from Bengal, during Sher Shah Suri's time.

Almora was a dead town after dark—no one was seen outside except the drunks; of which there were many. After all if there were no jobs, and there no desire to leave the town in search of one, then one could only become a drunk or an educated lunatic like the many lawyers who wore pith hats and mumbled some vague mythological arguments outside the Court.I think their think tanks required severe overhaul—but then these guys added to the spice and colour of the little town.

It was said that Almora was super saturated with educated people—literacy was on a high and if you threw a stone at any house– it would contain at least a couple of law graduates and some MAs as also some graduates. But many had died without seeing the trains at Kathgodam—such was the mental apathy in Almora—lack of adventurism!

Me—I am Captain Surinder Singh Sahni of the 6/3 Gorkha Rifles, and in a few days I am about to get married.

I keep my self informed about the people, flora and fauna around me wherever I go—makes life a trifle interesting! Actually I am wondering how to keep my bride happy in this desolate town—one really cannot call it a hill station---hill stations welcome you even though it is for the money in the wallet you carry—but in Almora things are different as though the town refuses to come out of the dark ages.

The sidewalks abound in bichu buti, a very interesting plant that has some acidic content in the lower part of its leaves and if you insist on touching it, causes a burning sensation which can last for hours. Imagine wiping your arse with these leaves and the effect would; be like one of those, Popeye the Sailor Man cartoons! The local women seem to cut the younger shoots off and boil them before making it a vegetable!

Along this weed grows another the weed called hashish or bhang and this lured the hippies or *flower children* to this region because no one in the local population was really bothered about how much or how often it is consumed—only the Army kept the troops away from it—the Nepalese did not favour the weed but the Indian troops knew the power it contained!

Sherni di Muchh, as one Punjabi soldier from the Artillery described it—the Moustache of the Tigress!

But there was a silver lining—Almora was located approximately thirty odd kilometers from Naini Tal and Ranikhet and a little further was Kausani—which was once a preferred resort for Mahatma Gandhi. So one could break away to these places if the need be. The journey to Ranikhet gave anyone a headache because the road had too many bends—but the scenery was breathtaking. One found excellent fish in the Kosi– I am a little illiterate as far as fish goes, but I know it is delicious especially the way the boys split it open removed the entrails and deep fried it whole, eyes and all!

We lived in the Deodar Hotel-there was no *deodar* which was a variety of pine, in the vicinity– but it provided sanctuary to the bachelors some of whom lived near the Mess. It had a lovely view but the disadvantage was that the CO lived above us and kept an eye on us.

Every morning we began the day with physical training—PT, which took the shape of a run for some distance as a squad, then a few limbering up exercises on the football ground followed by games designed to toughen us, and then we broke off. On some days we had drill practice instead, of PT.

We shouted out orders till we were hoarse and us tall guys had a big problem because ours was a rifle battalion and designed to march at 140 paces per minute; unlike the other regiments which marched at 120 paces per minute. Also we did not raise our thighs till the level of our belts—instead we turned and executed a smart movement designed to save time for *we were protectors of the flanks and speed was our forte.*

The Commanding Officer had declared that every night be declared a Dinner Night, except on Wednesdays, Saturdays and Sundays. This had an advantage in that everyone was in the Mess before the bugle call, in uniform, and after a drink or two went straight for dinner. Thus the Mess Staff could wind up and close the mess early. As it is there was nothing to do in town and there were not many people one could befriend for social calls or spend time with– there was a general reluctance to befriend us, as far as the locals were concerned since they were extremely conservative.

On Sundays we woke up luxuriously, sat outside and waited for the omelette competition—in which the *sahayak* who could cook an omelette with the maximum thickness was declared the winner. There were two points for consideration—one—the thickness would be measured in the centre two minutes after the eggs were presented —two-- that only two eggs were allowed to each participant.

So the boys went off into their sanctuaries and began beating up the eggs– some had put the onions and tomatoes cut into small pieces into them while others were waiting for the egg white to become fluffy before adding the slivers of onion and tomatoes, coriander, salt and red chilli! Some even added slivers of cheese to the mixture.

Pat was the only judge because he alone amongst the officers, knew how to cook.

Eventually the boys stood in a line and produced the omelettes—which were held in the right hand and the left hand supported or simply touched the right elbow as is the custom in the Gorkhas! Pat cut the centres of each after two minutes—most of them had raw egg oozing out—hence he disqualified them. These boys were told to press a fork to the middle and cook the eggs well at a low temperature. The remaining three were cleared for the competition and their thickness was measured at the centre.. The winner received a bottle of *rakshi* or rum which we knew would be cheerfully emptied within minutes of presentation—we all enjoyed the breakfast– and got ready for the Mandir Parade.

The *Mandir Parade* was held at the Regimental Mandir which was located in the wing of the main hall. Our Panditji was a genius and he used the power of the Sanskrit words, gift of gab, story telling and his melodious singing to mesmerize the simple audience! His chief musicians and singers were all the naughty boys of the drama party, who sang popular devotional songs from the movies—they were a popular lot and even the shy families of the men; who had come from Nepal, could not help but smile at their pretentious devotion.

Panditji's *natak mandali*– choir-made the mandir programme lively and the boys who were very devout would sway to the songs, interspersed with the Panditji's sermons and then would terminate with the Aarti; amidst beating of the gongs and also bell chimes all designed to attract the attention of the gods and goddesses!

Six Third Gorkha Rifles Ki Jai! Long live Six Third Gorkha Rifles!

Sache Durbar ki Jai! Long live the true congregation!

The distribution of Prasad, the holy sweets; by the boys and the flame went around the congregation and the Session was over!

Since the Company offices were near, the Pay Naiks waited to see if Company Commander *Sahib* was visiting the company or headed to the Officer's Mess.

At the Officer's Mess, the Mess Staff was waiting for the officers—menu for Sunday was always special and beer was always chilled! Special Cook Mahavir Singh was qualified in the culinary arts and had just completed his Army Special Cook course. He knew after an exhausting week, the officer's had to loosen up on a Sunday—so he had made chicken and rajmah, or kidney beans, as per the Food Member's instructions and rice for the rice eaters with tandoori roti for the rest! The 2IC had told the Food Member—the food must be cooked with care and must be tasty—but watch your daily messing—it should not cross the laid down limits as enunciated in the minutes of the last Mess Meeting. Back in those days the pay of a 2/Lt was just Rs 640/-! This was about $15.

Not kidding!

This Sunday, the bachelors had invited the family walas and soon they trooped in with the kids in tow. The waiters had been briefed and soft drinks were served quickly—the children ran to their favourite bachelor Uncles—for with kids there was a rule—

Ask a beggar– what is 2 plus 2—answer 4 *rotis*(somewhat like tortillas)!

Ask our kids—what is 2 plus 2 and the answer was always– 4 Five Star Chocolates!

The badminton net was up and some of the ladies challenged the youngsters to a duel. The more serious intellectuals set up the table for bridge and us lesser mortals got ready for rummy! The kanchas watched bemused and wondered what the fuss was all about! The 2IC rang up the CO and invited him and his family over—no he did not require transport– it was a lovely day to walk and his family would be in the Mess in 15 minutes.

Soon the CO arrived and after enquiring about everyone's health and after playing with the children, went over to sit with the 2IC and watch the bridge game. One of the younger officers got up and offered his cards to the CO, but the CO told him to finish the game.

There was a roar at the badminton game– Mrs Joshi was cheating as usual because she could never win otherwise. Anyway the point was conceded to her, and the game continued. There was a *pakora* break, then a *samosa* break and finally a soft drink break. Amidst all these breaks the Mess Havildar came to the 2IC and reported —

Shreeman Bhojan taiyar hai! The food is ready Sir!

2IC signaled that the ladies and children begin while they played one more round—the bachelors went in to help look after the kids and the ladies sat down in groups in the lawn. After lunch, some thoughtful guy had ordered *jalebis* from the wet canteen and though beer, gin and jalebis did not go together—who cared—so down the hatch they went.

We all decided to call it a day

The next day Major Sameer Shukla had to give a lecture on *A Battalion Attack in the Mountains* at 1200hrs, there was a class on *Radio Telephony Procedure*, courtesy Major Ashok Godbole, Major Ashwin Cariappa was to conduct a *lecture demonstration on Advance to Contact*—all this was to perfect drills for the coming *Exercise Kingfisher*. In the evening we had day two of the Boxing Championship! Companies had been instructed to get their act together by arranging all their mobilization gear for the Test Exercise being conducted by the Brigade Commander..

As we hastened to the lines, a couple of hippies lay sprawled on the track, below the road– probably on a high from hashish or brown sugar or whatever. Almora was quite a haven for these *flower children*; who liked the locals; because they never bothered with them. The woman was good looking, but she had starved herself by living on the smoky substitute for food, she lay spread eagled across her male companion, who had his arm around her midriff in a protective sort of way—her blouse had been hiked up exposing much of a beautiful breast, but she lay there oblivious to this fact in some strange hallucination. Many of them ended selling anything of value and as you went past Glory Restaurant, which they frequented, the proprietor would smile and say—

I have a couple of cameras but they are not for you!

The natives allowed these flower children to go gamboling around their countryside searching for the most potent of these weeds. They went into their stupors and did not know that they were making love or bathing in the nude in the streams attempting to wash off their grime. The locals tolerated them as though they were elves or gnomes or pixies because they harmed no one except to ask for a *chilam* or earthen funnel through which they smoked their narcotic illusions of fantasy!

When I asked one of these youngsters why he preferred such a life, he confessed that he was actually a painter in New York and in a year he made so much money, that he could lead a carefree life in the Kumaon hills for two years! When I asked him whether being filthy and dirty was part of the dress code- he said they did not really care, for in their flights of fantasy; grime was not charged extra!

They came in hordes—cannabis was the craze then and one marvelled at the number of ways it could be consumed till it began to consume you! The flower children did not know any ranking in social structures nor were there any taboos for mingling inter racially or for that matter nationalities too. You just latched on to someone with matching vibes. Their dress code was restricted to a top of any colour, the lower garment was invariably pyjamas.

Up in the hills above Almora someone had made cottages for German tourists and others from Europe who wanted to shed their tensions from a life of automation in every sphere. The cottages had no electricity and one had to use lamps to cater for light. Food was cooked in wood or charcoal fireplaces and one had to fetch water from a spring and also go and do your own purchases from the market for daily necessities. These people freaked out in this haven, sang, danced and even their children seemed to enjoy their jaunts in the hills and the frugal living style!

They just wanted to be left alone.

As I went up to the Company, the Subedar Major came up and told me that I had been detailed to collect the pay for the month from the State Bank of India on Monday and that a guard had been detailed. One was expected to proceed on foot to the bank– those were the good old days—one need not fear the prospect of being robbed, the people of Almora were very respectful and dared not invoke our wrath! Almora was a small town and the SBI Manager smiled as I entered, notes had already been segregated as per the instructions from the Subedar Major who had his benign hand over all the key people in the city. The KMOU busses would come to the unit lines whenever required and the boys proceeding on leave or duty loaded up cheerfully in front of their barracks while the driver was fed in the langar or cook house and looked after!

Next to the Alexandra lines, was the Tamta Colony—they were superb artisans and made beautiful pots of metal. They did not like the system of caste bias and were quickly offended when someone poked fun at them. One appreciated their work– it had actually nothing to do with their lineage.

Someone was selling chestnuts and advised me to roast them and eat them in a day or two or they would not last.

The Adjutant's messenger Bal Bahadur, came by– he was a cute chap, but we dreaded him because we never knew what his messages contained. As Major Shukla read the message and signed– he smiled!

Sign you jokers—I was expecting this.

It was a curt message that each company would prepare four patrols under the Company commander and JCOs which were to be submitted to the 2IC who was the Patrol Master. Tasks for each patrol were ready and maps specified in the circular were to be issued by the IO or the Intelligence officer. Boxers who were due to fight in the bouts today were excused the training.

There was no time to lose—Subedar Damar Bahadur was told to get a conference organized and all the JCOs were ordered to brush up their orders for patrolling, prepare their skeleton orders– a copy for me as well and then prepare their patrols, have these approved and I would give them a talk on the subject as well. The Pay Naik was told to organize the maps and Subedar Dal Bahadur got cracking with the skeleton orders, Cook was told to cater for dinner a little earlier than usual because the Company had to be ready in front of the Battalion office by 2030hrs.I sent for my sahayak and told him to have my gear ready as well!

Thus the serene and calm tranquil morning was galvanized into crazy actions—weapons had to be drawn and helmets worn—maps checked, route charts made along with night march charts with distances and magnetic bearings included and rehearsals done and the 2IC was unforgiving if you dared to come late!

As soon as we received our instructions we prepared our orders and briefed our patrols and after a cursory check by the 2IC, we moved out of the unit lines. All the patrols had been briefed that any activity on their routes was deemed to be suspect and enemy patrols had to be avoided at all costs. Skirmishes were also to be avoided and it was vital that the required information reach the 2IC at the earliest as accurately as possible. Those patrols which went traversing the hillsides were clearly visible while the patrols which clung to the shadows along the pine slopes were impossible to spot. Most of the patrols reached their objective simultaneously and then there was the sound of rattlers and bicat strips as the enemy discovered one of the patrols. A parachute flare went up as the enemy decided to illuminate the area. The boys were wise to this antic and froze in their tracks till the flare died its natural death. At that distance one could be mistaken by the enemy to be the stump of a tree, *unless you moved.*

The task given to the patrols were always in question form to which answers had to be found. To ensure that the message reached the battalion even if the patrol was ambushed, a get-away man was appointed by name. His job was to break away as soon as ordered and take the answers to the 2IC.

Their task completed, the patrols headed back by a different route and reported to the 2IC who debriefed them for correctness of their report and to glean any additional information that the patrol members threw up.

The next day, Lieutenant Choudhary, a cheeky little braggart who claimed to have blood lines to Casanova, a regular *Teesmar Khan*; was on his way to the ranges when he heard Captain Dahiya whispering to Tony. The whisper could be heard clearly if one was slightly attentive.

Tony you have to go alone to the temple. OK!

But Sir, how did you discover this place?

You know I dispersed the company and then returned via the shortcut to the Officer's Mess. Just short of the top, where the track meets the main road from Garam Pani, I saw her outside the temple wearing saffron. I need not tell you that she had a very voluptuous figure and it seemed as though she was beckoning to me. She seems to wear only a single garment– the saree, because she wore no blouse. The effect of her clinging saree and the outline of her breasts was a sight for sore eyes—the image is not easy to forget and rouses me whenever i imagine her beckoning to me.

In a trance I walked up and sat near her.

What do you want from me Devi–I asked?

She did not speak but began to remove my boots and bathe my feet in water. She then wet her saffron robe and cleaned my face and then thrust her heavy breasts into my face. I just do not know where she transported me to- heaven or hell but I woke up feeling truly rejuvenated.

God that woman knows how to please and making love seems to be an art as far as she is concerned. May have learnt it from some sage—perhaps? Experts in kamasutra—perhaps?

She bid me goodbye with her waving, requested me– no beseeched me to come whenever I wished– but I have never gone that temple again because I will be tempted to go up there time and again till i become a crazy lunatic. She said that she had a special affection for Army walas!

Who is she--? Asked Tony

She is some Pujarin of the temple who has taken a vow to be concubine for a certain period as a sort of penance.

Chaudhary saw the temple in his mind and decided to pay the Pujarin a visit after the firing was complete.

As he stepped out tip toeing with delight, both Dahiya and Tony began to laugh. The Mess Havildar asked if he might be of help.

Dahiya simply said-*Chaudhary Sahib aja late auncha– unko lagi bhaat kamra ma pathai dinu.*

Chaudhary Sahib will be late today—send his food to his room.

Serves him right, for he would never find any temple or a Pujarin—it was a joke on him.They would laugh at him at an opportune time!

Casanova—my foot!

FOR WHOM THE BELLS RING

The story ceases here as a narrative from my side; because it would involve using the letter- I, very frequently– and in the Army, persons who use this letter very often; are dubbed- - Eye Specialists!

Captain and Mrs Surinder Singh were married on the Pahariwala Gurudwara Sahib, (The Sikh Temple On The Hill, in Greater Kailash, New Delhi); with all the pomp and gaiety allowed sparingly, by the bridegroom. Preeti's mother was secretly pleased with her son in law's decision that there should be no extravagance of any kind. Outwardly, she sobbed discreetly and complained that Preeti was her only daughter and her son in law was not letting her spend in the manner she wanted to according to her family's status– rich businessmen.

Secretly, she had utilized the considerable savings, to buy a flat for the couple and would present it to them at an opportune time—Surinderji was right– why squander their hard earned money in frivolous expenditure. So after a few feigned protests she meekly succumbed to her son–in–law's decision. Earlier, she had tried to gift her future son in law—her *jawai-* to- be, some cash given as a ceremonial token, but he refused adamantly. So, when he was engrossed in a discussion with her relatives, she slipped the cash into his coat pocket!

Many of the guests in her primary list were removed, and included in the reception party which was a joint affair– guests from both sides were invited and Surinder had insisted that the cost be shared! This sort of a function had never been imagined and Preeti's mother wondered how Surinderji's parents had agreed to this– not knowing that Surinder could be very tough on such issues and no one dared to question him!

Surinder's parents were very proud of his decisions for it signaled a radical change from the old thought process! They agreed that it was pointless taking too many friends and people for a function which was very private, and there was no need to empty the coffers of their *samdhis* or Surinder's in laws.

Moreover it was a decision which could only be taken by the groom's family because in India the groom's family had the upper hand in the nuptial arrangements and the groom's father was King Almighty! In Surinder's view, his marriage should be as simple as possible. There was no place for unnecessary and wasteful expenditure. He would respect the tenets enunciated in the laws of Sikhism and according to the rules framed by the Shiromani Gurudwara Committee, according to which a marriage between a Sikh couple be solemnized under the Anand marriage rites, which fell in disuse due to the influence of the Brahmins and the Arya Samajis since the reign of Maharaja Ranjit Singh. The feeling was that the Sikhs be considered as a sect of the Hindus and therefore subject to the code of Hindu Law.

Darji was upset—*Beta*(son), why are you being difficult?

Surinder hugged Darji.

Darji—there is no need for a formal engagement, as long as a ring, a *kara* (steel bracelet)and a *kripan*(Small dagger) are presented in front of a *sangat*(congregation). Marriages should be performed within the means available to the bride's family. You should be quite happy that I am getting married—why– because Sikhism frowns on acceptance of the vows of celibacy, fasting, renunciation or the *sanyasin* state!

Darji laughed—*Putar*(Son) you can make anyone laugh—even a *murda*-a corpse!

So Surinder laid down his commandments:

One-Milni (Meeting)is allowed for it was a formal welcome and introduction of the male elders on both sides.

Two-Anand Karaj (wedding ceremony)should finish before twelve in the afternoon.

Three-He would ride to the Gurudwara where the Anand Karaj was being performed, on a ghori or pony.

Four-Lunch would be at a venue to be at the discretion of the bride's family. Refreshments were not required because there was no need.

Five-Flowers would not be showered on the bridal couple, after the fourth phera in the presence of the holy Guru Granth Sahib.(In Sikhism, the bridal couple circles the Guru Granth Sahib four times to solemnise their wedding, and the custom of kissing the bride does not exist)

Six-During the *pheras,* Preeti would walk without any escorts.(during the walk around the Guru Granth Sahib-now the living Guru)

Seven-There would be no speeches, lectures or recitals of poems.

Eight-He would not have the ritual turmeric bath—his Lux soap was good enough.

Nine- There would be a joint reception and guests from both sides would attend. Expenses would be shared Only close friends and relatives would attend the marriage proper.

Ten-Other social functions like *Munh Vikhai, Khichri* for the bride, veils, showering of coins over the bridal car were not permitted. Only mustard oil ceremony; to welcome Preeti home, would be performed by his mother.

Surinder was a tall six footer and was in good physical shape with what is called a vee shaped body, thanks to his regular exercise and his obsession with physical fitness. He wore a black suit and looked smashing in it. Vedi's in Connaught place always ensured that he got the latest styling and the suits were always delivered before time, because Masterji liked the discussions with Surinder—not many appreciated the Saville Row styles.

Preeti wore yellow—her suit was expensive and very heavy, but she felt that she should break from the traditional maroon and red dresses normally worn by brides. With a heavy chunni, she looked weighed down by her ensemble, but she decided to go through with it—after all you get married only once in this country. With her height of five feet seven inches, she carried herself well.

The ceremony proceeded as planned and finished at eleven oclock– an hour before noon as Surinder had wanted. Drinks were served and soon it was time for lunch. Preeti and Surinder ate from the same plate and were closely watched by their giggling nephews and nieces. The girls had already hidden Surinder's shoes as per the prevailing custom and Surinder had to pay a ransom to get them back!

The couple had their bags packed next evening for their move to the battalion, which had kindly sent two pipers from the unit band to the marriage. As the couple sat on their *Raja Rani* sofas during the reception (the traditional Emperor and Empress Sofas on which the bridal pair is seated for being introduced to relatives and friends), the pipers played around them swaying sideways to the melody and Surinder offered them large pegs of rum which they quaffed in one gulp without a burp!

It was very dignified and touching!

Surinder could make out from the discussions that the Reception– a joint affair had sent ripples across the congregation and given food for thought. While some came up to him in open praise, others felt that they did not know half the guests.

Get introduced- was Surinder's advice to the doubting Thomas's—get sozzled too!

The Surinders had no time for a proper honeymoon, because Surinder had to return to the battalion or paltan which was getting ready for *Exercise-Kingfisher*; and had to move out to the exercise location. Major Cariappa and Major Shukla were leaving right after the marriage ceremony, because there was a lot of work to be done! They were Surinder's best friends and had come to represent the battalion at his marriage.

The train journey to Kathgodam via Bareilly was an overnight affair and the last leg of the journey was made possible by using two railway engines because there was a gradient to negotiate. Surinder preferred to get off at Haldwani because a taxi would be available, and they would reach Almora quickly.

Meanwhile the Second in Command, or the 2IC, Major Udai Gurung had instructed the Senior Subaltern, the senior most Lieutenant- -Tony Fernandes to get his team ready and greet the newly weds—

--and it better be done well or I will have you guys up the gum tree—OK!

Tony was a powerful guy—as the undisputed leader of the Lieutenants and 2/Lieutenants, he was a force to reckon with. His task was to chaperon these youngsters into future officers for the battalion– instill pride in their hearts for the battalion, teaching them mess etiquette, regimental history, the Mess silver, history of each photograph, artefact, maintenance of the furniture, the method of keeping the Mess Staff trained, efficient and ready to cope with any eventuality—be it a normal Dinner Night, Regimental Dinner Night or for that matter a party in the Mess. The Wine waiter or *Abdar* had to know how to make a Pink Gin, Bloody Mary, Rum Punch or any other specialty of the Mess.

Tony always chose a new method to bring home his lesson.

Since it was taboo to take a lady's name on the table, Tony would breach the subject of movies and frown at the insipid movies running in the town to bait a youngster off guard.

No Sir—Meena kumari is very beautiful and she has a sexy voice too—almost like a drawl—

This was enough and Tony would order drinks for all and put the tab on the offender's name.

Tony also ensured that two dancers from the paltan came over to teach *Jhaunre*; that fast rhythmic and very stylish Nepalese dance form to the youngsters, help them write down the lyrics of songs which were the rage with the boys, and also teach them to play the *madal*—that Gorkhali drum which was a mandatory requirement for any function! The boys loved officers who could sing and dance with them at *Barakhanas* or ritual regimental get togethers.

Tony got the youngsters together, took them for Duty Officer rounds to ensure they were aware of the procedures and showed the new youngsters how to mount the Guard.

He never minced his words when he cautioned them that they must hold bloody still when they were challenged by the guard at the Quarter Guard at night, because the sentry had a fixed bayonet and could use it on them.

Why is that Sir? This came from Lieutenant Muthu.

A sentry gets charged up emotionally after he had shouted the customary warning—

Tham Kaun Aata Hai—Halt– Who Goes there?

Give him the password when he asks for it and allow him to cool down. Remember, he has a fixed bayonet at that time.

Only then enter the QG or Quarter guard.

And you bloody buggers, better not forget the password---OK!

So Tony got down to the present business with a serious note and gathered his henchmen around---

Ramesh---Go and send for the joker---I will brief him personally—on ahem--- the finer points-

Muthu—ask your Company Senior JCO, Subedar Pirthi Singh to arrange for a pair of drummers, one palanquin and a bullock cart. Pirthi is a local isn't he? Should be no problem for him and I want it done as reasonably as possible. *Chito! Quickly!*

Kirti—*Chorey*—you make sure that the bands are in place—I want two pipers to lead the procession playing a local tune and they should be dressed like the locals too! I also want a safai wala ready to cart away the-you- know- what-- in case the bulls have an urge.

Also make sure that the CO enters the Mess after the couple arrive—put a sentry at the gate to delay him-Got it!

Saikiya—Make sure the Bania makes the mirchiwali jalebi and ladoo for the bride, also keep a waiter with water and a soft drink ready for her after she has eaten. Sweets with a load of green chilli stuffed in it!

Joginder, Bhaaji—the tables for the food, arrangements for dinner are your responsibility—

The Surinders– Preeti and Surinder were expected at lunchtime, and arrangements for their temporary stay had been made in the MES Inspection

Bunglow just outside the Officer's Mess. Meanwhile, the Quarter Master, Capt Janki Das had applied for a married quarter for Surinder who had turned 25 years of age a few months ago and was eligible for one.

As was customary, Surinder had applied for permission to get married and his Commanding Officer had given his consent-- for Surinder was one his best officers, had a decent bank balance and was a very mature officer for his age.

The request began with the customary- *--I have the honour to state that I wish to seek your blessings*----followed by a brief description of his bride to be and her family.It was customary to send an invitation card to the officers through the 2IC, to ensure that you were eligible for a silver salver with the names of all the officers who had contributed to it.

Hukum pronounced it as– *shinining silver salva*!

In the evening, as the officers and children waited in the Officer's Mess, they heard the bagpipes and the excitement grew—the kids were keen to see the new Aunty. Surinder had anticipated this, but chose to keep quiet; else the fun of initiating Preeti into the family would have been lost. He was carrying a box of chocolates and a cake from Wengers, Connaught Place! Preeti was glad that she wore a salwar kameez oufit, instead of a saree when she found that she had to get into a jeep and then into a palanquin!

So with much fanfare, the couple reached the Mess, the palanquin bearers and the pipers were paid their bakshish– four bottles of Hercules rum and the games passed on to Tony's gang!

The ladies welcomed the bride with an *Arti*, a religious custom designed to welcome a guest and before she entered the Mess, a little mustard oil was spilt near the entrance door as an auspicious sign. Preeti was gushing with excitement– but more was to follow—

Suddenly a screeching of the tyres of a vehicle, announced the arrival of the Commanding Officer and his family. Lieutenant Colonel Randeep Singh Katoch, was from a small princely estate in Kangra, and was an alumni of Sonawer and the JSW or the Joint Services Wing, and had graduated from the Indian Military Academy. His family had been associated with the Army for generations and one of his uncles had been shot down during the Battle of Britain; won a DSO, and lived to tell some very interesting tales.

The CO, or the Old Man as he was affectionately called had a smashing moustache which required meticulous grooming every day and was the envy of every *kancha* in the Unit—where anyone who could muster six or more hair on either side of his nose was a potential candidate; for the appointment of RP Havildar or Regimental Police Havildar!

Mrs Katoch was a very graceful lady from Jammu and was the epitome of a cultured upbringing and had spent some time for her grooming in the French Riviera. They had two children– a boy and a girl. The 2IC, Major Udai Gurung welcomed them to the Mess and formally introduced them to Preeti.

The expression on Mrs Katoch's face was a complete giveaway– it said—

I like and approve!

Preeti and Surinder touched the CO and his wife's feet, an Indian custom, to seek their blessings and Mrs Katoch embraced Preeti and planted a kiss on her forehead. Not to be outdone the CO gave Surinder a warm hug, congratulated him, and praised him for his conduct of a very "revolutionary" wedding, about which Cari and SK had briefed him in detail!

After they were seated, Tony signaled and the gathering moved to the Band Stand where Panditji was waiting. Chanting something like Sanskrit--which sounded guttural but definitely was not connected to religious scriptures, the priest began the series of devotional and religious chants and procedures which solemnize a marriage according to Hindu rites. His *dhoti,* a white piece of cloth worn under the shirt; slipped a little because he was neither used to tying it nor wearing it!

Preeti was confused—she could make out that the events were not happening as in the many weddings she had attended, but her husband sat with eyes closed, as if he sought the blessings of the heavenly gods in right earnest! This and the fact that the CO and his wife sat opposite them with equal religious fervour added to her confusion.

Many of the ladies had not witnessed a marriage ceremony such as this, because they had got married during the paltan's field tenure, and as soon as they realized that the Punditji was a fake—they could not hold back their laughter' till a stern glance from the 2IC, put an end to the mirth and the solemn function began once again.

The couple began their ritualistic walk around the sacred fire and the marriage was finally over—two pipers emerged out of nowhere and on Tony's signal began to play a haunting melody sounding like Auld Lang Syne—and began walking around them----soon two buglers joined them and then two drummers—the cacophony was too much to bear for Preeti- --

At last the priest returned with the spiked sweets and Preeti's mouth turned on fire because of the green chilli, the sweets contained! Prem Singh appeared with the glasses of coke and the fire was doused. Panditji emerged again and put forward his donation thali or plate and Surinder gave him two hundred rupees!

To Preeti's surprise Panditji, saluted, did a fine about turn grinned and vanished, holding on to his dhoti which had dipped precariously and displayed the striped blue and white shorts he wore underneath! Similar discreet grins were beginning to spawn on the faces of the Mess waiters, though the Mess Havildar shot them a discreet, yet stern look which indicated his displeasure at their mirth.

Similarly Surinder dispensed bottles of rum to the band personnel, Mess Staff and the palanquin bearers!

Dinner was announced as soon as everyone left the bar and the newly weds were packed off in a jeep to the MES Inspection Bunglow. As she lay in her husband's arms Preeti tried to recap the events of the day and laughed quietly!

Penny for your thoughts—asked Surinder.

But Preeti had gone- --to the land of slumber- --with so many unanswered questions in her mind. Never mind--I have just joined the Army—plenty of time to unravel the mysteries of this new life, and a smile began to form on her lips inadvertently.

The ladies had told her that the Inter Company Boxing Championship was coming soon and it would be great fun!

Charlie was the company to bet on!

Charlie was Surinder's company!

EXERCISE TO EXERCISE

Life moved in its own tranquil manner at Almora.

The battalion moved from one exercise location to another and kept the ladies guessing—was this a peace station or was it a field area? As soon as the unit returned from an exercise location– orders were received that another exercise was ready.

This time it was a Test exercise. The Brigade Commander would put the paltan to a test and examine whether its battle drills and battle procedures were upto the mark.

It was rumoured that in all likelihood the Army Commander would also visit. So arrangements were made appropriately. Surinder came up with a great plan—many of the Umpires and the JCOs participating in the exercise were able to understand Nepalese, but not many knew the dialects. So the idea was that all the radio operators were to be in pairs– one a Gurung, the other a Magar! The transmission would be in either language for speed—of course the plan was fraught with danger because messages could get garbled while they were being transmitted or received, or while they were being conveyed to the second operator like the famous *Chinese Whisper*–but all is fair in love and war.

The intelligence officer—IO was instructed to make arrangements in such a way that the sand model was electrified—so if the CO mentioned- Start Point or SP–a lone blue light would light up, if he indicated Bounds then Red lights would light up, and blue lines if Report Lines were indicated. This was successfully created and the sandmodel was such a great hit that the Brigade Commander wanted this replicated in the Brigade. Our IO was a gem—Muthu was a wizard with maps and could remember the entire route in his head where the Almighty had even created a gyroscope; which helped him to maintain direction with ease.

So after the CO gave out his orders, the Army Commander took him aside and grilled him on battle procedure. When he was happy with his answers, he smiled—one of his rare smiles and patted the CO on his back—

Why were you absent at the reunion? Both of them were RIMCOLIANS—from RIMC, Dehra Dun.

CO looked him in the eye—Sir, I was attending an exercise.

Ok I forgive you– I was a little peeved, I like you all to be present at these occasions—it keeps everyone in touch. Ours is a great fraternity—where else can a youngster muster courage to see me in my office—only because we are from the same school?

Lets keep it that way!

With that he nodded and left for the helipad at the KRC or Kumaon Regimental Centre, where his chopper was waiting to fly him to Lucknow. The visit had gone off well and the Brigade Commander had to merely go through the motions.

Muthu had worked out his plan for the advance well. He gave out the landmarks which were essential before CO gave his verbal orders for the advance and asked in a brisk voice—Seen?

Major Sameer Shukla shouted– Not seen!

What have you not seen, Sir?

Where is this feature called Knoll?

You are sitting bang on it, sir!

The CO gave out his assessment of the situation and gave his detailed orders.

Everyone had a laugh—later Major Shukla called Muthu aside—I do not like smart alecks– you bum!

Neither do I, Sir!

The 2 I C, Major Rai told them to break it off and get ready for the advance. There was so much to be done, battle drills and also battle procedures came in to play so that everyone was doing his job without getting into the other's way. It was a legacy of the war which taught troops to economise on time and effort. *Who knew that this would one day be called Management and that American pundits would create business managers who would teach us what they learnt from us in the first place!*

Muthu despatched a patrol to a certain feature which would interfere with our advance, it was a hunch, he called it. So the battalion prepared for the advance—the vanguard crossing the Start Line or (SL) on time--, Bravo Company moved on the left flank to ensure that the enemy did not interfere with the rate of advance while the rest of the battalion moved as per the order of march. At every report line the vanguard company was changed.

Muthu was right– the patrol caught the enemy commandos fast asleep.

They were expecting no activity till noon and it was a rude shock for them to be awakened like this! The CO congratulated the patrol and Muthu received a pat; even Major Shukla gave Muthu a big hug—

Well done Muthu, you are an efficient little bastard!

Compliment indeed!

Muthu's plan had gone off so well that by noon they were within reach of the objective—for which the Brigade Commander had planned a night attack—this faultless movement, section and platoon attacks on snipers and ambushes were done as per the book and in the required amount of time allotted so the battalion was in time at the objective. There was a quick consultation with the Umpire who came over to state that that 6/3 GR had lost half its vanguard company and that the battalion would have to dig in for a night attack!

CO was furious—his battalion was being denied the prize merely to accommodate the Brigade Commander's plan which it appeared, was faulty in calculating time and space.

So the boys dug in and waited in the sweltering heat. Major Jones was the ASC representative-from the Supply Corps, and an Anglo Indian to boot, had slowly turned pink and then red in the heat. The Adjutant heard him mutter– *wish I had a chilled coke.* He signalled to the Mess waiter and when Major Jones opened his eyes he was staring at a genuine coke chilled as he liked it—it had been chilled in a *chagul*—a canvas bag for carrying water!

Thank you son– was all he could mutter and he hugged the bottle to his chest.

Everyone smiled as he rubbed the bottle on his face! After an agonising time the sun seemed like it was indeed going to move down in the West, so the CO got his Order Group together and gave out his orders for attack on the assumption that the enemy at the objective was estimated to be a company plus.

Muthu swung into action and laid out the FUP and companies were indicated landmarks by the company commanders– so that each platoon commander knew his objective well and could indicate it to his section commanders. At the appointed time assault companies moved in silently into the FUP and crossed the FUP at the allocated time. This was important because all timings were taken from this moment; including the time for the artillery guns to fire and the time they would stop firing and lay down fire at the depth targets, during the re organisation stage when the enemy could counter attack.

The necessary drills of reporting casualties, first aid were taken care of and ammunition was redistributed. The Companies began to convert the trenches to avoid casualties from enemy artillery which could be called in by the enemy– and get ready to repel a counter attack by the enemy. Each assaulting company fired it's *success signal–* verey lights or flares of different colours; and allowed the reserve companies through to go in for Phase- 2 of the attack.

Soon these companies fired success signals after catering to time required for the assault and the hand to hand fighting and the battle was over.

The reports were collected by the Adjutant and given to the CO who briefed the Brigade Commander. After an hour the codeword to close the exercise was received and then tea was quickly brewed and a small fire was lit; for it was quite cold in the pine forests with a cold breeze whistling in the pines--. All those huddled near the fire did an automatic drill, at which the boys grinned discretely. Muthu took out his water bottle which was full of rum.

The CO accepted a tot with water—Muthu—do this in the desert and you will be a dead man for sure!

I know sir! Before long the bottle was empty and Muthu just about wet his lips—but it made him happy to see that his gesture had brought a little cheer to the group.

As the fire was increased in intensity everyone wriggled away from the fire but when the fire receded—everyone squirmed forward and this ritual carried on through out the night with Muthu letting off loud snores sporadically, convincing everyone that all was well in heaven and earth—possibly in the underworld too. It was difficult to imagine that a short guy like him could muster so loud a sound—but it wasn't the snores which made the boys laugh with glee—it was Muthu's half closed eyes—with the whites showing, coupled with periodic muttering at two minutes intervals which sent them rolling on the pine needles. But they were careful– Muthu Sahib had a bad temper too--!

Dawn broke out and Muthu instructed the boys to wake up the CO and the 2IC with a cup of tea. The adjutant had passed instructions that the battalion assemble for a briefing by the Brigade Commander who would come in from Chaubatia. The IO and his staff carried out a de- sanitation round to ensure that nothing of informative value to the enemy was left in the exercise area—scraps of paper, toffee wrappers were burnt, for we knew that the brigade intelligence guys would come to their camping site looking for anything of concern which might be of use to the enemy. In our case it would be embarrassing if this was given as a security point against us. The Subedar Major had brought one change of clothing for us all and everyone looked fresh inspite of the exercise.

Major Ravi Krishnan took Captain Choudhary aside—listen, do NOT go to sleep during the briefing– OK! Be careful, because we all knew that our *Chora* could sleep in a second!

The Commander came to the podium and after the GSO3, had oriented everyone with the enlargement, the battle was indicated, the Brigade Commander, Brigadier Satnam Singh began his assessment of the exercise on which 6/3 GR had been tested:

—everyone knew what was required to be done.

The SP or the Start Point was crossed on time.

He congratulated the CO for his capture of the enemy patrol—CO looked at Muthu and smiled, indicating to him that the kudos were his and his alone!

He was happy with the planning, conduct and execution of the advance and the attack operations.

The deployment of the support weapons throughout the exercise was par excellence.

He was very impressed with the communications of the battalion especially that no one could guess from the intercepts of wireless communication as to– what the hell was going on.

This drew a big laugh from us all.

He then outlined the movement of the battalion from start to finish. What he and the umpires were impressed with was the following:

There was no talking or shouting in the battalion- excellent.

He was happy that the lessons he had indented to bring out were amply addressed.

Lastly he was impressed that the officers and men of 6/3 GR, were kept informed of the progress of operations and had taken part in the exercise with a lot of josh. He wanted to congratulate the Tiger(CO) for a job well done and to the men who looked like they were going into battle and not as though they had finished one.

So, a hefty tea was demolished with the sumptuous eats provided and as soon as everyone had finished burping, Colonel Katoch decided it was time to take leave and return to Almora.

We all moved to the boys and got their transport allotment organised. The battalion would leave for the Camp location where the *Panther* or

Quartermaster had lunch arranged. As we stepped into the Mess, a beaming Pandit was holding silver jugs of beer for us and some pink gin for the gin walas. Great guy—the Almighty made very rare specimens such as Pandit, when he was at peace with himself!

Muthu ordered a six egg omelette—which was going to be his lunch. Then he would sleep till eternity! Everyone heard him muttering away in his native Tamil and looked inside. There was Muthu chatting earnestly with a photograph of a good looking girl—his fiancée.

Relax– I am just giving her the latest sitrep(situation report) to keep her updated—so do guys mind--?

Everyone was in a light mood, jokes were cracked at random, and leg pulling was also abundant because the tension of the exercise was over. The CO was relieved no rabbit had popped up during the monotonous wait at the Forming Up Place—FUP, where the attacking companies waited just before being launched at the designated time.Our boys– inspite of their discipline could falter at the sight of a rabbit– even an *apsara* could be resisted, but not a rabbit!

The CO and the 2IC, left—they had to go to off to Ranikhet to be briefed about the exercise in which 6/3 GR was to be the enemy in a test exercise for the Dogras. Randy or Randhawa would bring the battalion to Almora. Randy was a fine chap but his Nepali was atrocious and every sentence he spoke was so heavily interspersed with Punjabi words that the boys found ways to pull his legs akin to a character called Santa Singh– probably a cousin of Sancho Panza or the proverbial guy we called Pat- of the Pat yarn series:

Santa Singh is sitting at the end of a bar. He sees a lamp at the end of the table. He walks down to it and rubs it. Out pops a genie.

It says, "I will give thee three wishes."

Santa thinks awhile. Finally he says, "I want a beer that never is empty." With that, the genie makes a poof sound and on the bar is a bottle of beer.

Santa starts drinking it and right before it is gone, it starts to refill.

The genie asks about his next two wishes. Santa says, "I want two more of these."

Then word came that the villagers had requested that a very large wild boar damaged their crops at regular intervals– could we sort out the bastard?

Subedar Min Bahadur and two of the boys went and laid a trap, in the morning they had got the monster– a magnificient specimen with huge damaged tusks. The bugger must weigh at least two and a half maunds!

As Subedar Min Bahadur went to play with the dead beast---he squeezed the genitals playfully.

He had no inkling that the beast's testicles were full of semen and he received a squirt in his face—result—the whole battalion could not stop laughing till their tears stopped and the look on Min Bahadur's face told the story in clear!

Randhawa or Randy came over and with his usual mirth made the statement of the day—

Oye- Shaheedan nu thude nain marde; nale becharyan de tatyan nu kadey vi dabaya na karo- -

Nahin ta akhan wich golian marange!

Never kick fallen warriors or squeeze their balls in vain!

Otherwise you will receive an eyeful!

INTER COMPANY BOXING CHAMPIONSHIP

In every Army unit, a list of holidays and a forecast of Inter Company Championships is published. This is generally based on the training directive issued by the Brigade Commander who bases this on the directive issued by division headquarters! The advantage of this system was that the companies could plan the leave schedules for their sportsmen and competitors in such a manner, that they were available for inter company events because these were contested with a intensity so fierce, that it would make Olympic Squads weak in their knees—such was the prevalent *josh* or *espirit de corps.*

Every company commander's ambition was to become the Champion Company Commander, because a flag post inside or outside the Commanding Officer's Office displayed the positions of each company in the Inter Company Championship and the Championship Banner would belong to the Champion Company for a year.

Surinder held a conference in his office—Charlie Company, to work out a strategy for the inter company boxing championship. The Gorkhas took naturally to boxing; as would an otter cub, to water. Their style of boxing was fair, according to the rules and adherence to the dress code was mandatory. The conference was a very secret affair and his Senior JCO(Junior Commissioned Officer)had placed a sentry outside to ensure that there were no spies from other companies lurking about.

Subedar Sahib—Hamro taiyari kasto cha? How is our preparation?

Subedar nodded and said—*Sahib, Taiyari to ramro cha, sapai weight ko lagi fighter ra reserve train gare ko cha, matre heavy weight ko lagi koi pani paye ko chaina.Hazur le OK gare bhane Tulsi Ram, hamro bhanche lai hal diyun?Tes ko diet ramro cha ani rati ma hamro coach le ali ali training pani gare ko cha, manche tagra ta chaina tara weight ko point pai jala!Keta haru khana pakai dincha—jab sama Tulsi fit for hundei na!*

In short Subedar Dammar Bahadur, had told his company commander that preparations were in order, but they could not field a fighter for the heavy weight but they had secretly trained Tulsi the company cook at night and had been feeding him goat's head;he was not a great fighter but he would get them the points for fielding a fighter for that weight! If he won then the points they got would be bonus! The boys had promised to cook the meals till Tulsi recovered from the effects of combat.

Surinder agreed—this had been smart thinking on the part of his Senior JCO.

The coach, Havildar Santa Bahadur called in the boxing squad– each reserve stood behind his fighter and had his gear in front of his feet. Surinder then gave the coach five pairs of the latest boxing gloves and shoes, socks, along with boxing shorts to give a complete look to his boxers.

A present from his family!

Show me the vests—these will have to be modified– Sante– get one of the boys to dye the vests yellow—for Charlie's colour was yellow, and have this design stamped at the back Alternatively tell the Wet Canteen Contractor Peshoriji to arrange for the vests to be dyed.

But Sahib—we do not have any funds in the Company funds!

Surinder put his arms around him—You stop worrying Old Man—just concentrate on the boxing—Ok!

Subedar Sahib laughed—The Company Commander would pay for the stuff! Great Chap!

The design was that of a gloved fist in a Victory Salute and Charlie written below it in bold letters!

Santa Bahadur then briefed Surinder about the strong points and weak points of every fighter and his reserve.

Surinder then told the boys to sit on the floor and stuck photographs of the great boxers of all time in various poses and with the help of his regimental cane began to explain the styles adopted by these fighters. He explained the points which were achieved by simply giving the opponent a strong jab on the target areas. The obsession with aiming for the face must go and similarly one should not attempt a knock out punch from the first bell! Combinations were a better way of tackling opponents and dealing KO punches. The boys listened– they dreamed of reaching the Services team—and who knows the Nationals—or even better, a shot at the Commonwealth Games—the sky was the limit!

He then explained footwork, balance, guard, presenting a limited target to the opponent and use of combination punches. I want you to play fair—no fouls would be tolerated. The idea behind these inter company competitions was to select a battalion team for the Brigade championship and subsequently select teams in every discipline for the division teams, the command and the services teams.

He outlined the strategy to be used by every fighter, based on his stamina and expertise or experience. Gurkhas were talented boxers and took to football and boxing naturally. But they had their failings– he knew that the boys were not afraid of blood and would smear blood on the faces of those who failed to chop off the heads of goats in one swing of their khukris, but when one of our fighters saw his own blood being spilt during a bout– he seemed to get effected and would lose heart. Similarly in football, the boys enjoyed the game while they were winning but as they saw more goals piling onto their team– they could lose heart.

So Surinder outlined his strategy in detail

He would see them in the evening and hoped that they would do well!

Sante—he beckoned to the Coach---have we got all the weights right?

Hazur! said Santé

Where did you get these from--?

Hazur—*hijo issue bhaye ko*—These were issued yesterday!

Surinder scanned the instructions quickly---the 2IC had not missed a single trick. Winners of Quarter Finals would get a point, winners of the Semi Finals two and winners of the Finals would get three points. Byes would distributed to companies by draw. Settling positions of teams which had equal points, duration of bouts, weigh-in, rules applicable if boxers weighed more or lesser than their required weight, Selection Committee, Jury of Appeal, officials, documents to be produced, age limits, medical fitness certificates, dress code for boxers, referees, judges and spectators and time for a final Coordination Conference were all covered in the instructions.

Winners of previous inter company competitions were not eligible---individuals who had represented the Battalion were similarly not eligible---present battalion team members were also not eligible--!

Have the six copies required by Battalion Headquarters been prepared?

OK—let me see them—now have them delivered in time, Sahib!

Surinder glanced at the list–

Light Fly—Not exceeding 48 kg

Fly-- Over 48 kg, not exceeding 51kgBantam— 51 to 54 kg

Feather--- 54 to 57 kg

Light--- 57 to 60 kg

Lt Welter 60 to 64 kg

Welter--- 64 to 69 kg

Middle--- 69 to 75

Lt Heavy--75 to 81 kg

Heavy--- 81 to 91 kg

Super heavy—over 91 kg

Damar Bahadur Sahib, please make sure that all the boxers and reserves are within the laid down weight limits during the weighing in—I do not want to hear any excuses after this moment—thik cha! OK!

Subedar Sahib nodded grimly—he could not falter on this issue!

And before I forget– I do not want to see story tellers as *seconds, (the two boys detailed to resuscitate their boxer during the time of rest)*—there is not a second to waste—tell the boxer where he is faulting and advise suitable corrective action while resuscitating him—got it!

OK, Boys I will see you at the ring—make the company proud—

Charlie Company Ho ki Hoi Na?

Are we Charlie Company or Not—Ho! Came the reassuring answer—

Surinder was satisfied and with a wave of his hand he left the office. Sahib—let us talk to Tulsi and see what he says!

Tulsi came out of the cook house into the Dining Hall—he was nervous—his clothes were soiled from the cooking, and the grease and he was perspiring.

Surinder put him at ease and after he had regained his composure, he put up the proposal to him—that he would represent the Company in the Heavy weight bout and that his exposure to any excessive beating would be prevented by the seconds throwing in the towel!

Tulsi looked at Surinder and at Subedar Sahib and then burst into a big smile—*Thik Cha sahib!* Three words said it all! Surinder solemnly shook hands with cook and told Subedar Sahib to take care of the formalities! It was difficult to get heavy guys in the paltan because the Gurkhas were either not bulky enough or their bones were lighter.

Surinder had learnt that Admin Company was fielding their washerman and he was an old man—not very fit.

So Tulsi would have to be motivated and spruced up.

Back with Preeti– he gave her a run down about what to expect—advised her to take cues from the CO and 2IC's wives, who were mature ladies and would behave appropriately during the function. The lunch was a formality because Surinder wanted to supervise things at the Company end—he gave her a big smile, kissed her cheek and told her that she would be picked up by the other ladies in organized transport.

At the boxing ring– the arrangements had been made by the battalion team and the ring was well lit. L shaped tents had been pitched up company wise to enable the families to watch and the boys sat with a keen eye registering everything which was happening A few whispered their queries to one another because the inter company boxing event had not been held in the paltan's field tenure.

As it grew darker, the lights came on and now the CO and ladies were seated while company commanders huddled separately to get a better glimpse of the fight. The Subedar Major came over to sit beside the CO, and the MC or Master of Ceremony came into the ring to announce the event and caution the spectators about cheering manners! The Time Keeper and his staff sat with the gong and the referees took their place.

Everything was in place and as the MC finished, the Referee walked into the ring.Maxi Bhatnagar posted as a GSO3 in Jullunder was visiting the battalion on his honeymoon and he had been roped in as the Umpire!

Simultaneously, the boxers who were waiting in the wings entered amidst a roar of encouragement from their companies and the families of those companies. Surinder and Sub Damar Bahadur were not so concerned—it was a fight between Alfa and Bravo Companies—what concerned them was actually the weaknesses and the strong points of the winner of this bout, because their boxer would be pitted against this chap! Damar Bahadur Sahib nodded to the Company clerk-- Pay Naik Shyam Bahadur, who handed a clipboard to Surinder with the details of all the fights of the evening detailed on it so that Surinder could make annotations against the boxer's name.

Nothing could be left to chance.

The boxers were facing the crowd which was yelling itself hoarse—the officer's wives were yelling too and so were the children!

The referee turned to call the boxers and cross checked their gloves and gear—sent them back to their corners. Time keepers staff had taken their place and the announcement began—Seconds out of the Ring-- First Round– and the gong made a humming sound—the fight had begun. Those concerned were watching– those who were coaches were calculating the points for and against. Seconds were sitting tense while the boxers circled for an opening punch. Suddenly the boxer from Bravo let fly a barrage of well aimed punches and the Alfa Boxer lost his balance and fell—there was a roar of approval. The boxer from Alfa regained control and swung a left hook followed by a full blow to the chin with all his strength. The Bravo boxer was lifted from his feet and the bout ended—for he never could get to his feet!

Preeti could not help it– she leapt to her feet and clapped for the winner! The senior ladies smiled—the boxing bug had got her too!

The next fight was a Charlie versus Delta fight. Surinder looked at Damar Sahib—*hamro Dale lai defence tagra garnu parcha ani afno reach ko pura faida lenu parcha sahib!*Damar Bahadur Sahib nodded and looked at Santa Bahadur who raised his hand to indicate that he understood. Our Dal Bahadur must keep his guard in tact and take full advantage of his reach.

Charlie was fielding a very lithe and fast boxer called Bijli by the boys-lightning-- but his actual name was Ruk Bahadur Pun. So the boys started the ritual chants

–Ruk Bahadur Pun– hamro kura Sun, which meant

- Ruk Bahadur Pun, listen to what we say!

Bijli! Bijli! Bijli!--

There was a hush in the air as the boxers faced off and it appeared that both of them were sizing each other! Suddenly Bijli struck and gained three points. The crowd gasped---again he lashed out and drew blood from the Delta boxer's nose. The more the boxer tried to clean the blood the more messy his face became and the ladies began to look away. The bell saved further embarrassment and the seconds quickly patched up their boxer. Every time Bijli scored, there was a loud sound because everyone had become quiet now, and the sound was deafening.

In the second round Bijli took a few more points and hit a couple of punches on the Delta company boxer's nose causing more bleeding—the Referee stopped the fight and requested the doctor to have a look. At the doctor's nod of disapproval he called the boxers and Bijli was declare the winner.

Surinder shook Damar Bahadur's hand and smiled—it was their first win.

At the other end Preeti had shouted so much that she had lost her voice!

Charlie Company had two more fights that day—one was Tulsi's fight and the second was that in the Light Heavy weight. Surinder was not so worried about this fight, because Sohan Lal Gharti was a very tall heavy and athletic boxer– one could call him stylish in a way and he was very quick in sizing up his opponent.

Tulsi, cook, gentle giant was quite another matter—would he hold?

Anyway as soon as Charlie won the fight after Sohan Lal Gharti knocked out his opponent with a fine combination of three punches—eyes were on Tulsi. Santa Bahadur was busy coaching him and giving him tips on what to do.As Tulsi entered the ring, his stance changed and he was no longer the figure of gentleness– in his place stood a strong contender ready to fight for his company—even Surinder and Damar Bahadur Sahib were taken aback! He stood tall, jogging lightly and banging his fists to the beat. As he looked in Surinder's direction, he raised one glove to show his confidence!

A fighter in every way!

The Admin Company washerman entered the ring and one could make out his dismal body language before the fight– he had already lost the fight—Tulsi also sensed this. As the boxers faced each other Tulsi let fly and before Hira Singh knew it he had been lifted from his moorings and was on the canvas! As everyone roared—good sense prevailed on him and he decided to let the count begin—the referee began the count and Hira Singh got up after it was over—Tulsi had won and Charlie carried him on their shoulders! It had been a great day—Charlie had done well and created a new boxer this day!

Someone started singing—

Charli ko bhale le– poti payi na mayale!

Charlie ko bhale ta—auncha chap samauncha--

Surinder and Dammar Bahadur congratulated their coach Santa Bahadur! The next day would be tense because Charlie had four fights again. A lot depended on wins, because if Charlie won these bouts the others would not be able to catch up with them—Surinder took Subedar Sahib and the coach to the Mandir for some thanksgiving and to pray or success in the coming days. Panditji smiled because other companies would get to know that Charlie Company had paid a visit to the Temple and soon the others would follow suit!

It was always good to have the Goddess on your side before a competition!

The next day the bouts began and excepting for Pirthi Lal, all the other boxers, Top Bahadur, Lila Bahadur and Hom Bahadur won. Pirthi Lal's fight was very technical, both boxers were good and knew exactly how to gain points and keep score, but the referee reprimanded Pirthi too many times with the result that he lost heart.

Surinder did not protest because he felt it was bad manners to do so.

It promised to be a tough fight in the Finals. The Charlie Company leadership was tense because the Delta boxers were homing in for the kill too. Tulsi had taken them by surprise but they had made up by winning as many points as Charlie, and who knows they might have an ACE up their sleeve!

Surinder told Subedar Sahib to keep an eye on Delta. As he turned to leave, there was little Bal Bahadur, the Adjutant's messenger with a circular for him—he was to leave immediately for a cipher cadre being organized by the Brigade Headquarters---underneath was an envelope addressed to him.It was from the Adjutant—

Hey relax—I know you will miss the boxing finals, but the CO has fixed up accommodation in the Brigade Mess and a jeep is waiting—take the missus along—one of the boys for the Map Reading Exam will act as a sahayak. Yenjoy yourself for a week!

Surinder was just not amused but CO must have tried to get him off, and made it easier for him with the extras. Preeti would love a change– he would get to know her better and of course Bhoopi Dalal from the Dogras, was there with his charming wife Tania, and their lovely two year old daughter.

Chaubatia was a beautiful place.

There was no choice and so with a heavy heart he got his order group together and briefed them in detail about the patrolling exercise due that evening, the detailed preparation for the Boxing Finals and of course the reminder that minute to minute details must be given to him about the matches—he would phone from the brigade exchange at 2100hrs sharp.

Preeti was surprised at the sudden change in plan so they packed quickly and left in the jeep. It was dark and there was no choice but to take some packed food along—Surinder had one packed for the driver as well and soon they were going down hill towards the Kosi river from where it was all uphill to Ranikhet and then Chaubatia. Classes would begin early next morning so they slept as soon as they had changed. Surinder arranged for Preeti to meet him for lunch at the Brigade Officer's Mess and then they walked down to Bhoopi's place– the Dalals were expecting them.

Oye Sardar– tu shadi kar baitha? To-- uska kya hoga? You got married– now what is the fate of the other one?

Preeti—looked at her husband's face then at Bhoopi's face and finally at Tania who burst into a smile—

Preeti– *inko seriously mat lena--Yeh course mate milte hain na to aise hi baten karte hain, sochte hain ham confuse ho jaingi*---Do not take them at face value, when these course mates meet they indulge in this sort of nonsensical chatter designed to confuse us---

Bhupi—*tera kissa Colonel Ahlawat ki chori se nipat gaya ya Budha tere ko goli marne par tula hai—chori to sunder thi aur tere pe marti bhi thi— uska abortion*—(What about your affair with Colonel Ahlawat's daughter, or is the Old Man set on shooting you?No matter what—one has to admit that the girl was a beauty and madly in love with you—abortion--)

Now Tania looked at her husband who appeared to be squirming. Surinder punched Bhoopi on the arm—relax Tania—Bhoopi could not plan an affair with a buffalo, let alone Col Ahlawat's daughter– that girl was something---

As it grew dark, Surinder wanted to go to the exchange to get news of the boxing—

Relax—Surinder, don't get into tension– my neighbor is the *Sparrow* (the nickname for the Brigade Signals Officer)and we will get the call at his place—this was excellent.

Promptly at 2000 hrs the call came through and Surinder burst into a huge grin– Charlie had won! The details did not matter now– winning was enough!

So, a drink was in order, then came a lovely dinner which Taniya had cooked and the evening was over.

In the kitchen– Taniya asked Preeti—what did you make out from Surinder's talk—you think Bhoopi could have--?

Preeti laughed—you– a veteran so so many encounters are asking me this question? I think Bhoopi Bhai Sahib is a very simple person and Surinder is simply pulling your leg.

As they were leaving, Bhoopi asked Surinder—Listen, You can ride a Bullet can't you? So take my bike and after an early brunch tomorrow—take Preeti to Naini Tal—there is a short cut to Garam Pani from Ranikhet, and from there you go to Bhowali and move to Naini Tal– an uphill climb—aur petrol tank bhar ke bike vapas karna! Return me the bike with a full tank OK?

Bloody *kanjoos*—miser

Dekh le agar phir chahiye to full karke vapas kariyo—

Look—if you want the bike again—you better fill her up—

Next time I will, Taniya's parents must have bought the bike for you—you *bhikari*-pauper—

Bhoopi laughed heartily—how well we know each other—I got the bike so that I could take Taniya for a drive—slave for life!

Taniya, what did your parents see in this chap—I sometimes think–how did Bhoopi become an officer—come hand over the bike key!

In the morning, Surinder kicked the bike into action. It roared into life and Surinder was happy with the well tuned and well kept bike. As they turned to drive off the messenger from the paltan waved to him—there was a message for him.

It was from Colonel Katoch.

It simply said- Congratulations—posted to 39 Div as Staff Captain. You have to report after one month- leave granted!

Surinder was happy—he would get time to look after Preeti. So with a song on his lips, Surinder took off for Naini Tal. Ordinarily he would have driven faster, but now he drove carefully because of Preeti's first trip on a bike. The fruit at Bhowali and Naini Tal was gorgeous—peaches plums, apricots and Japanese fruit which did not appeal much to her because of its pungent aroma. Naini Tal was beautiful and the lazy trip in the local boat was great– Preeti did not want to walk too much—her feet became swollen.

They stayed the night in a nice little hotel, watched the lights over the lake at night and planned to return next morning.

As they approached Garam Pani, they stopped at the local dhaba and had some pakoras, puri with tomatoes and potato gravy, with yoghurt raita containing shredded brown cucumber with a tadka of raw mustard oil and rye seeds! It was delicious and they were hungry too. They turned to Raniket to the left—the right turn of this fork would have taken them to Almora.

Another cup of tea and they were home in their room at Chaubatia! Preeti had enjoyed the trip and it was their first contact with the pines–she loved the smell of the oil from which she learnt that turpentine was manufactured. The people were simple—women aged quickly because they worked so hard while their men joined the Kumaon Regiment and other units in the Army! Some had even ventured to join the Air Force or the Navy!

They returned the bike to Bhoopi– tank full of course and since the cadre was over-it was decided that they would return to Almora next day. Bhoopi was happy to hear about the posting and wished them luck. So on arrival at Almora, in a couple of days after he had dashed off his introductory letter to the AQ and the DQ, Surinder was excited to find two DO letters—one from the AQ and the second from the DQ. Both the officers welcomed him to Yol Camp and the DQ wanted him to let him know details of their arrival—in fact he had chalked out a plan for them. A vehicle could be arranged to pick them up from Pathankot but he wanted them to savour their trip to Nagrota and come by the narrow gauge train from Pathankot– the last of these trains which would vanish when the Pong Dam began construction.

Meanwhile a lot had to be done at the battalion end too. Army Headquarters, MS Branch functioned in strange ways as far as postings were concerned. Their motto was if a guy was from the South, then post him North and if he was from the East then post him West—good for national integration!

Charlie Company decided that they would celebrate Surinder's Bara Khana too and they wanted to make it the last event before he left for his posting. The JCO's Club wanted an evening with him as well and there was his dining out from the Mess too.The flat had to be handed over and the luggage was to be packed. Preeti was expecting her first born and everyone cautioned her to be careful while travelling. So they left for Kathgodam and there on to Delhi because Surinder had a couple of days leave and his joining time too.

In Delhi, Preeti was pampered and spoilt by both the families.

Despite the objection from their families, Preeti and Surinder left for Yol Camp by train to Pathankot and got into the narrow gauge train which would take them to Nagrota, the rail head for Yol Camp. Nagrota was a small sleepy town and the only successful business it seems was one of tea and *pakora* stalls. The Station Master greeted Preeti with a *Namaste*, for he could make out that these good folk were going to join the Army garrison at Yol Camp.

Their first view of Yol Camp from Mile 53, - -*Tirvinja Meel*, was lovely and the Military Policeman gave him a smart salute as their jeep halted at the Traffic Check Point or TCP.

As they moved off, Surinder was curious—why had the MP saluted him so smartly? The jeep driver laughed– Sahib– he knows that it is your prerogative alone to issue vehicle permits as the SC'Q'or Staff Captain Q Branch, and it is your signature alone which will allow any vehicle to pass his check point—So—in a way you are his Boss!

Surinder smiled—a unique way to inform him that this was a great privilege entrusted to him

They reached the DQ's house and were given a warm welcome by the family. The DQ was Major Kuldeep Singh from the ASC– The Army Supply Corps, and Mrs Kuldeep and her daughter fussed over Preeti with girl talk while the boys tried to hog the eats.

How was the journey? Comfortable?-asked Kuldeep.

I would say– a trifle awkward because I had my legs outside the window– but the scenery was beautiful and picturesque.

I have arranged a Guest Room in the Divisional Mess, and you can stay there till you are allotted a house. I spoke to the Station Staff Officer and he has assured me that there is no problem in getting married accommodation. So after you complete the formalities, go over and meet him, collect your allotment letter and speak to the AGE (B& R).Shift in only when you are fully organized. You will be staying in the Red Eagle Colony for now.

Surinder thanked him, and Kuldeep invited him inside for a drink--.

As it grew dark, Mrs Kuldeep called them over for dinner. You both must be tired– and Preeti needs to rest. I will take her to the gynae tomorrow—she needs to get her check up done.I know the Lady Doctor– there is nothing to worry about. You have a lovely road to walk on– use it because Preeti needs exercise.

Surinder and Preeti thanked them and left for their guest room. As they lay in bed—Surinder silently said a prayer for the Kuldeeps for taking care of them!

Kuldeep had suggested that he report to the office in time so that he could be introduced to the AQMG with whom an interview would be arranged, and if he was lucky; his interview with the General would also be arranged.

Meanwhile the DQ would introduce him to the other staff officers.

A Son Is Born

Preeti liked Yol Camp.

The place was beautiful and peaceful, the officers of the Headquarter were very considerate and friendly according to their rank and status. Branch heads kept their officers together and the ladies seemed to do the same. True, there was healthy rivalry, but the aim was to get on with the job at hand and make the GOC, (General Officer Commanding, a Major General) feel that he was running a fine outfit, enable him to look after major issues like operations and training, and keep him away from the mundane aspects of routine nature. In the Indian Army, the GS Branch or the General Staff Branch considers themselves superior to the others, while Administration is generally taken for granted!

Ho jaye ga!—meaning—it will take care of itself!

Surinder found himself learning quickly—there was no formal training—one saw an issue, dug up the pages of the connected files, read the minute sheets and directions and carried on from the last noting. If you did not understand procedure, the dealing clerk put up the references-Army Orders or Army Instructions, on the subject; for you to read and interpret intelligently.

The AQ, or the AQMG, was a large portly officer, Lt Col Ajay Verma, and the only problem was that his mind sharp, as it was on administrative points, worked at a complete tangent when it came to other issues. If you asked him for leave, he would attach so many tasks for you to do, that it was not worth going home for your own specific work.

And he loved to eat.

If he was leaving from a party, and someone said,

Sir, what do we do with these fish fingers?

Verma Sahib would return to the embarrassment of his wife, and casually polish off what was left.

It was the same thing at the club—he would saunter in early examine what was being served, eat a plate or two and if some unit representative asked him to sign, he would give a dirty look to the man and which said– *write that off, Man—don't bother me, it was my duty to king, country and division to taste the snacks!*

Surinder received a buzz from him on the intercom—come over, said the AQ.

Find out what is a buzz or a buss—you know those European ladies do this when they greet you—

Sir that is a BUSS, it a touch of the cheeks, on both sides of the face while the lips pucker up into a kiss like formation, and sometimes a kissing sound follows!

Are you sure, Surinder?

Yes Sir. any problem Sir?

Nothing much, the new Army Commander has a French wife and sometimes she greets you as per the European custom—one needs to be prepared!

Don't worry, Sir. You let her do her part– you go along, only– don't make the kissing sound!

The AQ laughed, the tension was broken and he was told him to run off!

So, in his routine job, Surinder grew in stature and found that his skills in writing minute sheets had improved considerably and they returned from the GOC with a complimentary remark! Kuldeep was also pleased that he had learnt intricate jobs of Q Branch efficiently and he handled his counterparts at the Brigade well. From Major Kuldeep he learnt the art of handling an ASC battalion and how movement was planned by road by working out road capacity and thus working out convoy schedules using set formulae. The Audit guys taught him to demand the correct amount of funds and distribute them to the formations according to their holding of large and small fire places—*sigri* as it was known those days!

The phone rang and he casually said—Surinder!

The voice on he end was a lady's and she just said– *Surinder Bhai Sahib*--Brother—just bring some transport and come—your wife needs to go to the Military Hospital—it is time.

Surinder jumped consulted Major Kuldeep, who told him to reach home– his car would be there in five minutes. Preeti had packed her clothes and one small suitcase for the baby. At the MH or Military Hospital, the nurses took Preeti for a check up and admission formalities were completed.

The Senior Sister smiled and advised Surinder to return to the office—there was time.

Let us see what you get in this lottery!

The call came from the hospital after lunch, the nursing officer literally shouted—come over, its a boy—and don't forget the sweets!

Surinder thought– so much excitement over a boy seemed warranted– on the contrary she would have meekly informed him in a hushed tone that it was a girl! Typically Indian enthusiasm for a male child—one who would carry on the lineage and torch the mortal remains of his father!He would have been equally happy if it had been a daughter!

Anyway, it was great news and he went up to the hospital with the sweets and the baby's suitcase—God bless Preeti– she has packed everything so carefully. Surinder beamed at her and gave her a loving kiss on her forehead for giving him this lovely gift. Then he took the little bundle of happiness from her and gazed at him in wonder as the little one unconsciously caught his hand with his long and delicate fingers, and smiled.He wondered whom would the little one look like– but he knew that babies change several faces before they decide to keep one of them.

Welcome to the family little one—we will make a great team– you me and your wonderful mother—perhaps I will learn more from you than I will be able to teach you, because you are thirty years ahead of me already!

He handed over the little one back to Preeti for safe keeping—it was October and a little chill had crept into the air. Beeji is coming tomorrow, so i will breathe easier. And he held Preeti's hand lovingly for she had been through a great ordeal—in India– people said that it was a second life for a woman after she had delivered a child. They had no words except admiration for their creation; for parents think that they alone have created a miracle—which was true.

As they examined and admired the little one, the Ayah, or the attendant maid came over and pressed a small black bindi or dot worn by Indian women on their forehead; behind his ear to ward off evil from the boy! She looked at Preeti and warned her not to feed the child when visitors were around, and also to give her husband Surinder the bottle of honey so that he could put some of it on the baby's tongue! Surinder took out his little Braun camera and began clicking photographs for all he was worth—the excitement was thick in the air and quietly he pinched himself to convince himself that he had truly become a DAD!

Preeti signalled Surinder that he should give ayah fifty rupees. Ayah took the money and thanked the child and blessed him. May he be an illustrious and famous human being and make you both proud!

Soon there was a flurry of activity as all the officers of the headquarter turned up together to see the little one and congratulate Preeti and Surinder. There was genuine excitement and the ladies pressed cash into the baby's hands as *Muh Dikhai*—or first gaze of the baby and his welcome into this world and the family. Blessing were abundant and Surinder kept offering sweets. The AQ looked at him—this will not do *Beta(* Son)—we look forward to a proper party with lots of delicious eats!

They went as quickly as they had come—everyone wanted Preeti to rest. There would be time for fun and laughter later. Surinder reluctantly parted from Preeti and requested the ayah to take care of Preeti and sleep in her room. The ayah nodded—she would be with Preeti till she was discharged!

Surinder had a song on his lips and his feet seemed to dance on their own, a light breeze was in the air and it was a wonderful scene. Surinder stopped in his tracks and looked up at the heavens– and though he was never a seriously religious guy, he said a small- Thank You, to the Maker, for this gift he would always treasure.

As Surinder reached home, Mrs Sharma accosted him—Captain Surinder– *kitne pound ka baby hua?* How many pounds did the baby weigh at birth?

About seven lbs-said Surinder

The baby is definitely weak—my girls were both nine lbs each.

Surinder was exhausted, but despite this he asked if he could sit on the chair in the lawn and requested for a glass of water. As he finished the glass of water he said—

Mrs Sharma, in Kanpur there is a large mandi where chicken and other birds are sold and adjacent to it; some keep eggs for sale.

One fine day, a large car drove upto one of the vendors and a very well dressed portly gentleman stepped out.

He asked the vendor to show him eggs and also indicate their prices.

The old Muslim vendor looked at him showed him an egg and said– 4 annas.(25 paise. annas were used as currency before India switched to the metric system and to paise. there were 16 annas in a rupee)

No this will not do– show me something bigger.

So our vendor showed him a bigger egg for 8 annas.(50 paise)

Show me something bigger—so the vendor produced a fairly large egg for a rupee.

Not satisfied our friend asked the vendor to show him something still bigger and ceremoniously placed two rupees on the counter.

Without blinking an eye lid our vendor opened his drawer took out two rupees and placed them atop the first two and said–

No thank you– I do not want to kill my poor chicken!

Mrs Sharma blushed, ran inside and never bothered him again!

Mummy came over in the train from Delhi and Surinder brought her home from the station. On arrival, she took charge and wanted to proceed to the hospital immediately. Surinder smiled for there was a saying– *asal se sood jyada pyara hai*! It meant that the interest is dearer than the principal. Beeji kissed Preeti and looked lovingly at her grandson, thanked her children for this wonderful gift, and proceeded to fall head over heels in love with her grandson; with whom she struck up a long and affectionate conversation!

She was a graduate– one of the few women who studied in 1941, in undivided India; and was a fiery orator during her time and a member of the Students Union, till her father a senior officer in the Audit Department requested her to resign her membership—lest he lose his job. The British were bent on their policy of subjugating the minds of the Indian populace, she explained and she laughed; because– young children in 1935, had to recite the following verse, with fervour during the Coronation, or Tajposhi of Emperor George V:

> *JUG JIYE SADA BADSHAH-- Long live the Emperor*
> *GEORGE PANCHAM KHUDAYA-- His Majesty George V*

But there were naughty ones who said :

> *ABC, tu kithe gayi si?-- ABC, where did you go?*
> *EDWARD mar gaya, main pitan gayi si.-- I had gone to mourn at Edward 's funeral!*

Beeji was in a very happy mood and as she showed Preeti the gifts she had brought for them, she told them the people in the Punjab had struggled against the British. The people called those who were Government servants– TODI! So they chanted loudly on the streets:

> *Inqualaf jinda baad—long live the freedom struggle*
> *Todi bacha Hai Hai- -A curse on government servants*
> *Angrezki hakumat taba kar do- -Destroy the British Rule*
> *Desh ka nara– JAI HIND!—the country's slogan is– Long Live Hindustan!*

As students they had participated in the khadi movement and worn khadi much to the chagrin of their parents, because her father was a senior government officer and her brother was a King's Commission officer in the Medical Corps, who did not want any problems from the British. But there was the better side too—there was no corruption and in one isolated case where a lawyer was caught accepting a bribe of a measly 100 rupees there was hell to pay! She bemoaned the fact that this gentleman had no place to hide after this incident, but today one does not seem to care even if one is caught stealing thousands of crores!

In 1943, their servants--a pair of brothers who were absconding; after stealing from their house. These rogues, were caught in three days and all the stolen articles including their dolls were returned, by the Police—all this with an apology from the *Thanedar*!(SHO)

Beeji had interesting anecdotes from her younger days and could liven up the conversation. She had seen good days becoming bad when partition took place and she had seen the misery affected by the move to Delhi forced upon the family, but she was a practical soul and preferred not to dwell on this aspect too long—one had to move on. She adored Preeti, who loved her like her own mother and their camaraderie made Surinder happy.

At the dining out party of the ADMS; the Medical Advisor at Division Headquarter, Col P K Sarkar(in jest it was said– *Pee Ke Sarkar aye hain,* or (His Lordship has come after drinking)– the GOC, Major General SK Dogra, shook his hand and congratulated him on becoming a father.

Remember, you have increased your duties manifold and making him your best friend will become your first priority- said the General.

The division was moving out on an exercise and so as per schedule the lorry earmarked for the Q Branch arrived and everyone loaded up. The lorry driver moved out to take his designated place at the convoy ground. They moved out and Surinder enjoyed the lovely scenery during the journey in the hills till they suddenly emerged into the plains! After some forty kilometres, sign posting indicated that they had reached their destination. The lorry had shelters on the sides, the office came up almost the same time as the accomodation for him and as the Q Branch set up a proper office to begin work, it was time for supper. Surinder moved out with the GSO3, a tall lanky officer, Captain Ranjit or Ronnie, set out to scout for a suitable source of drinking water.

Sikh officers acquired nicknames in the Army– so Grewal became Gary, Randhawa became Randy, Sandanwalia became Sandy, and so did a few non Sikh guys like Saxena became Sexy, Bharadwaj became Birdie, Mandhata became Mandy, and also Sandeep became Sandy too and so on—what the heck—it made sense.

They found one next to the camping site and this was examined by the JCO(Junior Commissioned Officer) from the Engineers, who pronounced it fit for use. The farmer had a tube well and told them that they could have unrestricted use of his bore well as long as they left him some diesel when they broke camp! Seemed to be a fair deal—sez you! But the farmer was not satisfied—he had instructed his little daughter to get some lassi or butter milk and some *sarson da saag with a few makki di rotian*(Cornmeal unleaven bread and vegetable from mustard leaves and stems which was considered a delicacy in the Punjab) and humbly offered them to the three officers and the driver. He insisted that it was an honour that their olive green uniforms had graced his fields! From somewhere a couple of charpais or cots were produced and all the *fauji* guys(army guys) swore that this was one of their best meals—it was laced with love and affection from the poor farmer, with a big heart!

Ronnie gave him a bottle of rum.

They returned to camp and when the day's work was done they went to sleep. As Surinder hit the sack, he said a silent Good Night, to his little family which was now his responsibility! He longed to hold them and with these thoughts he dozed off.

The exercise lasted for a couple of days and then the code word to break camp was issued. The vehicles lined up again as per their lanes and took their place in the convoy! Surinder's vehicle driver was a chatterbox and regaled him with stories of his time in the Army, strange experiences he had been through and strange customs he had witnessed in the border areas where he had served. India was a big country and the government apparently had not established contact as the Army had done.

He told him of Morang in Himachal, ahead of Shimla, where polyandry was practiced.

Surinder understood that this practice had nothing to do with the locals of that region claiming lineage with the Pandavas, the five brothers who had one wife– characters from the epic– The Mahabharata. It was simply that cultivable land was scarce in the mountains and to prevent fragmentation the people had found succour in adopting polyandry! All the children born from such marriages were termed as the children of the eldest brothers. There was a surplus of unwed females in the region and therefore children born out of wedlock were accepted as part of the village progeny. The story was that during a Mela, or get together a group of brothers kidnapped the girl of their choice and took her to their house where she lived with them and if she passed the stringent tests, she would be brought back to her father's house and then married to the brothers! All her children would be the legitimate children of the eldest brother.

But sometimes the bride came to a family, one of her husbands could be a small baby, and as he grew up in age– so did she and it was difficult to find the young boy consummating his wedding night with an old woman!

And so such husbands wanted to marry someone their age! That's when trouble began to brew!

He also told him of a convoy which had halted at a place called *Khatra Dhang*—and the drivers had gathered to brew tea for it was cold.It was a small slippage at first, and then all hell broke loose as all the vehicles were covered in mud. All of them were carrying ration for the troops. The Army then decided to build a road over the convoy instead of recovering them because the cost factor was not commensurate with the effort! One could even now see portions of this convoy sticking out from below the road—a very grim reminder to all drivers!

The golden apples of this region were legendary for their colour and sweetness, but could not be ferried across the river in small steel baskets. So the locals made a local brew called *ghanti* from it! Wild apricot grew in abundance and when you walked through the villages your feet sank into the mushy fruit which had fallen from the trees. The locals collected the inners, broke out the almond shaped seeds and extracted the oil from them which was handy for massage, hair oil and also a cooking medium.

They called it *chuli ka tel.*

The region also grew hops for the beer industry!

With such chatter, they reached home! But it dawned on Surinder that India was indeed a great country—with great diversity—if only we had been blessed with good governance and sensible politicians—instead of those who were uneducated, criminals and believed in the policy that–

Charity begins at home!

Their first Bajaj scooter arrived soon and the little family would get on board and go for a ride from Yol to *Tirvinja Meel* or Mile 53, wave to the MPs there and proceed to Gaggal, then turn to Dharamsala and have an ice cream. There was this quaint shop which ordered Kwality Ice Cream probably from Pathankot for people like Surinder. After the ice cream they would head back to Yol Camp via Sidhbari and drove up the slope to their house.

Petrol was a rupee a litre and lasted for a long time, till the OPEC countries played Merry Hell into the economy. It was difficult to survive and at times he was forced to draw petty amounts from his account. Surinder's pay as a Captain was now Rs 850/-.

The small cantonment also boasted a cinema hall run by the Canteen Stores Department The manager told Surinder of an interesting story. The drummer who went from village to village to announce the arrival of a new film played so beautifully on his drums, that many of the village women wanted to marry him because they went into a trance, when he played.

He had accumulated six wives so far!

It was a terrible time for those with salaries!

Back home Preeti realised that she had to attend a wedding in the family—it was one of those- must attend types. She needed a suitable wardrobe too and this could only be accomplished if her cousin cooperated. So Surinder bunged in his application for leave, despite the issues raised by the AQ, because, he had to go.

Leave was sanctioned.

He asked his six foot four inch sahayak, Mohar Singh, a Guardsman, to look after the house in his absence. Initially, Preeti was scared of him, but gradually she found that he was a gentle giant.

Pat came the reply—*Sahib tu ja– main yahan aise bathun jaise aande pe murgi!*

Sahib you go—(sic) sans worry—I will sit here like a hen sits on her eggs!

Then he went upto Preeti– *Mem sahib—mere jaise jawan ke bagair baju ke sweater ke liye kitni uun lage hai?*

Preeti told him that it would take approximately ten ounces or so—she had no clue herself.

Thik hai ji-aap mere liye oon leti aana aur ek sweater bana dena!

Ok you buy the wool and knit me a sweater.

Preeti was horrified. She hastened to her mother and discussed the issue with her—her wise mother decided to get a professional to do the job. Mohar Singh had ordered her to make one with a design– so that is what the professional was requested to do.

When she reached home Mohar singh tried on the sweater and beamed at her appreciatively.

From that day she was his best friend, guide and philosopher—he would open his heart to her and take her advice on matters personal.

One day in a lighter vein he told her of this woman in the Bihari village, a soldier's wife, who went to the Bank for a small loan. The manager asked her to sign. She looked dumbfounded.

Woman do you write to your husband?

Yes, I do but the Postman writes the letter for me.

Do you sign it? Yes, I do. said the woman.

Then write whatever you sign, over here.

So the woman held the pallu or corner of her saree in her teeth and scrawled

Tumhar Chumban ke intejar mein (Waiting For your kisses)

Tumhar Phulwa (Your Phulwa)

The Cantonment Bazaar was a long barrack type affair which had refugees who had settled down in the place and prone to speaking pure Punjabi. For a price, especially before a party one could give the vegetable vendor a list of stuff required for a party and you could have whatever you needed, delivered to you. A small poultry farm provided the fowl and milk came from the village through their maid servant.

JB turned up at Yol as the Officer Commanding of the workshop. His wife Manjeet was a happy go lucky girl who seemed to fit into JB's clothes and everyone had a whale of a time wondering who was wearing whose clothes. They also had a mood meter which indicated which of them was getting horny or was already in the mood. Sometimes they played rummy and the loser had to offer himself to the winner! Once when Preeti asked Manjit why they had not expanded their family—Manjit laughed and said– listen, in our house we cannot even make yoghurt leave alone a child– maybe it's the *jaag*(the small amount of curd which is mixed in warm milk to set the yoghurt) is defective—hinting at something else very similar.

Jb's house was full of caricatures by Italian prisoners who had been lodged there. Some seemed accomplished artists. Obviously the prisoners liked their stay in Yol Camp because the place was lovely and one could see the scenery right upto Kangra.

By now they had company in the form of bandicoots– large rats who managed to frighten the cats away!

JB and Manjeet wore each other's clothes in turn– a uni- sex type of arrangement and since bell bottoms were the rage of those days– their clothes looked appropriate on them unless of course the trousers were shocking pink or turquoise in colour!

Handa was posted in the Sikh battalion based in the cantonment and PSC Nair, dubbed Pussy Nair was posted in the Artillery Brigade Headquarter as the GSO3.Surinder enjoyed playing a hard game of squash with them and during the break remembering old times.

Pussy's wife did not know a word of English or Hindi, so the ladies found a way to communicate with her. She was very affectionate and won everyone with her smile. Life was fun with four course mates together, till

Ronnie turned up in the Engineer Regiment. This made it five and it was a comforting feeling to be together.

Major Kohli from the Maratha light infantry was posted at Dharamsala in the NCC(National Cadet Corps) unit there.One day he told us a very interesting anecdote.

His small staff comprised of soldiers of the Sikh Light Infantry– a couple of JCOs and NCOs.One fine day he caught them in a disused shed, brewing liquor. Immediately, under the supervision of the senior JCO he had them locked up.In the evening, he heard a knock on the door and was surprised to find the wives of the soldiers outside.

Sahibji, Have you locked up our husbands?

Yes! said Major Kohli– looking very embarrassed.

Please do not let them out because they were brewing that stuff at home and went to that shed only because we would not let them brew it at home!

When they left, Major Kohli decided that he had taught them a lesson and that they should be let them out now. He therefore passed suitable orders for them to be released.

Once again there was a knock on the door and this time the culprits were standing outside with a bottle of some pale liquid.

Sirji, can we come in? they pleaded.

What is it?

Sir we know you are very annoyed with us, and you have every right—whatsmore you can give us a slap each to round off the request. But we have a boon to ask of you. We made this stuff with great love and affection—we do not know what to name it, but it is not only potent stuff, but it has chicken, almonds, dried prunes and other delicacies like cinnamom and cardamom.

Sir, we would be honoured if you tasted the stuff.

*Kohli could not resist a laugh from these loveable and incorrigible rogues, and had a drink—and he swore it was better than a scotch—wish he had patented the damn recipe!**

*Such jokes lose their flavour when they are narrated in English—they make you laugh your guts out only when narrated in Punjabi!

GAMES GENERALS PLAY

Yol Camp was a small cantonment and was perched on a hill side with a water source from the Echo Khud above the Cantonment. The GOC was an avid golfer who was always dreaming of hitting his perfect shots as soon as it was time for lunch. Then, without wasting time for lunch, he would change and drive off to the Golf Course, which was at some distance; and join his foursome, who had to be in time, because they knew that the General was very prone to irritation, if they teed off later than the appointed time. The General subscribed to the famous theory, that good generals only commanded divisions and corps or armies in their spare time– for prime time was spent on the Golf Course; where one could propound one's theories to his staff and they could present their views candidly and without fear!

It was also a game he reasoned which could be played well or otherwise; in one's head, because irritations, tension and anger was clearly reflected in the manner that you swung your clubs at the helpless ball—a very unpredictable creature which could change its ideas during the course of its flight; indicating the state of the turbulence in your mind! You were therefore playing against yourself and not against your opponents. Above all, you could beat the shit out of the ball, if it represented someone who had been unduly unfair to you and satisfaction came in the form of a lofted shot, appreciated by one and all—all you had to do was to doff your cap and take a bow.

And, you never forgot to collect your golf winning money no matter how small it was.

So it became a tradition– all the heads of the arms and services bought golf sets, wore beautifully coloured shirts and two toned golf shoes with spikes; and stood waiting in all their splendour for their chieftain to take notice of them. To be invited to play in the General's foursome, was an honour and soon they learnt that it was impolite to win and very correct to be humble when they fired off a lovely shot, but applaud vociferously when the general hit a *wunder by thunder* shot! Some even honed their skills at losing simple putts to allow the Old man a win, but the General was no fool and made a mental note of such follies as he called them, while writing their Annual Confidential Reports.

Once in a while, a picnic was organised at the Golf Hut, where the ladies indulged in putting competitions, at ten in the morning. The golfers participating in the Golf Tournament teed off in the wee hours, so that they could take a break for breakfast and applaud the putters.

The tournament lasted till lunch, after which there was a lot of beer to drink followed by lunch with an exquisite cuisine.

Then there was the prize distribution and after which everyone went home happy that they had done some reasonably constructive work—liaison with families– some chit chat with the staff and of course showed their golfing armour to one and all, and; their newly acquired designer golf sets to the General!

One evening, it was confirmed– the General had received his posting orders.

The new GOC was an infantry general with a keen interest in hockey. He liked his commanding officers and their officers to play troops games and did not encourage elitist games like golf which were designed only for a privileged few!

Woe is me—every golfer took his golf set, sat with his sahayak, both armed with a toothbrush each and cleaned the golf clubs, before mothballing them for future use; sighing wistfully every few minutes or so!

Regimental tailors were summoned and ordered to make black shorts for everyone– *jaldi jaldi*—quickly, because there was no time and word had reached that the new General would like to play a game of six a side hockey– his team of officers would be the top brass at the division headquarters versus the rest. The sweet meat contractor was instructed to have some *jalebi* (–that concertina type of thick Indian noodle, which was later immersed in sugar syrup after it was fried and used the principle of osmosis to absorb the syrup)ready for the match. He would also make some pakora and the three cornered favourite– *Samosa.*

All the station ladies and children were invited to witness the match and other officers were ordered to attend. The six a side ground was decked up as though a jousting arena of medieval days had been established, with buntings and coloured flags and a pipe band in attendance.

The General arrived wearing his black shorts—he was from a Gorkha

Rifle battalion, and his strong legs and fit body indicated that he was used to a tough regime– his body showed no signs of fat anywhere.

An outdoors officer!

As the referee whistled, the teams entered the ground and the GOC's team looked like a ice hockey team from the USSR. But the bravado did not last long because one does not really exert one's muscles in golf—whereas the officers from the divisional troops teams were very fit. It was agonising to watch the division headquarter team trailing by a dozen goals while there was ample time to go!

The agony ended finally as the referee blew his closing call and the GOC realised that he had been rather harsh on his officers—they needed exercise and he therefore ordered all of them to report for physical training with the troops so that they could shape up in time for the next match! Word had spread and the fixtures in his visits to the brigades featured hockey matches instead of golf as had been the custom hither to fore!

The pipers played and did some fancy footwork marching and playing in figures of eight and in circles and in columns like their performance during a band competition and then the drummers gave a demonstration of their prowess and had everyone clapping for them– young and old!

There was change in the air—instead of lonely ladies walking in groups, amidst a loud cackle of laughter when one of them let off a joke– a naughty one of course– the scene was now replaced by one of husband and wife walking in pairs– the officer wearing a sweaty tee shirt indicating that he had just come from a hockey match!

A group of girls from a Jamia College was standing together during a break when one of them asked;

Listen Jamila– do the men folk crack dirty jokes like we do?

Said Jamila– Don't you worry Leila—they do too, but our standard is considerably higher in this field.

I say Jamila– what if we were cracking our dirty jokes and a male overheard us?

Arey Leila hona Kya hai—uske kaan khare ho jayenge! Oh if he overhears us, his EARS will get erect!

Leila crossed her arms and touched her ears—Main na janti thi– use kaan kehte hain! I never knew that– Ears was the name for IT!!(Sir Penis)

A few months passed and everyone looked fit– the GOC's team was now considered a strong team having donated its flab in exchange of solid muscle, for it was time for the Annual Confidential reports to be initiated. Someone in some vague corner must have been a shammer (a lazy bum) because his prayers were answered and a posting order came in announcing that the GOC was to move without awaiting his relief to a posting in the Northern Sector– to replace a GOC who had been injured in a vehicle accident. *Fuck you Charlie*—this was the second change of a GOC in the last seven months or so—there was no time for farewells— there was just no time.

And so we said *Au Revoir* to our GOC of six months and waited with abated breath for what the wind would blow in. There was no long wait and a brigadier waiting for his slot was promoted and appeared one fine day without warning to out little town.The Military Policeman at Mile 53 rang up his Commanding officer and told him in gasps, that the new GOC had just crossed his post with his wife, and was headed for the Headquarter Officer's Mess in his blue Ambassador.

The message was relayed to the Colonel General Staff and from there to the AQMG and both of them scrambled post haste to receive the general while the Military Police sent a pilot jeep to escort the GOC to the Mess, and a driver to drive the General's car. The GE was instructed to quickly open the Flagstaff House so that the GOC could visit, in case he wished to. The Mess Secretary was ordered to have Number One Guest Room reorganised, a message sent to the Station Commander and the Reception Committee was ready. The pilot reported the progress of the GOC and soon he arrived at the Mess.

The General settled for a glass of beer and someone asked the lady whether she would like a coke. She requested that a glass of wine would do and took many by surprise– news travelled fast; there was a sudden demand for wine which was lying surplus in the Canteen, (because no one wanted it)—and in no time dry, sweet and the bottles of bubbly were gone! The senior officers and Messes were getting ready for the welcome dinners. The more enterprising officers began teaching their spouses to acquire the art of drinking wine much to their discontentment; because in Indian households wine is taboo for the ladies, except the liberated ones!

The next day during the morning tea– the Colonel GS asked the GOC whether he would like to play hockey or play golf. The GOC looked at him and said that neither of these appealed to him– he was addicted to squash—did anyone play squash?

Up went a couple of hands and the GOC smiled.

By afternoon an officer who knew what a squash ball and a racquet looked like, was despatched to Pathankot secretly, with explicit orders to purchase them in bulk, because one never knew whether this GOC could just complete his full tenure!

After a few weeks the casualties of the game were visible—some were limping– a sprain is it—some had their arms in a sling and others had a pulled muscle or a torn ligament! To top it up the GOC suggested that the next party be organised at the club where there would be a water polo match between the division staff and the division troops.

Everyone groaned because most of their stalwarts were already sporting plasters and slings. Surinder suggested that the units of the div troops be milked for their team which was agreed to.So the match started with all the non players and the ladies watching. Everyone laughed when someone received a dunking without realising the poor guy's misery. Anyway the div staff won by cheating a little and everyone trooped to the toilets for a shower and a change.

That was when Surinder realised that his wedding ring was missing.

He tried to recapitulate on the circumstances and realised that he had been standing near the staircase twirling his ring after the match and that was the time it could have slipped off his finger, a little wrinkled and shrunk after the prolonged stay in the water. He spoke to the keeper at the pool and indicated to him the exact spot where the ring had gone down.

Next morning, as he went to the pool, he found the keeper grinning from ear to ear and flashing the ring. Surinder was relieved and gave him fifty rupees which was a big sum those days. Gold was about two hundred and fifty rupees per 10 grams then.

As he narrated the story to Preeti, she showed her annoyance by pouting– a gesture which could not be ignored—so Surinder kissed her lips till she burst into laughter and pretended to beat him up.

PROMOTION

As Surinder completed his second year at the Division Headquarter, he realised that he had become very good at his job—he could devise excellent solutions, and short cuts for tricky administrative problems and could put them into action swiftly. This obviously pleased the AQ and his DQ, who could relax knowing that Surinder was capable of handling issues on his own and coming to them only if things were beyond his control.

It was fun working with the AQ—

Whenever Surinder presented him with a brilliant draft, the AQ would change the commas or full stops without changing the text. Then he would look at Surinder and say—This is how you make a draft– not the amateurish stuff you guys put up. It is really so simple.

Surinder would look away and laugh when he came back to his office.

It also made Surinder very confident! One brilliant minute sheet which he sent to the General came back with glowing remarks, but the AQ said nothing in particular. When Surinder asked him whether he had liked the comments—the AQ remarked:

Listen Surinder– if I have not criticised your work, it means I have liked your effort—don't go fishing for complements!

Little Jaskaran had started to walk and his inquisitive ways were very difficult to fathom—like Preeti had found him in a puddle and trying to put his finger into the 15 amp socket. Slowly the two of them learnt that Jas was more dangerous when all was quiet on the western front, because then you knew he was into something extremely naughty or interesting! Once he gave Preeti a fright when she caught him trying to catch a baby lizard! Another time was when she found him trying to go down the stars head first—only her quick thinking saved Jas from a serious misadventure.

The next day, Surinder was pleasantly surprised when at the get together at ten every morning, in the tea room, the GOC told him that he had been posted back to his battalion. Very soon, Surinder also received a demi official letter(DO) from his 2IC, welcoming him to the battalion and congratulating him on picking up his rank of Major! This was great news and as a senior Major, he was now posted to Support Company. So, in the evening, Surinder broke the news to Preeti and told her they were going back to Almora—many of the officers she had met had gone—some on postings and some commissioned during the Emergency, had not made it through the Selection Boards. These two years had gone so fast that he had not noticed.

That evening there was a party in the club, in honour of a visiting senior officer. The Gorkha battalion at Dharamsala had sent their jazz band which was very good and those little fellows could belt out English, Hindi and Himachali songs by the dozen. Surinder and Preeti danced till they were dizzy! Surinder was very nostalgic and began to miss his own battalion jazz band which was equally good if not better.

Anyway, the 2IC of the ASC battalion sent him some wooden crates, Major Ramachandran-Ramu, from the Engineers sent him a painter, and a carpenter and soon Surinder was preparing for his move to the battalion or paltan as it was affectionately called. They had increased their luggage many fold since the birth of Jaskaran. Preeti did a survey and gifted Jaskaran's unwanted clothes away to whoever wanted them for they were almost new.

They were to be dined out and were the guests for the evening. The GOC and all the other officers welcomed them to the Mess and inquired about his paltan and everyone vowed that they would keep in touch. At the end of dinner, Surinder was presented the Division Headquarter momento by the GOC, and a short speech followed. Surinder in turn thanked everyone present for the honour they had bestowed on them and thanked the General for the momento presented to him. The General, knowing that Surinder was from the Gorkhas, and that most Gorkha officers learnt the language and songs, requested Surinder to sing for them.

Goreto Tyo gaon Ko– was a very lilting song about a guy who is unable to find the small *pagdandi* or track to his sweetheart's village-cause he is drunk!

Many of those present did not know that a Sikh officer could sing a Nepalese song so well and congratulated Preeti—who felt happy at the compliments! What they did not know is that singing was encouraged and was part of growing up in a Gorkha paltan—and the boys loved it! Then a chair was brought and Surinder sat on it and while everyone lifted the chair out of the Mess and sang

–For He's a Jolly Good Fellow, he's a Jolly Good Fellow– so say all of us–

He was thus dined out of the Mess!

The next few days were hectic because everyone knew that packing was tough, so a long list of invitations was given to Preeti; in fact those who could not invite him home were trying to arrange packed dinner for them and soon they moved to the railway station at Pathankot from where the broad gauge train would take them to Delhi and from there to Kathgodam. Surinder had some joining time so he decided to break journey at Delhi and spend some prime time with their parents– very eager to see Jaskaran. But such time passes quickly and it was time to leave for the paltan. Two vehicles were waiting for them at the Kathgodam Railway Station– some stores had been delivered at Bareilly by the Quarter Master, the returning one ton and three ton vehicles were told to wait for Surinder Sahib.

With the tarpaulin half rolled up, the vehicle was readied for Surinder's little family and the vehicle rolled off.

Bhat kata khane hola Sahib? Where would you like to stop for lunch?

Havildar(Sergeant) Dal Bahadur asked Surinder.

*Garampani ma rok dinu, ani keta haru lai bhannu bhat ko paisa dinu pardai na—(*Dal Bahadur-- Please stop at Garam pani—and tell the boys that the lunch is on me)

With that he handed a hundred rupees to the NCO(Non Commissioned Officer).

This was a group of eating joints near a natural source of drinking water and located next to an ancient temple. The menu was basically the same they had eaten when they had gone to Nainital by Bhoopi's bike!

It brought back very pleasant memories of their stop over at Garam Pani!

They went straight to the Officer's Mess and while they had tea, Havidar Gam Bahadur saluted and told him that he had taken over the married accommodation earmarked for him in the new block and would be waiting for him there. A working party had also come from the Company, to assist them in settling down. The flat had been washed thoroughly and essential condiments had been stocked by Captain Muthu and his wife.

Muthu has been posted as the MMG officer after qualifying on the course.

At the flat, Muthu, his wife and Subedar Chand Bir his Senior JCO were waiting for him. After exchanging pleasantries, Mrs Muthu took Jaskaran from Preeti and discreetly told Preeti that she was on the family way too!

This was good news and Surinder jabbed Muthu in the ribs—So,

Intelligent Man(Muthu had been the Intelligence Officer or IO)– you have been very hardly working!

Muthu had a big grin splashed across his face.

Meenu– Muthu's wife was an Army brat and her father had retired as a brigadier. She was well well versed with Army protocol and had prepared dinner for them. So as soon as they had changed they went over to Muthu's place on the first floor. Muthu filled Surinder in with the gup shup of the paltan over a whiskey and they laughed—it was good to be back home! A lot had happened in his absence and he was happy that Charlie was doing well. He would always have a soft corner for the Company no matter where he was posted.

The CO was likely to be posted out and the 2IC would take over the paltan. Though the succession was within the battalion, Surinder knew that he would miss the CO who had guided him throughout and groomed him for the Staff College entrance exam. He had been fair in his assessment of the officers and had never let one isolated incident affect his judgement in writing the confidential reports of the officers. He had led a good team, trained them well and each officer was fit to face any challenge. In fact each officer proceeding on a course was given time to train and was tested before he went to the course. The same applied to the JCOs and the NCOs who went for their courses—the net result was that there was a glut of these guys who had received instructor's grading.

While there was training, he was also careful that the men and their families had some recreation– so the families and their husbands were sent to the Chitai Temple where arrangements for their picnic lunch, had been arranged. So while the boys struck up their madals, or drums, everyone joined in for songs from home; beneath the pine foliage which stretched as far as the eye could see, while all the local women passing by held their *chunris* across their faces and giggled.

News of their impending move to Ladakh came in. Their NMB had also been intimated—NMB stood for NO MOVE BEFORE, an approximate date by which all arrangements for the move needed to be completed. The Advance party had to be prepared and briefed in detail. Orders for handing/taking over weapons and barracks and engineer stores, telephone cables, ammunition and stores were being prepared. Lectures for briefing the troops on the hazards likely to be encountered in snow bound and extreme cold climates. Most of the troops were not used to living in such cold climate and needed to be acclimatised as well.

Inspite of detailed briefings and precautions, the boys of the Advance Party were duped by the outgoing battalion.

The Kanchas were shown the huge heaps of firewood and goaded to weigh one of them. The weight surpassed the purported amount considerably and the boys were happy—only to discover later that the other heaps of firewood had rocks underneath. Similarly they were shown telephone cable and requested to measure it. Since the cable also surpassed the estimates the boys took it over. Then it was discovered that the signallers of the outgoing battalion had been unwinding the cable shown and re-laying the same cable else where. Similarly they took over barrels of kero oil which appeared perfect, but in winter these barrels began making thumping sounds because water in the barrels had frozen. The water had sunk leaving the oil on the top!

The Quarter Master was dumbfounded, there was nothing he could do because there was no malafide intent on any one's part. They had been taken for a ride—*a donkey ride at that.*

Pulmonary oedema was one of the biggest challenges. The next one was frostbite and chilblain, after which we had snow blindness. There was another problem of trying to speak on the radio if it was very cold and a cold wind was blowing. The tips of our fingers grew numb with the cold and then the fingers froze. One could risk losing his fingers if you tried to thaw them out or you even risked leaving patches of skin on your weapon if you tried to hold them with bare hands.

Cold injuries were as bad, if not worse than burn injuries.

The boys learnt that you did not step out in the cold after a couple of drinks—for that could invite pulmonary oedema, because one's lungs filled with water and you had to be evacuated by helicopter where you were put into a compression chamber to get the water out of your chest..

Snow blindness struck in the later part of the night, with eyes burning and water streaming out of them. Minor cases took a day to heal, but serious cases could take more than two days with excruciating pain and a risk of permanent damage. All this for not wearing your snow goggles in the sunlight after snow fall or even in the moonlight, because on a clear night moonlight reflected off snow crystals and had the same effect on one's eyes— after all it was reflected sunlight!

The CO had made the wearing of snow goggles on the forehead, wearing of rubber boots and keeping gloves in the pockets mandatory. Result—no cases of frostbite or snow blindness. There were a few stray cases in the brigade, of barracks going up in flames due to carelessness;

and a couple of cases where a few soldiers had been careless and had to get their limbs amputated after gangrene set in!

Thus it all boiled down that the key word was carelessness!

The Advance Party and the battalion carried out regular acclimatisation everyday for the mandatory period and short cuts were prohibited. Slowly, the boys learnt the nuances of combating problems of extreme cold and life went on as usual. In a blizzard, icicles formed on the copper telephone lines and the WD cables and these broke under the sheer weight of the icicles. As one left the highways and began an ascent or descent towards his destination, one found tell tale markers of deep yellow urine designs made by unknown artists who had discovered their shrivelled *John Thomases*, and braved an attempt to cajole them from layers of clothing to the biting cold outside and take a pee!

As the Medical Officer recalled, during one FFI inspection, one of the JCOs was exasperated to find that his monstrous penis, had shrivelled to such a miniscule size that he could not find it! And then came the myth that one became impotent in the cold, prompting the CO to despatch a team home and this team returned beaming– a sign that they had been successful in their endeavour and that all was well!

One fine day, there was an eerie sound in the middle of the night and the sentry was worried– but the Surinder explained to him that this was the sound of the ice on the frozen lake breaking up or developing large cracks-it was definitely not the *Bokshey* or Boogie man!

In the morning after a little exercise the boys played cricket with frozen brinjals and returned them to Cook, for preparing their afternoon meal after he had successfully thawed them! The cook was trying to make friends with very attractive blackbirds– some with yellow beaks and some with red ones.

One night as Surinder was returning from the Battalion he found Major Sarma, an Assamese officer, trying to extricate, one of his medium guns, whose tow truck had skidded off the road. The cheerful gunners– all South Indians– a motley crowd of Tamils, Andharites, Coorgis and Malayalis were fiercely proud of Sarma and were trying to extricate their vehicle from slipping down further. Surinder and his boys joined in to assist in extricating the vehicle. Another vehicle was hooked up in tandem, and slowly the vehicle which had skidded was pulled back on the road after the gun had been safely unhooked. Both vehicles moved backwards till they were safely on the road.

As soon as their vehicles were safe, Sarma led them in a very spritely gig in celebration of the event!.Surinder joined in because Sarma was a good friend and always gave him a cup of tea when he crossed his unit location The sight of these soldiers dancing in the snow like ghouls in the middle of the night in the beams of the vehicles would have raised the hackles of other ghosts in the neighbourhood! But the prize went to Sarma, an Assamese-- for singing a very popular Tamil song from a popular Shivaji Ganesan movie.

On another occasion, Surinder was moving up to his location in a one ton vehicle, when it started slipping on the ice and as it slithered about fifteen yards or so, the driver became jittery, but Surinder encouraged him by placing an arm on his back and told him to sit still, and control the steering carefully. Suddenly the vehicle hit an obstruction, swerved its nose towards the mountainside and came to an abrupt stop.

Surinder came out gingerly and found that the left wheel 's non skid chain was entangled in a jagged rock frozen in the ice. The right rear wheel was spinning in the air about two feet off the track. Slowly the men got down and it was discovered that an innocent stream which was discharging water on the track, had frozen during the night and caused the vehicle to skid. The boys were great at building sturdy stone structures, and soon Jack Robinson– a nice rest for the right wheel was constructed. Then with their picks they cut tracks for the other three wheels and slowly Gunjaman engaged the four by four gear and launched his vehicle, back to the road. The boys reverently thanked the jagged stone for saving their lives before clambering into their truck!

It was great fun watching the weather gods at play. Initially small motley clouds appeared, like sheep grazing on a huge plain, soon merging to become a large single blanket of clouds through which some of the taller peaks were visible. Then this blanket rose steadily till it rose above us and settled at a higher altitude. It would grow warm and then came the soft snow flakes sailing down rapidly, till they had covered everything in sight. It was now dangerous to meander off the original tracks, because what looked like a flat piece of snow covered land might suddenly cave in and you could land in a hole!

As you walked to your destination especially where it was wooded, you saw spoor of deer and other animals especially musk deer which was very valuable. There were markings from the feet of many birds especially peasants– these were dull looking creatures and not those with bright plumes. Surinder learnt to distinguish some of these signs from boys who were used to similar surroundings back home. This was a bonus and Harish one of the younger officers, had literally written a very interesting piece on the flaura and fauna prevalent on his route of patrolling, which fetched him a pat on his back from the Brigade Commander.

Surinder's post was way up at approximately 14, 000 feet from where he could peek into some of the Chinese defences. Behind his living bunker was a drop covered by black boulders and a lake lay at the foot of the rocks. This was their water source– prohibited for washing clothes, the water was meant purely for drinking. Someone had fuelled the story that the black boulders oozed *shilajit*– a legendary aphrodisiac which enhanced one's sexual libido. Surinder wondered about this but he did realise that this water which they drank without adding any medicine or bleaching powder caused their stomachs no ill effects and gave them all a very healthy appetite and another advantage was that there was no need to keep burping the whole day!

Surinder really missed was his family—Preeti's warm caress and the happy gurgling laughter of his son Jaskaran. As their pact decreed, he dashed off a letter a day to Preeti whether he received one or not and Preeti did the same. The Company runner always checked for Surinder's mail from the office before starting for the Company knowing that Sahib would be waiting anxiously for his mail. Sometimes he would have ten or more letters for him. Surinder would then put the letters together date wise, kissed and began reading them– enjoying every bit of them because Preeti was a natural story teller! Such treats always regaled his spirits and rejuvenated him—melancholy never came near him! He longed to be with his family, and worked himself to exhaustion to avoid such thoughts from entering his mind lest his judgement on routine matters get warped.

Subedar Lok Bahadur was an excellent JCO—he had excelled in all his sports, done extremely well in professional courses, and was an accomplished organiser of the cultural requirements of the battalion during Battle Honour Day and Dushera. He was quite a flamboyant guy too, popular with officers and all other ranks. But he knew that he would become the Subedar Major of the battalion, in his turn. Sometimes the best of men suddenly germinate a worm called *ego*, in their brain. Lok Bahadur had done this and after the initial germination, he had nurtured this worm till it was fully grown and had begun to affect his decisions.

One day as Surinder went to address his company in the Langar, or Dining House, Subedar Lok Bahadur kept him waiting for twenty five minutes in spite of receiving three hints from the CHM that the Company Commander had arrived. It was snowing and Surinder's face was totally covered with snow as he waited patiently for his Senior JCO to give him the report.

When Subedar Sahib eventually reported to him the report was thirty minutes late. Surinder told Subedar Sahib to check the time. He then told the JCO to take off his watch, which had been issued to him, and hand it over to the CHM, so that it could be examined for accuracy. Subedar Sahib was no fool and he realised that he had gone too far.

Galti bhayo Sahib! I have faulted Sir.

Kina Bhayo Sahib? Why did it happen Sahib—Asked Surinder.

Ma Keta Haru lai CO Sahib ko inspection ko vishay ma briefing gari raha ko thiyo, Sahib. I was briefing the boys about the CO Sahib's impending visit.

Briefing to mero kura ko pachi pani honu sakne thiyo? Your briefing could have been after my talk to the boys?

*Lok Bahadur had nothing to say.*He looked at Surinder as if to say– so what are you going to do about it?

*Surinder knew this was a show down.*He would have to tackle the issue firmly without losing his nerve and by showing a very cool temperament.

He calmly continued—Sahib, You are my right hand. If I order my right hand to break a morsel of food and put it in my mouth, but the hand disobeys and shoves the spicy food into my nostril then I want nothing to do with this hand– it needs to be severed and I should learn to use my left hand! I order you to pack up your stuff, go with your Sahayak to the battalion headquarter and report to the CO with my compliments.

With that he turned about and went into the Dining Hall to talk to the men who had heard every word.

After the talk, Surinder found Lok Bahadur waiting to meet him.

Yes what is it sahib?

Sahib, bahut thulo galti bhayo, malai maaf gar dinu—ainda koi yesto kura Hazur ko samne aunde na!

Sahib– I have made a grave mistake and I assure you that such an incident will never happen again!

Surinder understood the loss of face Lok Bahadur would suffer. He told him to behave and return to his duties.

There was no problem in the Company thereafter.

When the time came to write the annual confidential report– Surinder called Lok Bahadur and showed him his report, which was outstanding except for the one line which said;

The JCO needs to curb his ego which is likely to come in the way of any future promotion.

The CO called Surinder and said:

Surinder, I know you are a fair judge of character, but you must realise that we will lose a good Subedar Major if your report is sent up.

Surinder did not dwell on the recent trouble he had experienced, he merely said that it was his opinion that Lok Bahadur was not suitable candidate for being appointed as Subedar Major, which in his view was a very important rank in the battalion.

Surinder, I am your CO, may I request you to rewrite this report please?

Surinder nodded, saluted and left– he knew that the CO was making a very big mistake, but was blind to Lok Bahadur's faults.

Only time would tell.

Later he learnt that Lok Bahadur had landed the battalion and himself into serious trouble after being promoted.

Was I to blame– the question haunted Surinder for a long time!

The snow set in and Surinder found that his pyjama and kurta was worn out. He paid a visit to Peshori the unit civilian contractor, who gave him a fine cup of tea.

What brings you here Sahib? inquired Peshori.

Peshoriji, I need two sets of pyjama kurtas urgently. said Surinder.

Sahib—I have run out of white poplin and the only bale of cloth I have is this orange coloured one which Panditji got for his Mandir requirement. There was no choice, so Surinder got his pyjama and kurta stitched and wore it next evening.

No one commented, but by the next week end everyone was wearing similar orange coloured pyjamas! When he went home, Darji told him to get rid of the stuff.

Next morning he was surprised to find Preeti wearing his kurta—and she gave him a big naughty wink, which made Surinder laugh till his tears rolled!

Once you got used to high altitude, life was not too bad. The thought of putting or checking if anti freeze mixture had been added to the water in the radiator came automatically and one checked whether anti skid chains had been tied on the tyres. Ashok Bose had come back to the battalion from his stint at 39 GTC with a beer belly. It would soon vanish Surinder bet himself—in about three months..

The evening passed in the Mess with music till the CO and the senior officers turned up. The conversation fluctuated from topics of general interest to those relating to the activities of the next day, because come snow, hail or sleet, training slots had to be complied with. Everyone looked at the food with distaste.

No one was hungry, because the tinned food caused you to burp and fart the whole day. The AFD or accelerated freeze dried meat, gave off a pungent smell like dried prawns. Too much tea from powder milk gave you constipation—so they looked for anything fresh—even green chillies. Just fry some garlic pods in butter, put the concoction on rice and eat it quickly before it became cold.

A retired General had gone to the Military Hospital to get a sample of stools tested. After a couple of days when he went to collect the report, the young major, a lady doctor, looked at him curiously and said-

Sir, we feel that you should reduce your intake of powder milk!

Young Lady– bristled the Old man– this sample belongs to my grandson– get it? I have no need of the stuff!

All officers coming from leave were ordered to bring sweets and greens while returning to the paltan. It made everyone enjoy a couple of good meals– coriander, onions, carrots, green chillies, spinach, cauliflower, cabbage and leeks were the hot favourites.

The conversation veered to politics and the CO was surprised to find that the knowledge of politics and political parties was very scanty. Not one of the officers had ever voted or even bothered to check his name on the voters list. The CO explained to them that this was very wrong and they need not dabble in politics but should learn about the political system prevailing in the country.

Shukla who had not spoken so far said—Excuse me sir, but don't you think that our political system was doomed from the start?

Why? asked Tony.

Because the Congress which was the biggest, strongest and most respected party decided through the Constitution, to allow all and sundry to operate a party of their choice and so a large number of regional parties were created in the opposition—not one national level party came up in the opposition and Panditji won because of his Chacha Nehru image and because of the lack of a cohesive opposition. The net result was that the Congress base widened and the other parties fought a bitter battle in their own states with the Congress. This was a divide and rule story in earnest. It was also because of the status of Uttar Pradesh which was the key in the symphony. Any party which captured UP, would always win the majority.

You seem to be very upset with politics- said Godbole

No I am not upset—we have only a few good leaders and unfortunately when you vote for a party– it is not these leaders who implement policy but their party decides the chosen path. So why vote for any of these fellows who are only out to fill their own and their party's coffers. This not my voice alone—it is the voice of the people. Everyone knows this, everyone admits it in private but no one wants to do anything about it—it is as though nationalism does not exist in this country.

I was in Patna once and as i sat in a rickshaw, the rickshaw puller spoke about politics to another colleague of his who had hailed him. I asked if people in Bihar were politically conscious and the rickshaw wala told me

Yahan to bacha maa ka pet men hi politician ban jata hai.Problem to bahat aakarr na hota hai, kyon ki etna partia dekh kar confuse hojata hai. What he was implying was that politics was in the blood but the confusion occurred because there were too many parties!

Aap kisko vote do ge? Whom will you vote for?

Ham to Congress ko vote na denge! Yahan tak to bhara hai na, indicating his throat– dusra to petwa se shuru karega. I will vote for the Congress because they are full upto their throat.The others will start from the stomach.

It was unanimously agreed that the need of the hour was that there should be a change in the Constitution to say that there should be one ruling party and two in the Opposition only.Regional parties needed to be replaced.

Cariappa summed up– Actually the concept of liberty as prevalent in France, USA or in England; is alien to us because we have never seen bloodshed or a civil war– heads have not rolled because we got freedom through satyagraha– one fine day we woke up and found ourselves free—the only people who went through a holocaust were the people of Punjab who received and sent back trains with the mutilated bodies of the dead! Similarly the partition in Bengal saw something akin to the slaughter in the Punjab—which was worse. I am quite sure vested interests brought about partition—imagine our status in the world, had we been one unified India instead of the truncated nations we now are. there was no need to kill the thousands who perished during partition in Punjab and Bengal. I can imagine what a great country a unified India would have been! Our ancestors were screwed by the British royally– they never knew what hit them.

It reminds me of the time when a noted violinist, sitarist and a famous mridangam player from the South, asked a village Sarpanch why the people of Punjab had no culture.

Said the Sarpanch– Oye who says we have no culture? Don't you see our agri--culture– we have been fighting so long with the invaders; that we don't have time for these other shu shas– get it?

Can anyone stop his feet tapping to the bhangra?

Randy spoke up– you know in Gandhiji's speeches, I believe he spoke of the the *Muslim bhais* and *Sheekh log when referring to the Sikhs.* Could he could have saved Bhagat Singh and his friends from the gallows if he had wanted to; but then it was hinsa versus ahinsa!

All it required was one fast! One wondered what was in his mind then!

Angels passed and there was an eerie silence.

So much for a lesson in politics

The Mess Havildar saluted-*Bhojan taiyar hai Shriman*!

Dinner is served and this broke up the silence!

EXERCISE CUNNING FOX

The signal came from Brigade Headquarters—it simply instructed all the Commanding Officers to report to the Brigade HQ, with their Intelligence Officers and an NCO from the Intelligence Section. Col Rai, Captain Muthu and Havildar Dal Bahadur went over to the HQs. While The Commanding Officers met the Brigade Commander and the Brigade Major before the briefing, the GSO3 had called the IOs to brief them about the map settings. They were to collect any maps which they did not have, the overlay for the exercise setting and the location of friendly forces. The enemy forces were laid out only up to company level. The battalions would have to find out the exact locations themselves. Certain features actually on the ground had been shown as non existent on the maps in order to bring out certain lessons. Transport had been earmarked for the battalions and would reach them appropriately. Practice ammunition was to be carried but on reaching the exercise areas, it would be held centrally by the battalion QM.

Detailed instructions would be issued by the Brigade Major and the DQ, as soon as direction came in from division HQs. Battalions would in the meantime make necessary preparations and carry out necessary training so that everyone knew what was expected of them during the exercise. Lectures were to be suitably organised during training and demonstrations should be designed to bring home the procedures for various manoeuvres.

As, the CO returned to the unit, he realised that he had hardly spent more than a month with his family without being roped into a sand model discussion, or called as an umpire or invigilator, or for writing an exercise or even officiating as the Brigade Commander, since he was the senior most of the three battalion commanders! But this was part of life—and he had chosen this path!

It was tough, on the families but he knew that his wife would try to keep the unit families—both officer's and men's families happy and occupied. He had briefed the Subedar Major and Punditji that the men's families must be involved with religious functions as well as in competitions and welfare activities so that they had no time to think of their separation.

The CO called Surinder separately—Surinder, take one JCO and five Havildars from the Adjutant and report to the BM before the exercise; because you are going to be the umpires. Take a good one ton vehicle and spare jerry cans because you will be acting independently. Please explain details to the men so that they know how to fill up the Umpire's forms.

Surinder called his group and briefed them separately on their role and the need to be fair in their assessment of the situation prevalent on the ground or painted by a senior umpire and how to resolve any disputes which might occur. Equipped with their white arm bands and the white flag fluttering on their vehicle Surinder's group reached their destination, after they had been briefed by the BM. The vehicle was tucked into a slope near the canal while Surinder reported to the CO of the battalion he was to umpire on. There were strict instructions that his group was to maintain its distance from the battalion.

Surinder went on ahead on foot to study the map for the next day. There was a small foot bridge across the canal on the map and ground, but it was non existent on the ground for exercise purposes. Surinder wanted to see how this was being implemented. As he reached the place, he found a soldier from the Sikh Light Infantry; literally pleadingly with an old woman, whose goats were being pushed back from the footbridge.

Dadiji (grandma)—said the soldier—This bridge exists on the ground, but General Sahib has declared that it does not exist for the purpose of this exercise.

Said the old woman..See—I can touch the bridge, the goats are restless because they are tired and you have the nerve to tell me that i cannot go to my village?

No Granny—if I let you go they will chop off my head!

Granny was in no mood to listen—to hell with your head—I have no use for it—as it is it is dirty—looks like you have not bathed for a week or so! Now move aside because I am getting late.

But the soldier would not budge.

Look you are stopping me from crossing and letting those guys go because they are yours—shrieked the old one!

The soldier turned in the direction the old lady was pointing and saw a group of Sikh soldiers crawling across the foot bridge on their stomachs as though they were swimming!

Halt! he cried. Who is your senior—come forward!

As a lanky NCO stepped forward our soldier inquired in Punjabi, from him, as to why they had tried to cross the bridge—when orders had been given that this bridge was non existent?

Oye Khotya! You donkey! mocked the lanky NCO—do you think we are fools; have you seen us walking—No, no—we are swimming across—we know there is no bridge!

Our soldier was in a quandary—the NCO was right—they were actually doing the motions of swimming! And then there was this old woman breathing down his neck! Why argue on two fronts—better to get rid of them!

OK—you swimmers can cross---old woman—you stay put till I get orders!

Surinder could contain his laughter no more!

After he sobered up, he walked over and called all three parties together.

Is this old woman part of our exercise? He asked the soldier.

No Sir!

Then let her go home, She has no lessons to learn.

... and the old woman looked gratefully at Surinder, whom she mentally thought was the incarnation of the wise king Solomon or Harish Chandra, as she shot a dirty look at our soldier, who was now looking quite deflated.

And as for you—you think you are very smart are you? Let me teach you guys how to swim—get into the canal and swim across he ordered. He knew the water was very cold and no one was keen to swim– perhaps some were not even swimmers.

The NCO caught his ears—Sorry Sahib– I simply could not resist the urge to use the bridge; and I thought that I could outwit this stupid sentry—how could I imagine your presence here sir--please excuse us!

Surinder thought that this lesson was enough—he ordered them back across the bridge.

Soon they had set up camp and got a hot meal organised—on exercises one always feels hungry—maybe it was the water you drank from the canal that was responsible. Next morning the messenger from the Garhwalis came to fetch him– CO's orders were slated in the next 20 minutes at 0930 hrs, Please be seated at the sand model before then. Surinder finished his breakfast and joined the others at the sand model. Soon the Commander arrived and the CO gave out his appreciation of the impending situation. After the orders were over the Commander gave out his assessment of the orders and highlighted some flaws which required to be corrected. He was happy to see that the officers and men had an enthusiastic look about them and were raring to go.

He wished them good hunting and left.

The troops were dispersed for their final preparations and Surinder joined the CO to clear his own doubts– he was due to appear for his Defence Services Staff College Exam and needed to get his ideas in place. The CO was happy to see his interest and cleared all his doubts as best as he could. The Battery Commander was also glad to be of help in assisting to clarify the artillery lacunae; and soon they were ready for lunch.

Surinder distributed his NCOs to the company and specialist platoon headquarters and fixed a time to meet on a daily basis. Each of them would paint the picture given to him and report reactions to him on the forms provided.

The sniper fired at them from close range—they were actually blank rounds and bicat strips—to be considered as rifle fire. Considering that the company was in range and there were some troops lounging carelessly in the open—Surinder had to declare two casualties. The Company commander reacted swiftly and despatched a section to hunt the snipers. The snipers did not expect that their route out would be cut off so quickly and both of them were captured.

There were smiles all around.

Later the company on the flank and the one in the vanguard needed replacement and after replacement the companies fell back. The vanguard ran into fire from a feature overlooking the road, and since there was no time to lose, the vanguard company commander decided to attack. The abruptness of the attack and its ferocity caught the enemy by surprise and in their hurry to bolt, they left many important items behind—a pair of magazines, a compass and a map folder marked with the detailed plans for the next day—a bonanza.

At night the battalion got ready for the attack uphill. the requirement was for two objectives to be taken simultaneously. and so the Intelligence Officer had two FUPs readied and lit up behind which the reserve companies were ready. The movement was through narrow spurs offering little frontage. The Garhwalis were a hill people and the uphill movement was no problem for them. The Battery Commander had put his fire plan into motion and the companies advanced steadily towards their objective. Then the moon emerged from behind the large cloud covering it and the enemy swung into action. The sound of bicat strips representing rifle fire, number 90 grenades depicting mortar fire and gun cotton slabs depicting artillery rounds began to break the tranquillity of the night, but the attacking companies had over run the forward elements; with their battle cry of *JAI BADRI VISHAL*-- ringing in the ears of the enemy, who had fled.

The attacking companies over ran their objectives, began the process of reorganisation they fired their success signals in the form of verey lights to indicate their success to the battalion commander who then ordered that the reserve companies pass through and complete the attack as also carry out exploitation to ensure maximum gain. The Battalion Headquarter also moved up after the leading companies. The Brigade Headquarter was also given periodic reports to enable them to understand the progress of the battle. The next wave went in and after some time presumed to be the hand to hand fighting fired their verey lights. They proceeded with the process of reorganisation and exploitation and finally prepared their report on casualties, ammunition expenditure and redistribution of ammunition while their *bulas*-as the Garwalis are called akin to *kanchas* in the Gorkhas, began to convert the enemy trenches.

The exercise proceeded as per plan and soon it was time to part company– the umpires had made a number of friends and they were treated to a Garhwali Barakhana—a sort of farewell and when Surinder picked up a piece of *kachmula* or raw meat, he found he just could not eat it while the Garwalis went about it– chomp chomp chomp! Then one of the officers saw his discomfort and asked him to spit it out! They all drank rum with the men and each company soon burst into song. It was very touching to see the men together and realise that in time of war this camaraderie was necessary to wield the lot into an invincible homogenous team. Surinder missed his own unit and especially his own company.

He had run into Mathews, Beniwal, Sandhu and Singhal– his course mates from the NDA and they yapped about old times like little children! It was great to meet course mates—there was so much to catch up on!

Mathews told them an interesting anecdote.

He was returning from the Weapons Course and as he entered his compartment, he found it occupied by an old lady who appeared to be quite sick and her daughter—a very pretty girl of twenty. They had the lower berths and as he shut off the lights and put on the night light everyone went off to sleep. Somewhere in the middle of the night, the girl shook him awake– her mother was not feeling too well.

So, as a gentleman he helped her out with the old lady, gave her medicine and tucked her to bed with a sedative.

As he tried to climb up to his berth, the girl signalled for him to join her on her berth.

So Mathews did as he was requested and soon one thing led to another and he found her making passionate love to him. He was a complete virgin and had no experience of sexual matters– .The girl undressed him and led him from one height to another, and after his initiation rites; he grew bolder and took control.

While the old lady struggled with her sedated slumber, Mathews learnt a thing or two about the birds and the bees, and realised that he had great potential! It was heavenly and they clung to each other as if possessed till it became dangerous to remain like that because dawn was breaking. Reluctantly they parted company and he climbed onto his berth but his eyes were glued to her large and firm breasts which she had left deliberately uncovered after their bout of unabashed pleasure and was aware of the effect they had on him– staring back at him with their small erect nipples.

She looked straight into his eyes aware that they were focused on her bosom. They had not spoken one word—for there was no need—the urgency for both had overridden this requirement, so he had not even asked her name and though he had given her his card with his address– there was no communication thereafter!

This left him perplexed—maybe it was just a one night stand as far as she was concerned!

Mathews grew quiet and we understood because such events are rare and were akin to Bollywood dream sequences–as if they never really happened!

Men never really understood the woman's mind– even though they pretended to.

A big sham!

Come Mathews– Just be happy that you went through such a treat—nothing as remotely connected happened to me so far damn it—can I shake your hand for luck—might rub off on me you know? asked Sandhu.

We all laughed and hugged Mathews, who was beginning to smile a little!

Come on man– at least you had a good time while we have had no luck so far!

De secret of life is :

Two eggs for breakfast, two pegs for dinner and between two legs at night! What a life it wud be—no?

Beniwal, clown that he was- --got us to hold hands; and in a sober voice prayed for Mathews, who was feeling very embarrassed:

Lord! Comfort our dear Brother Mathews for his body and soul are in torment—though his soul tries to forget the follies of yesterday– his body parts which gets roused even by thoughts, yearn for a repeat of what he experienced– hear his cries of anguish Lord!

Come on guys– I don't think i will forget that night in the train so easily, but what the heck it was one very lovely incident!

Lets drink to that– Amen!

Hey..what is the lightest thing in the world----even a thought can raise it!

Soon they parted company.

Back at Almora, Surinder got into the groove and appeared in the Staff College entrance exam, keeping his fingers crossed. He had got Support Company honed into a fine team and taken all the competitions in his stride and claiming the Banner for the Company. Life continued as usual, exercises, training, lectures and demonstrations and documentation, not necessarily in that order.

CO had arranged a party.

This one is on me he said, Surinder can invite us later

Surinder was quite taken aback..

Relax Surinder, you have made it to the Staff College!.

That was good news because this was his first great achievement in the Army.So Preeti would have to begin packing soon.

Then after his course, he would have to complete a Staff tenure at a brigade or a higher headquarter.

As they reached Wellington a pretty place in the South almost near Ooty in the Nilgiris, the Staff College ensured that everyone was kept busy from dawn to dusk except during brief sojourns when there were parties or central functions.

There were telephone battles which kept them on their toes.

It was a great time but the year passed before they knew it! Their posting to a Brigade headquarter was expected but it came as a field posting. Preeti and Jaskaran went home to be ferried between Surinder's house and Preeti's! Life became hectic as she had to attend all the functions in both families.

She continued to write faithfully as she had done earlier.

After a couple of months the Brigade Commander accorded permission for allowing families at the headquarter location. *The threat from the terrorists was very much alive; but one dies only once; was the theory propagated by the Commander.*

Preeti enjoyed her visits to the Brigade– she would take over the menu and work out the details of the dishes to be prepared during get togethers. Since she was expert at cooking herself; she guided Cook and taught him the inside story of cooking. She taught the cooks to make chicken pickle and was horrified to know that it had been polished off in a couple of days—all five kilos of it!

Jaskaran was spoilt by the sahayaks and by the officers as well. They heeded every whim and fancy he could dream of. Since she was a very nice person, everyone missed Preeti when she left and were excited to see her return to this God forsaken wilderness. And that is how Surinder completed his tenure in field. There was a lot of strain– handling five battalions in operations was no mean joke for a Brigade Major. But there were ways of handling situations automatically by developing shortcuts which came with experience and thorough knowledge of the terrain and the modus operandi of the militants. The Commander liked his style of working, which gave him more time with the battalions and a chance to see operational planning and execution at its best.

One evening a message came in from Division headquarters that five dreaded terrorists were being infiltrated into their area. The Pakistani artillery opened up and everyone knew that this was a ploy used normally by them to send in the infiltrators. Forward units were warned and patrols stepped. One patrol reported seeing a group of infiltrators looking like foreign mercenaries; holed up in an abandoned house. A party was despatched and the infiltrators challenged– suddenly there was a heavy volume of firing from the hut. It caught the young lieutenant squarely in the chest and killed him instantaneously. The major ordered his party to return fire and soon they heard the sounds of some infiltrators who had apparently been hit. One of the holed up infiltrators tried to make a break for it, but the machine gunner; lying in wait for such a possibility, caught him in a burst of fire and almost cut him in two.

The other infiltrators tried to return fire in desperation. The Major ordered an HE round from the Carl Gustaf to be fired and the hut was blown to smithereens. There was a search and some body parts were assembled together. They seemed to be foreigners– mercenaries from some Arab countries and each was armed with a Kalashnikov rifle with ammunition in abundance. Probably a couple of Afghanis too. There was a cache of supplies and weapons concealed in a hole dug into the floor of the hut. Some maps were found with vague markings on them and which required detailed examination.

The report was finalised for Division Headquarters and the GOC rang up the Commander to congratulate him on his success. He was sorry for the youngster who was killed in the encounter, these were the backbone of counter insurgency operations– brave fearless and highly motivated—but what a waste of life! Such encounters became a way of life in the brigade and Surinder learnt to cope with them.

Eventually it was time to go back to the paltan. There was the usual farewell in the Officer's mess and one with the troops before he reached Jammu to catch the train to Delhi!

Preeti deserved a medal for the trips she made to this desolate but beautiful country.—he thought to himself while in the train.

LOVE ME-- LOVE MY DOG

Surinder was amused when the General's wife rang him up and asked him if he had any new books. They were both voracious readers and fans of many renowned writers assuming that books by these authors would conform to the same literary content as their earlier work. So they read them all. Surinder had an agreement with the senior lady—*read de new book and pass it on to me and vice versa!*

All of a sudden, her calls stopped.

One day Surinder met her in the club during a social event and asked her whether she was in good health because he had not heard from her for quite some time. The lady laughed—its a surprise– you will find out when you visit us on Saturday.

Then she was gone.

Come Friday and as Surinder was about to pick up his files from the General's office, the General asked him–

I say Surinder, I know it is late in the day to invite you to my house with Preeti for dinner but would you consider it—i have invited some planters and thought you might want to meet them. What say you?

Surinder's reply was simple and to the point—

Sir, being invited to your house would have more meaning than being invited to the White House—Preeti and I would be pleased to come.

Good! said the General. You are hereby ordered to look after the tea planters—some of them are snobbish guys-will you be able to handle them? Come down a little earlier OK?

There will be no problem whatsoever-said Surinder.

Surinder and Preeti reached the GOC's house and were greeted– while Preeti was whisked away by the General's wife, the General took Surinder's arm and showed him around the house which was tastefully decorated and full of memorabilia collected over the years. He showed him where the whiskey and the drinks were kept and indicated the mess waiters who would serve the guests. Surinder nodded to the waiters and had several drinks prepared in advance so that each guest would have his drink within minutes of his or her arrival. Soft drinks were Preeti's domain and he did not want to get involved at that end.

As the guests arrived Surinder was introduced to all of them and he in turn offered them a drink. There was a lot of back thumping and loud hellos reverberated in the house as the ladies and gents met each other raising questions by their eye brows– asking– *how the fuck are you here—you sonofabitch*—but outwards smiling as if they were truly happy at seeing each other!

Surinder smiled—this must be the same all over the world I am sure!

As the evening progressed each guest latched on the person with whom he had some social or professional connectivity because this was a good opportunity to discuss subjects of mutual interest. Surinder ensured that the waiters read his signs and ensured that the right drinks went to the right people.He found Suresh Mahajan was quite frank on his views about life and he had a wealth of knowledge on the local flora and fauna, as well as the locals. He was willing to share his knowledge and educate Surinder only if he promised to visit his garden with his family. A promise was made and both became friends– Preeti and Sunita Mahajan also hit off well and found many things in common since they were both Delhi girls.

Then came dessert and an aperitif and the evening came to an end, because some of the planters had to drive back quite a distance to their gardens.

As the guests began to leave the general's wife stood at the door with a cute Labrador pup and everyone exclaimed– *cho cweet* and kissed it on its forehead. Surinder realised that this was the surprise behind the General's wife being out of communication. When it came to his turn, he picked up the little one and returned it without the expected kiss!

There was a discernable frown and then laughter—he had got away!

Later the Aide de Camp or the ADC had told him that the pup had been christened- Lady!

As time went by– Surinder realised that the pup had grown and one fine day as he was to accompany the general's entourage for an inspection, it was found that the pup could only be accommodated in his jonga—which was no problem because he was basically a dog lover. Lady was the perfect companion and she went to sleep as soon as she bedded herself in. Soon the reached the Artillery Brigade Headquarters and halted. The General beckoned lady and she descended from the jonga to meet Master. But as she gingerly put her paw on the steps of the jonga the band Master who had received his cue signalled the drummer who came down both arms akimbo on his drum and so did the cymbalist. Lady was startled out of her wits and before anyone could say Jack Robinson—she took off like an arrow into the thick undergrowth. Some of the men and officers ran behind her because she was heading towards unchartered territory and could get lost.

The band master was apologetic—it was all his fault and he broke into tears. While he was being reassured, Lady emerged from the bushes with all sorts of thorns and odd greenery stuck to her beautiful hide! But nevertheless she was happy to see her master and lay down quietly at his feet and began to whimper as though she was frightened out of her wits. So the next thing was that the programme was interrupted and the General sat in the guest room with a team of assistants trying to clean Lady's coat from the thorns and other greenery stuck to her. A good brushing and she was as good as new! The poor officers and men who had followed her into the undergrowth emerged later– some with torn trousers and others with boots and trousers wet with grime where they had waded through the swamp. Lady gave them a couple of barks as though she was telling them– *thanks for helping me– now go and clean up like good boys!*

The ADC had proceeded on leave and his replacement was Capt Rai who had not been introduced to the General's family so far.

He had also not met Lady.

In the afternoon the General told his staff to arrange for him to visit one of the forward brigades. Since he was a keen shikari or hunter, he had trained Lady in the fine art of retrieving game during his jaunts in the woods. Late in the evening he was returning from a visit to one of the units when the officiating ADC received a call from the General who wanted him to bring Lady to the airfield at four in the morning, because the General would reach the airfield directly from his duty station. Capt Rai hesitatingly picked up the phone and spoke to the General's wife and informed her that the General wanted her to be at the airfield at four in the morning.

Madame blew her top-

Has the General gone mad? she asked in anger.

Then in a kinder tone she asked Capt Rai to repeat the conversation he had with the General.

That cleared the fog and she realised that the ADC had no clue that the General was actually referring to Lady their labrador!

That induced a fit of laughter and slowly she wiped the tears from her eyes.

What a story this would make when her friends heard about it.

The first lady enjoyed her drinks and smokes too and therefore preferred male company. She preferred to discuss sensible subjects rather than those related to the kitchen or a wardrobe. For her drinks she only trusted Surinder who knew the exact quantity she required, and so Surinder waited for her discreet signal if she desired a drink. Some people enjoy their lives and she was definitely one of them. Not only was she an attractive person, but she had a personality which was magnifique!

Often she rang up Surinder in a husky voice– Yes Sir?

Its not Sir, Surinder—its Madam! And a hearty laugh would follow.

Any new book?

Yes maam!—and Surinder would get one in return!

Of Training and Associated Matters!

The Indian Army has only two type of stations– peace and field.

Peace stations are those where a battalion came down after its stint of two or three years in a field station to enjoy a bit of rest, link up with families and resume training. In some formations peace stations are tied up with training schedules with their own and neighbouring formations as well with the result that the battalion has no time whatsoever for its internal training requirements.

Indian troops traditionally prefer to keep their families at home in their villages. The children saw their father only two months in a year when he came on annual leave or when he was sanctioned some casual leave. The winds of change had started like a breeze, but it had slowly but steadily increased in intensity. Soldiers or jawans had begun to feel that it was wise to take interest in the education of their children and so the Army had begun to construct married quarters for the families for the troops, which were earlier undersubscribed. Priority of allotment often went to cases where the lady was suffering from a medical problem requiring immediate medical attention or where a jawan had no children and the couple could be examined for fertility issues.

With this change came the need for entertainment and also for shopping Since many stations were far from the city, formations often had a cinema hall where movies could be screened and the same hall could double up for training films and lectures. Often units also bought their own projectors and arranged for films to be screened from local resources.

As far as shopping was concerned, the Canteen Stores Department allowed units to run their own retail outfits in the unit lines. Unit Canteen in charges would demand items preferred by their troops at wholesale prices and collect these from bulk depots. Liquor was also sold through these canteens and profits were used for welfare purposes. Profit to be charged in terms of percentage, and rules for utilisation of these funds were categorically laid down.

In some units which were remote or where it was inconvenient for the families of the troops to go to town some units had arranged a vegetable shop or a shop where dals or lentils could be procured. Then of course was the unit bania or contractor who was able to fulfil the essential requirements of the unit especially with reference to tailors, blacksmith or a halwai or sweetmeat expert! He also kept the accoutrements of the battalion, the cloth required for various purposes and some other items of daily use which did not conflict with the inventory of the unit run Canteen!

He was supposed to arrange for almost anything and accompanied the battalion in peace or field with his entourage. In addition he was supposed to have an entourage of tailors who could stitch the uniforms, understand the sequence of medals and arrange to supply everything from paints and stationery as well as targets for the firing ranges at short notice—in fact he was Superman! Not only this– he would have to arrange the stitching of women's blouses and petticoat like ghagras for functions like Dushera and Raising Day celebrations, and arrange bras for the boys to wear along with their costumes.

No– I would not like to take his place because it was a tough job.

Choudhary and Saikiya were going for a training cadre and they took the risk of travelling in the front seat together, a *no no* in the Indian Army which forbade two people sitting in the front seat along with the driver. Sure enough the MP at the check post hauled up the driver and took out his pad for writing the report. Chaudhary walked up to the MP and realised that this guy was from his village. He accosted the MP a tall six foot and hefty Jat, and asked carelessly—

Bhai tene Maharaja Ranjit Singh ke bare mein suna hoga.?

You must have heard of King Ranjit Singh who was a fearless one eyed soldier statesman

To Ranjit Singh aaj is sisiley mein kahan pahunch gaya sahib? How has Ranjit Singh figured in today's matter Sir?

Bhai Kabhi Kabhi woh duniya ko kani ankh se dekhta tha. Sometimes he viewed the world with his bad eye..

Aisa kaun bolta hai? Who says this?

Yeh mere aur tere gaun wale bolte hein!

Aap ka gaun kaun sa Hai? Which village are you from?

Wahi jahan tu paida hua tha– meri Haveli ke piche.? The same where you were born-right behind my mansion.

Arey aap Chaudhri Kirpal Singh ke bade bete ho?

Are you Chaudhary Kirpal Singh's elder son?

With that he touched Captain Choudhary's feet and the matter was closed.

Chai piyoge Sahib? Will you have some tea?

Abhi to jaldi hai—aate waqt tere paas rukenge. No, we are in a hurry, but we will stop on our return trip.

Saikiya smiled and both got into the front seat. Driver Dai also gave a big grin– it was rare that you were one up on a MP!

The Commanding officer decided that the battalion should get cracking and complete its internal cadres both promotion and training so that the battalion was ready for any competitions which would be announced soon.

Surinder was made in charge of the Ummedwar Cadre, where riflemen are promoted to Lance Naiks. It was considered an important step in the promotion chain because one could weed out those boys who did not show any potential for leadership. These boys were young, extremely energetic and showed great potential for further promotion. However they could all not be promoted but if they failed to make the cut they were given a second chance since they fulfilled the criteria.

Surinder was trying to teach them fire control orders and this had been coined into a acronym called GRIT.

G—Group

R—Range

I– Indication of target

T—Type of fire

While explaining the subject Surinder found that the boys stared at him with beady eyes and when he asked—*Bujyo*—Understood? Everyone shouted at the top of his voice– *Bujyo Sahib*! Understood Sir!

When he questioned them then he found very few had actually understood.

He used another ploy.

Boys have you ever been to Paltan Bazaar in Dehra Dun?

They all had.

Now imagine Santa Bahadur and Durga Bahadur are walking behind three good looking girls—one in white(Syeto) one in red (rato)and the third in black(kalo).Near the Bata shoe shop fifty metres away.

There was rapt attention at the mention of the girls.

Since he had their complete attention Surinder continued—Sante's mind is set on the one in rato.

Now he has to indicate her to Durge'–

And then he wants to wink at her.

So as in today's lesson—when Sante digs his elbow in Durge's ribs, he is addressing his Group—or Number 1 section– Got it? A victorious shout went up! They had indeed understood.

Now, Sante' tells Durge' Pachas meter Bata ko dukan ko chau ma! This is Range– Got it– again that shout amidst laughter.

Now Sante says Sunder keti rato salwar kameez ma! Beautiful girl in the red dress! This gentlemen is– Indication of target! -- they all shouted.

And then Sante says—if she looks back– WINK!

This is Type of Fire!

Big laughter!

Now he was satisfied that these crickets would never forget and he began to devise lesson plans for them accordingly! When he told Cariappa about this in the Mess, they had a good laugh and Cariappa decided that he would try something similar in the Naik to Havildar Cadre which he was running at his post.

Similarly, Support Company was carrying out cadres for intake of freshers for their Mortar, Recoilless Gun, Machine Gun, Pioneer and Signal platoons. Not to be left behind, Admin Company decided to invite volunteers for their Band and Motor pool. So the training was organised on similar grounds for all except the Band, Motor Pool and the Mortar Platoon.

Subedar Min Bahadur Gurung looked at the volunteers and spat on the ground.

This was a bad sign, which meant that he was not entirely satisfied with the kettle of fish his net had caught. He knew everyone wanted to be a driver, but Min Bahadur had other things in mind—would he drive safely with stores or men, would he become a speedster and a rash driver, would he be steady or reckless in his driving. These questions continued to plague him before he gave his report to the MTO, Captain Gulab Singh Dahiya. He could not throw out anyone till he had given him a fair chance.

When Captain Dahiya took the report, the two of them surveyed the volunteers and made a game plan.

Subedar Sahib-get them organised into sections.

Subedar Sahib passed his orders and the NCOs from the jeep 1 ton and the 3 ton sections made the volunteers stand according to height– the tallest for 3 ton, the medium for the 1 ton and the shorter guys for the jeep sections. The NCOs took the boys at the double to where two derelict vehicles were standing. The ground was large and mistakes were permissible. Each of the potential driver was put through an aptitude test in which he sat at the wheel and the rest pushed the derelict. Those who passed were segregated and the rest were returned to their parent companies.

Phase One was over.

Meanwhile Subedar Gharti had assembled the volunteers for the Band platoon. He picked out those with pleasing faces because these would be the faces which would fetch them points for smartness and turnout in any competition. A couple of tall and well built boys were chosen for the *dhole* or the drummer, another group formed the pipers, some went to become buglers and some for the side drummers and eventually the band was assembled.

Don't touch my number one set– unless i tell you to- he snarled.

A second set was produced for the trainees– but only to look at. The drummers were ordered to cut twigs from the trees nearby to be used as sticks. The pipers were issued chanters and the potential buglers were issued old bugles which had something or the other wrong with them but could be used with rudimentary modifications—referred to as *jugad!*

Similarly the boys in the Mortar and Pioneer platoons were picked for their toughness and intelligence. This was a difficult combination to find but with so many gods to assist, miracles are just waiting to happen. For the Mortar platoon carrying base plates and gun barrels was important while the Pioneers had to lay minefields, low wire entanglements, and perform many other engineering tasks.

And so the training began in right earnest.

A look at the potential drivers indicated their intense concentration, because they all wanted to qualify—it was a very good opportunity to own one's own vehicle– a taxi or a truck after proceeding on pension or become a driver for someone as part of re-employment. Some were naturals, while some struggled hard to steer their vehicles and all of them were watched by the hawkish eyes of the MTO and the MT JCO and the section commanders.

Each of the finally selected boys were ordered to get hold of three bricks and three sticks each. The bricks were to denote the clutch, brake and accelerator, while the three sticks were for the gear lever and the 4x4 gear lever. To the onlooker this seemed quite strange but the potential drivers were now ordered to take their places in the cabins of their vehicles. They were instructed to take hold of the steering wheel with the left hand only after a small prayer. The next step was to start the vehicle wit an imaginary key push the gear lever to one and let the clutch go slowly before changing the next gear. They were also expected to wave the right hand up and down as a cautionary advice to vehicles behind them that they were about to move off!

Translated into Nepalese the words of command were as follows;

Start up!Arey, Chabi ghumaonu, ani sath ma awaj pani garnu!(Turn the key and make a sound as if the vehicle has started up)

At this command there was a flurry of action and a loud vibratory noice to indicate that the so called vehicles had started up.

*Check garnu keta haru ko khuta– dahina accelerator tira ani bayan khuta clutch tira honu parcha.*Ensure that the driver has his right foot on the accelerator and left foot near the clutch.

*Dahina hath ley march ko ishara deno ani clutch dabauno.*Give the signal that you are marching off with your right hand and press the clutch completely down.

Aba gear lever ley number ek gear ma halnu ani gari ley ahista ahista march garnu. Now shift the gear lever to one and march off the vehicle slowly!

Awaj badly gara– gari no i gear ma cha! Change the pitch of your vehicle's noise because it is now in gear one!

Now change the pitch of your vehicle's noise as you shift to second gear-- -and thus our boys put their vehicles into top gear and drove off into the highway!

Surinder looked at Dahiya who was staring stoically at this performance, without a trace of a smile and realised that this was a case of the famous *no mistake syndrome.*

Dahiya– when will you allow them to get near a vehicle?

Sir they will smell or touch a vehicle only after they clear this preliminary test. said Dahiya.

As Surinder moved off to the Band platoon he admired the ingenuity of the MT Platoon for devising this sort of training because many a Commanding officer had been sacked because of too many vehicle accidents in his battalion and the resultant loss of lives or stores.

The Nawab and The Begum

Every small town has its luminaries, ghosts and scandals!

Almora was definitely not an exception. Nawab Ali Haider was a nobleman from Lucknow, where his palatial mansion stood near the *Bara Imambara*. He was quite happy with his harem tucked away in his haveli, his nauch girls in the *bazaar*, where he was well known for squandering money at whim—in short he was a debauch old philanderer given to all the possible vices of those times. This took a heavy toll on his health and mental facilities. His Begum had brought up the children well and given them an excellent education to the extent that the elder children had been sent abroad and returned as doctors, lawyers and astute businessmen. Bibi smiled and enjoyed the vision of her family as they discussed politics and imagined that someday these children would be taking part in the governance of their state.

Her world was shattered one fine day when she found that Nawab Sahib had purchased; for a paltry sum, the beautiful daughter of a beggar. The wench was beautiful beyond description, tall, lithe, exquisite and seductive, with a pout like Brigitte Bardot and when the beggar women disrobed her daughter; to show Nawab Sahib the wares for his inspection—he almost fainted after seeing her beautiful and full figure. In anticipation of having sex with her despite the poor attire she had come in, the poor Nawab had an enormous erection, and had to calm down his champion with many promises.

He was certain that this girl came from nobility—she must have been lifted from some wealthy family—but it was none of his business. Payment was made and the servants instructed to make arrangements for her stay–without the Begum's knowledge. But Bibi's informers quickly gave her the news. She called in her eldest son Sohrab, a respected lawyer and posed the problem to him in the most direct manner that she could. The implications– family honour, future of her children and their ambitions in politics were vital issues and so were the proposals for her children from the elite families of Lucknow—which would now be defunct, after all who would want their progeny to marry into a family with such a scandal.

Sohrab acted quickly.He went to see his father, humbly explained the implications to him and made him a proposal. Nawab Sahib listened to his wise son—the family would state that their *Abu* had proceeded to Almora, to convalescence from tuberculosis. He would stay with a few servants in the cottage which the family owned at the outskirt of the town, behind Dr Bosi Sen's experimental farm. Of course the entourage would include Mariam Bi his newly acquired playmate. Money would be delivered to him every month through a courier.

This was an excellent arrangement and was acceptable to him if the financial arrangement would encompass Mariam Bi after his death. Sohrab agreed, and as the Maulvi declared Mariam to be his legally wedded wife, the Nawab took leave of his family whom he would never see again. The elder Begum refused to meet him—she felt she had tolerated him enough already.

So In the Nawab, s black *Humber Super Snipe*, a stylish English car, the small group left for Almora at the crack of dawn. The rest of his group would come by train to Kathgodam and from there by bus. By evening they were at the cottage and the keeper had got their meal prepared. Nawab Sahib was not hungry; he was in a frenzy—he bade them good night; and sought his bride for the delights he had day dreamed about all week.

As he took off her clothes he realised that she was his wife now and respect should replace lust, for she was available whenever he wanted unlike the women in the bazaar. Her body was perfect and so were the most intimate parts of her anatomy—he could never imagine any woman so flawless—he knew so many of them intimately. As he began his exploration she shuddered and clung to him fiercely, biting his shoulder in ecstasy.

Allah! Could this be actually happening to him and he laughed because it was true. And because she was not versed in the art of love making, the Nawab, gave her the experience of her life time—riding her like an expert horseman till she moved forwards, backwards, sideways and reared up at his slightest pressure! On her part, Mariam realised that the key to power over the Nawab lay in mastering the intricate points that she was being instructed in. Who knew it might be the very art, that would help to sustain her in comfort for the rest of her life. So she did as the Nawab bid her and enjoyed herself, as she slowly drained out the old fart.

For the Nawab, he was as close to *jannat*(Paradise) as one could reach while one was alive---and he thanked God for being kind to him in his old age!

It was simply great—it was sex for breakfast, for lunch and dinner—the *khansama or chef* was fed up with the food going waste even though the servants had a feast. Nawab Sahib was in Paradise and so was Mariam; who felt lucky to have learnt about sexual delights from so learned a teacher and soon she had mastered every game plan in his book. She loved every new move that he could invent and gave him as much pleasure as she could—after all he owned her very soul; and this was a great life after the horrendous and miserable life she had travelled so far, never sure when she would be gang raped, abducted or abused, but the beggar woman deliberately rubbed her face with grime to make her look unattractive.

Nawab Sahib began to look younger, shed flab, began to look handsome and in the summer, the two would go for a drive to the Kosi bridge at the fork where one road veered off to Hawalbagh while the other took a steep turn towards Ranikhet. The wind whisled in the pines and the dry pine needles were not very comfortable, but the duo forgot all their discomforts because they had each other.

Dinner would be laid out with silver cutlery and English crockery, with a sherbet for Begum Sahiba and some wine for the Nawab—what a life it was– one thought it should never end! As the water of the Kosi river gurgled past them one could see the temple behind the bridge all lit up and even though the Nawab was virtually an atheist, he nodded his thanks to the Hindu Diety within the temple walls.

God is omnipotent and omnipresent; it was all he believed in.

One night, the weather turned ugly—the winds rose in velocity and the pines creaked with the strain of bowing to the demands of the wind. The Nawab felt a little discomfort, and Mariam sent for the Doctor. Dr Joshi knew that the Nawab's time had come and took the Begum aside. The Nawab will not last the night, please send a courier to his family. Take a stock of your assets too, before there is a spree of stealing. Mariam in turn called her trusted guard Deen Mohammed and asked him to gather all the silver and precious artefacts into her room before they vanished, while she tackled the servants. Khansama who doted on her, was requested to gather the servants in the drawing room where she addressed them. She told them that she would keep on living at the cottage, after Nawab Sahib departed, and if anyone was not keen to continue serving her, he was free to go. For those who wished to stay, she would treat them well and pay the same wages.

The servants had a little conference of their own and discussed their future threadbare. Some were truly homesick while some preferred the slow sluggish life at Almora. Of the homesick variety, a few requested a few days leave in order to settle their personal affairs, get married and probably bring their spouses with them. Mariam gave them their dues and was quite relieved when they returned as promised. For those who did not return, Mariam said a silent prayer for them because they had served the Nawab well in his life time.

She buried Nawab Ali Haider in a beautiful corner near the cottage so that she could speak to him when she was troubled and pay homage to her mentor. *Mali,* the gardner was instructed to ensure that the grave was well looked after and had the best seasonal flowers available—a row of *nargis* or narcissus was laid all around the grave because the Nawab loved these beautiful flowers. But she was all of twenty five years of age—and in full bloom—good food and grooming had made her a tall, well endowed creature who could persuade the most rigid of males to fall madly in love with her. There was a waiting list of suitors wanting an audience with her, and Deen Mohammed screened them carefully after discussing their assets. She did not want to settle down yet—for she had never really felt free, and so a few years of independence would do her good.

Mariam instructed Deen to arrange for a few essentials.

A teacher- who could teach; her the intricate art of playing the sitar and singing along with it.

An English teacher- preferably; a retired teacher from the girl's school.

A handsome gigolo who could give her company when she was lonely, but one who knew his place—one on whom Deen could keep a discreet eye on.

Deen bowed and within a week, had his mistress learning English and French from a retired Anglo Indian teacher, from Naini Tal, who had settled down in Almora. In the early morning, her staff was pleasantly surprised to find her busy at her *riaz*—practice, and everyone discovered that their mistress was not only a beauty; but a talented singer who seemed to be a daughter of the muses.

Deen found Ronnie by chance near LR Shah, drunk, upset that he had lost his money in a game of chance and melancholic because he had lost interest in the sixty year old woman who was keeping him. He was a very handsome rogue, but penniless, came from a family whose fortunes dwindled when they were forced to convert to Christianity—Papa Bear had developed a craving for eggs and chicken and was thrown out by the family. Ronnie was stunned to see his new mistress and could not get over his excitement as she unveiled her assets to him the first time of their union. Here was another slave repeating to himself– God has been kind to me—he does exist even for sinners like me! He cried when it was time to go home at the crack of dawn. Was she happy with him? He had a lot to learn from her—his foreplay needed honing and his lovemaking had to be regulated so that he could reach the finishing line—a line denoting her complete satisfaction.

Since they also needed a good driver for the car, Deen found one in Ranikhet—a taxi driver called Majnu, with a body like a rake, one known for keeping his taxi in excellent shape and the most valuable asset was; that he did not get involved in the conversation and kept to himself. Slowly, he was given access to his mistresses chambers when Ronnie failed to turn up or when she was annoyed with him. And one day she invited them both into her bed.

Very very big mistake!

Ronnie did not get along with Majnu and slowly the desire to get rid of the competition began to germinate in his mind.

Meanwhile Deen who sensed the brewing trouble in Mariam's world, found an Italian Count, unable to pay for his boarding and lodging, but too proud to part with his stylish clothes. Count Luigi was a handsome man, tall, well built with the face of a Casanova and down on his luck. Deen paid his dues, picked up his suitcases, hired a coolie and took the Count with him to the cottage. Mariam fell in love with him and the Count was allotted accommodation to stay at the outhouse, but spend time with the mistress. Deen was happy and with Mariam's permission Ronnie found that he had been replaced—but rewarded handsomely. Majnu was put in his place and Mariam's affairs were once again under Deen's control!

Count Luigi taught Mariam the European style of love making and she realised that her tongue had many uses; besides, creating words or utilising the taste buds for culinary or gourmet requirements. And so Mariam, the good pupil began to learn once again and the Count was delighted with her progress.She was better in bed than many of the noblewomen he had bedded and she used a combination of the Indian and the European styles together to allow him to scale new heights. He decided to marry her and take her to Italy with him. The issue was money—and how it could be obtained quickly and without much fuss. A courier was despatched to Lucknow with a message that the Count and the Begum wished to meet Sohrab at the earliest; to conclude a suitable arrangement.

Sohrab was surprised to find that his step mother could converse in English, French and Italian with ease and was well versed in the muses as well. A fantastic improvement from the woman he has banished to Almora.

He wished them well.

Sohrab listened to the Count's proposition—assuming that Mariam was expected to live for a long time—the Count wished to request that a sum of sixty instalments of her monthly pension be paid in bulk with the proviso that there was no further payment to be made. The cottage, car and the silver were hers; to dispose off and she would leave the country forever. Sohrab out of compassion requested the Count to be legally wedded to the Begum before they left for Italy, and a quiet wedding was arranged according to Catholic rites. Sohrab added as his wedding present two tickets to Rome for the couple. Mariam was overwhelmed with Sohrab's generosity and held his hands tenderly.

The Count kept some of the capital aside for use in Italy, and with the rest bought beautiful etchings, *chikan* bales from Lucknow, silk from Benares, gold and silver ornaments– items which would be easily sold and provide him a quick return for his investment. So without much ado the couple took the train to Bombay and flew to Italy, to start a new life. They promised to send for Deen Mohammed, because a man loyal as he was would not only be an asset but be a star attraction amongst the nobility of Rome! Not only that—he might even become a source of additional income– for Mariam would manage his affairs!

Ah, so you are probably wondering where the battalion came into this story. It transpired that the District Collector, Shri Rudra Pratap Singh– privy to all that went on in his district, felt that the Begum could be a Pakistani spy and over drinks had suggested to the CO; that one of his officers investigate the goings on at the Nawab's cottage, by befriending the Begum. After all she seemed to have a never ending supply of money!

The CO kept puffing on his pipe, broke it open to clean out the accumulated tar, pretending that the pipe was choked, refilled it from his tobacco pouch, then lit it and inhaled deeply–and as he blew out the blue smoke, he looked the DC in the eye and said two words summing up the entire incident.

Bad Idea!

Then the Mess Havildar saluted the 2IC and shouted—*Bhojan taiyar hai Shreeman*!

(The meal is ready, Sire!)

BATTALION COMMANDER

Surinder was now the 2IC, which the British coded as the *LAMB*, because he was a very vulnerable guy. So all Commanders at any level were called *Tigers,* the 2IC was *Lamb,* because he was at the mercy of the Tiger, and could not take Command decisions without his permission! In fact their tenure was a precarious one. They could scuttle their careers, if they were not working in consonance with the CO's wishes.

Somehow, this was not the issue in the Six Third, because Colonel Rai was a third generation officer, his father and grandfather had served in the Third Gurkhas and he had been a 2IC too. He understood Surinder well and knew that he could sit back and enjoy his command as long as he did nothing to upset Surinder's apple cart! Moreover, he trusted Surinder's judgement and knew that he would always take a decision keeping the battalion's interests in mind. The biggest advantage was that in field areas there were no ladies and therefore life became easier, everyone wore uniform and moved only in military vehicles no one could flaunt his private vehicle here! There was no need to go to the hospital with the wife or the kids. The families had been resettled in separated accommodation at Dehra Dun and were being looked after.

The only major task was now to look after the men and their operational tasks. The enemy facing them was wily and therefore they had to remain on their toes. Complacency was not allowed to set in. In a few places they were within hailing distance of the Pakis and the simple Gurkha johnnies were subjected to loud laughter and jibes from the Pakistani soldiers. One fine day the discussion went like this:

Sathi, aaj kya banaya hai langar mein?

Comrade– what is cooking in the cook house?

Hamare cook ne to gosht banaya hai, thora bhejen?

Our cook has prepared beef for us—should we send some across?

Arey– tum to gai ki puja karte ho, na? Tum kaise khaoge?

Oh– You guys worship the Cow– how are you going to eat the stuff?

Arey Sathi– Fire karne ki ijazat tum Indira se loge– hamare to jeb mein hai!And a cackle of dirty laughter!

Listen Comrade– you need Indira's(Gandhi) permission to fire—but our permission is in our pockets!

Then one of the Gorkha Seargents yelled out– *Chup karo sale Suar ke bache!*

Shut up you sons of pigs—*this because the Pakis did not eat or even touch a pig which was considered unclean!*

Then all was quiet on the western front!

In the evening report Muthu requested that Naik Budhi Bahadur be sanctioned leave, because he had lost his father. Col Rai felt that Muthu was being emotional, because Indian families take the death of close relatives very seriously and he was using the same parameters for Naik Budhi. A couple of days later he noticed that Budhi was digging a pit in the company cook house. So Muthu enquired from him;

Budhi, timi chutti gaye na?

Sahib, ma tapai le dusain tira request garun la.

Kina?

Yesto cha Sahib, Mero aru dui bhai cha. Maile janam bata bhete ko chaina. Baba ko bite ko chithi pandhra din bitiyo. Ayle to sapai kaj khatam kare hola. Malai hazur lai pathayo bhane, Dushain ma gaye ra bhai haru lei bheti aunla—duita jurwa cha ani British ma cha!

Budhi explained that there was no point in rushing home because the letter from home reached him after fifteen days in transit, all the rites associated with his father's death had been solemnised. If he could be permitted to proceed on leave during Dushera, then he could meet his twin brothers whom he had not met for a long time since both were in the British Gurkhas.

A very practical mind—thought Muthu. That day he decided to become a Gurkha in his mental make up too. He decided to throw sentiment into the Paki bunkers, cleanse his soul from emotional thoughts and use a practical approach instead.

As he walked towards the view point—he saw one of the new recruits Bal Bahadur, looking through his binoculars to where a few cattle were grazing on the Indian side of the LC or line of control. Bal Bahadur did not know that Muthu Sahib was standing behind him– he kept shouting for the youngster accompanying them to push the cattle away from the Indian side towards the Paki side. Muthu asked him—

Bale timro awaz eti dur ta jandai na—Your voice will not carry to such a long distance

Said Bale'—*Doorbeen bata to najdik ai lagcha!*

From his binoculars he could see them very near! said Bale'—

Simple minds—beautiful guys– they could do anything if they were convinced that it was the right thing!

Muthu narrated this incident to the CO and the officers in the Mess and everyone had a good laugh.

Then Col Rai told them of three Adjutants who had met during a get together. Each of them narrated incidents to prove that his johnnies were simpler, but the point was not resolved.

Then one of them yelled—*Dhane' yo das rupya ko note linu ra bazaar bata eyota FIAT gari liyera auno!*

Take this ten rupee note and get me a FIAT car from the market!

Dhane saluted and ran off. *Hazur*! he shouted.

The other adjutant not to be outdone yelled—Ghane'

Ghane stepped in—*Ghane mero office ma jano ani check garnu ki ma tya base chun ki chaina!*

Go to my office and check whether I am sitting in my office or not!

While these three were laughing, unkown to them, the first two sahayaks had hidden in a bush and they called Dumare—Ei Gaunle! Hey– from the same village!

Aaj ke bhayo? Maile to agi ni bhane ko thiyo ki timro sahib ali lato cha!

What has happened today? I had told you earlier that your sahibs are slightly wonky!

Dhane laughed and said—CO Sahib must have seen some potential in him, that he chose to make him the Adjutant and there is a calendar from the contractor next to his bedside with Sundays and holidays in red colour to indicate that these are holidays. Today is a Sunday, how do you think am I going to buy a FIAT Car when the showroom is closed?

Ghane was laughing so much that he had to be pacified. My Sahib wants me to see whether he is sitting in the office or not! Just imagine– we have reached the moon and we have achieved such technological expertise—so should you not try and keep up, in your own humble way? Arey! Just pick up the phone give a ring to the Duty Clerk and ask—*am i sitting there?*

Now that's simplicity for you!

Surinder told them of another:

Two burly Sikhs were going home on leave and were sleeping on the lower and upper berths. There was a huge army box with a number painted on it lying in the passage and causing agony to all the passer bys—children were getting hurt, sarees were getting torn and so the passengers decided to do something about it.

They woke up the soldier on the lower berth.

Please get this box of yours into the baggage compartment—it is causing too many problems.

The soldier opened one eye slowly and promptly closed it and said—No!

Despite repeated requests the answer was always NO! Period!

Eventually the Railway Police was summoned at the next station and they pulled the poor soldier outside on the platform. The exasperated passengers—male, females and children began to beat the soldier. After a while the soldier told them to stop. Then he began to laugh—Arey! Why in God's name are you beating me?

Because you refuse to pick up your box—said one of the women

Bahenji– why should I pick up the box when it does not belong to me?

Then, the passengers noticed the other soldier on the upper berth. They charged in and began shouting at him.

What is the matter? He enquired innocently.

Why don't you remove your box?

Cooly he replied—because no one told me to do so!.

The battalion moved again– this time to the desert. Life in the desert was another story. At night temperatures were so low that the bottles of HALO shampoo cracked and broke, the bottles of hair oil too and in the afternoons it was stinking hot—one could have his lunch if there were no flies which bred copiously. The Mess Havildar had placed fine netted camouflage nets kind courtesy the armoured guys, on the entrances. In his opinion the flies could not fly through the holes in the net but they actually got confused by them, thanks to their compound eyes.

No one disputed this theory because it actually worked.

The other creature which caused some of us the jitters was the fast centipede which was known as *kankhajura*—reputed to make a bee line for one's ears. Scorpions were plentiful but we never saw one of the black ones– these were whitish or yellowish. Near every mound of earth one found myriad holes and tiny mice playing nearby. It was common for rat snakes to be in the vicinity because they were prey for them. Many of us who wore woollen pyjamas to ward off the cold at night never got time to discard the bloody things and when the sun came up it made life miserable. The desert had only one succulent shrub and the seeds of this shrub were like a two pronged affair—if they managed to get into your shirt or pants, it was fairly bad.

The water point had been set up adjacent to the canal and water was being supplied to the troops from the canal after necessary bleaching. Most of the boys had amibiasis at the beginning which eased later. As they exercised, one of the boys went to take a pee in the canal and just as he was about to unbutton his fly, his Havildar Sahib slapped him on his behind—

Silly bastard—this what the troops drink- OK.

The sheepish soldier pointed and Havildar Ganga Prasad was horrified to find a dead camel lying in the water. He vowed that he would not drink the water, but there was no choice– next morning he drank tea and slowly succumbed to a drink of water! Tonight he would have a drink to kill all these germs that were going into his tummy—and tonight there was plenty of meat and he would drink some rum to dislodge those little bastards from his tummy!

The tanks from the armoured regiment arrived early in the morning. Companies were allotted to the squadron which had brought eight tanks for the training. The squadron commander was a jovial guy who took one look at the overawed crickets in front of him and since Cariappa had told him to explain the basics in the most simple manner, he tried to do his best and interspersed his talk with a few jokes. The boys began to relax and enjoy their introduction to the tanks.

Soon the boys were quite familiar with their role and then came the grand finale when the tanks ran over their trenches. the faces of the boys glowed with excitement as if to say—*it wasn't too bad, was it?*

As the leading vehicle moved out from the Start Point at the appointed time, next morning, there was dense fog. As the vehicle picked up a little speed– thirty kilometres or so—there was a commotion, as though the vehicle had struck something. Subedar Dal Bahadur jumped out of the vehicle and found three sheep writhing on the ground– apparently they had been hit by the one ton vehicle in the fog. The shepherds came running in panic—Subedar Sahib thrust a few hundred rupees into the hands of the shepherd who looked relieved and grinned.

With a single flash of his khukri. Subedar sahib severed the heads of the animals who were in agony and after the blood had drained out—put the carcasses into the vehicle and caught up with his company.

A practical man– he hoped God would understand and forgive him for this action of putting the sheep out of their misery—and in the evening the Company would have meat! The battalion went in for the attack and then after the exercise was called off, the Company cooked the meat with a little sing song session facilitated by a little rum.

Surinder was passing by and the company Commander, Ashok Bose invited him over. As the boys belted out a few of his favourite numbers and Surinder danced with them, he realised that he was very fond of these soldiers, his comrades who had come from so far away to enrol in the Indian Army. Some of them had risen to the rank of Lieutenant General!

Surinder returned to Brigade Headquarters next day and passed the Sikh battalion Motor Pool getting ready for their CEME Inspection. They had opened the wheels from their jeeps and the burly guys had picked up the jeeps and placed each of them on four barrels so that they could spray paint them. They gave him a loud salute and requested him to have a mug of tea with them.

Surinder took a rain cheque and *told them that the tea would in any case stink of paint, petrol and grease!*

They laughed heartily and Surinder proceeded to the Brigade Major, to try and pick his brains for some lacunae which persisted in their plans. The DAA& QMG came in and gave Surinder a big hug—

Sir, The Brigade Commander saw you coming in. He wants to meet you.

The Commander as the Brigade Commander was called, shook hands and rang up Col Rai.

Udai, The results are in– Congrats– Surinder is through!

Surinder was relieved—Preeti would be pleased! And so would Darji and Beeji– not forgetting Mumma and Papa-- his in laws.

Col Rai requested the Commander to give the phone to Surinder.

Oye Khalse—what is keeping you in the Headquarter? Come back to the paltan– we have serious things to discuss– over some serious drinking too—be prepared to be drowned in beer!

And get ready to prepare for my farewell too! My posting has come too—I am going to the Centre as the Deputy Commandant!

Surinder walked back slowly to the battalion– he was in no hurry—he wanted to think and as the cold wind hit him in the face his mind began to register the fact that he was going to take over the battalion! He wanted Preeti to share the news with him, but inspite of the best effort of the FPO or the Field Post office, and the excellent CBPO, or the Central Base Post Office his letters would reach only on the third or fourth day.

3

THE CHANGE OF GUARD

The battalion returned to it's permanent location in field.

Since the Commanding officers were required to complete the process of handing and taking over charge, before the departure of the outgoing CO, a series of essential events had to be planned for the occasion. A battalion had arms, ammunition, documents, transport, stores-regimental and government issued and many more items to be taken on charge by the new incumbent, who was then stated to have taken over. The operational role also had to be handed over.

There was a series of conferences and discussions. The Adjutant and Quarter Master began the process of handing over and taking over between the Commanding Officer and the Second in Command. Essentially, all the stores of the battalion were on the charge of individual officers which included the Company Commanders, so papers were drawn up and this was done separately for the documents, arms, ammunition, vehicles and other government stores and separately for the regimental stores and funds. Manpower management, training policies, promotion policies and training cadres were important issues and required briefing especially in field areas, since the LOC or the Line of Control had to be physically explained and handed over in writing as well.

In addition, a series of social functions also had to be conducted in honour of the outgoing CO which would be replicated later for the new incumbent.

The Adjutant issued detailed instructions covering all the events and responsibilities were allotted as well.

The CO designate would be briefed by each Staff officer in the presence of the outgoing CO, so that any queries could be addressed.

There would be a Dining out for the CO in the Officer's Mess and a similar function in the JCO's Mess. A special *Barakhana* or a Regimental Celebration would be held in honour of the outgoing Commanding Officer.

There would be a Special *Sainik Sammelan* where the CO designate would be pipped with the rank of Colonel, by the outgoing CO and the Subedar Major. There would be a cup of tea with the Officers and JCOs followed by a ceremonial Group Photograph.

The CO s would proceed to the Mandir, to receive Durga Mata's blessings, then move to the Quarter guard and return to the office to sign the Official Handing / Taking Over documents.

Meanwhile an elaborately decorated jeep; would be waiting for the outgoing Commanding Officer, to be pulled by all the officers, JCOs and men ceremoniously; to loud cries of- *CO Sahib ki Jai*, bidding him adieu from the battalion which he had commanded! The programme was deliberately designed to ensure that the CO became sentimental and nostalgic because the paltan was bidding God Speed and farewell to the man who had guided their destinies during his tenure; and to remind him of his association with the troops, officers and the battalion itself.

Preparations began for the Barakhana in earnest. This was the Subedar Major's function and he would not tolerate slipshod arrangements especially for this function. The Quartermaster had ingeniously arranged for goats to be issued to the companies for the function. The Companies also received their share of rum for the evening. Enterprising companies like Charlie Company had arranged for chilled soda and ice for the guests.

No beer or whiskey was to be served unless requested by the outgoing CO, because rum was the troop's drink and with the troops all the officers drank rum except for the tea totallers who were seen holding on to their glasses of juice.

When everybody had been served their drinks the Subedar Major came and addressed the gathering.

Respected Colonel Rai, Colonel Surinder Singh, Officers, JCOS and my brothers in arms.

It is a sad day that we have gathered here today to bid farewell to our beloved Commanding Officer Colonel Rai Sahib!

In one of my eyes, I have tears, for I lose a very good friend and father figure whose generations served our Regiment.

In my other eye I have happiness, that Colonel Sahib will not be very far from us– since he will be going to the Centre at Benares; and we will be able to interact with him and seek his benign blessings.

Also our 2IC Sahib, Colonel Surinder Sahib is taking over the battalion in which he was commissioned!

I now request that you all join me in a toast! We seek Durga Mata's blessings and hope that she will guide Colonel Rai Sahib in his new appointment at the centre.

Jai Gorakh! Jai Hind!

With that he joined Colonel Rai and the officers and JCOs in a drink to commemorate the event. A few drinks later the entire group of officers and the Subedar Major began the round of the Companies. As they reached A or Alfa Company, the Company Commander and senior JCO came up to welcome them with the tray of drinks and snacks following behind. The Commanding officer had to reduce the quantum of drinks being offered because he had six companies to visit. The snacks were delicious and made just as they were made at home by the boys—hot spicy and delicious.

Gorkhali Chutney was– Til or sesame seeds ground into a paste, to which tamarind sauce was added for the tangy taste, pieces of boiled potatoes and radish with green chillis.

Bhutua was made up of chopped pieces of heart, lungs, stomach, and intestines, cooked in spicy hot chilli.

Khoon Andra was blood sausage cut in salami like slices and deep fried with spices to taste.

Liver cooked in spices and tomato.

Boiled eggs with salt and red chilli.

Potato fingers.

Pakoras– vegetables like brinjals, potato and spinach coated in ground black chick peas and deep fried, without which no party can hope to succeed!

The menu for the troops was almost similar and had been circulated well in advance so that it could be prepared in advance. The Quarter Master had arranged adequate goats for all the functions well in advance.

Colonel Rai would take a small portion of rum offered to him add a little water and salute the company. The boys would request him to dance with them to the popular tunes in vogue and then the group would move off to visit the next company—it was a ritual of bonding– some of the boys would have tears in the eyes as they danced reverently with Colonel Rai, which made him sentimental too because he may never see them again.

They began with a jhaunre:

Lahure Dai nachauna lagyo– soldier boy started to dance--

Ramdhi ko pani jhain sa la la

Then came Khursani bari ma—in the chilli patch

And later—Naini Talo—Oh Naini Tal—(a hill station in Kumaon)

Followed by Saili Maili ma bhanchu kasto cha(my darling– i will tell you what Darjeeling's like--)

Sapai le bhanchan Darjeeling ramro, ma bhanchu kasto cha

Then again—Bida Hone Bhaisakyo bela– pheri bheta hola kin a hola!(It is time to part company– will we meet again or not--?)

Naik Santosh Kumar the Company dhobi or washer man came up and offered his glass to the CO and requested him to take a sip from it and then came Havildar Moti Singh the Safaiwala who did the same and the CO took a sip from his glass too. Surinder watched from the side and the Subedar Major was on cue by his side to ensure that none of the boys caused any undue embarrassment to Colonel Rai, out of excessive love or sentimentality!

Truly this was love in the first degree and the real love for his troops showed in the moonlight! *The eyes of the CO were moist and he was getting nostalgic just as the Subedar Major had hoped he would! The battalion kindred spirit is such that each officer in the battalion begins to love the men under his command and this feeling runs deep—sometimes deeper than it is with real relatives. would, because one must shed tears for the boys, who considered you their God and are going to be separated from you in a couple of days.*

As the CO reached the last company his eyes were red rimmed from wiping away the tears which flowed of their own free will, but he was not ashamed, in fact he was proud of them because they symbolised his grief at the separation.

It was late and so they proceeded for dinner. Colonel Rai could not eat, but he indulged in a little of each dish so that the cooks were happy. Soon it was time to leave and a very tired Commanding Officer returned to his billet and his sahayak helped him to change. He was asleep as he hit the bed, dreaming of the madals, singing and *Ho Ki Hoina* of the boys of his battalion.

The next evening was the Dining Out in the Officers mess. All the Officers were ready to receive the Colonel as he arrived with the CO designate. Everyone was keen to be with the CO because he had been a *Father Figure* to them all and had guided them to the best of his ability during his tenure, granting them leave whenever the situation demanded even if the situation in the battalion was critical, detailing them on courses with adequate pre course and training them in various operations of war, taking care of their personal and command requirements in the battalion, which was one big happy family!

The best thing about him was that he had never been unfair in his decisions even if they were difficult.

There was a lot of leg pulling, some jokes peculiar only to the battalion, and some words of wisdom. Colonel Rai had been a good CO and he was very popular in the battalion. Such commanding officers are missed and revered by all ranks of the battalion.

As the drinks flowed, the time for fun and revellery began in earnest.

Dahiya sang a ragni– *Arey cycle wale mane bitha le—arey aadey tak le chaal re main thaki soon'!*

Raj sang—*Oh mere So– narey—so-narey– from Teesri Manzil*

And then he could not be stopped because he loved a captive audience.

Then came Chetri who sang– *Timro gaye ko geet ma– and Tyo pari gaon ma ramaillo thaon ma bajyo madal--*

Randy sang– *Pretty Blue eyes—*

Then someone sang– *mera lal dupatta malmal ka—oh jee!*

This was followed by– *aj diye rati raho mere mitra– a very touching Dogri song.*

Finally—*Bida hone Bhai sakyo bela– pheri bheta hola kin a hola?*

Everyone had heard these songs many times and in every party– sometimes in tune and sometimes out of tune depending on the state of intoxication the singer was in, but no one cared because we were after all a family and though there were many fights, woe to him especially from another battalion if he dared to criticise the battalion or any of the officers—he would be beaten black and blue!

As the evening came to a close—it was time for dinner.

After dinner, everyone assembled in the Ante Room for the farewell speech. Surinder was a powerful speaker and spoke of his association with Colonel Rai, and the Colonel's personal attributes and his achievements in the battalion. He prayed that the Colonel would find satisfaction in his new job and rise in rank. He then handed Colonel Rai the battalion momento to remind him of his association with the battalion because Colonel would henceforth enter the battalion only as a guest. Colonel Rai then presented a beautiful silver momento to the Mess, with the names of his ancestors who had served the battalion. It was a beautiful piece and a very fine gesture!

Colonel Rai also spoke to his beloved officers and thanked them for the momento he had received and which would remind him of his association with the battalion. He was grateful for the chance to command the battalion in which he had been commissioned. He would do all he could to look after the battalion's interests at the Centre.

Mi casa su casa—my house is your house he said and if any of them came to the Centre they should walk in and his wife and he would look after them, like their own children. The youngsters arranged a chair and Chaudhary seated the CO on it. Then Tony, Randy, Raj and Saikiya picked up the chair with the others lending a hand to dine out the CO from the Officers Mess with them all singing:

For he's a jolly good fellow, for he's a jolly good fellow,
For he's a jolly good fellooooooooo,
and so say all of us!

The party was over—the paltan had a new man at the helm and Colonel Rai would henceforth be treated as a guest in the Mess. Such are customs of the service.

Colonel Rai got a call from the CO of 1 Assam, Colonel Siama—Hey Man– *tum hamko miley bagair kaise ja sakta hai?* How can you leave without saying goodbye to us? Come over in the evening for a drink—OK, Rai sir?

Colonel Rai promised to see them but only for one drink.

The Assamese officers were a cheerful lot like their troops and soon they were singing while someone produced a guitar. Then Colonel Rai thanked them for their hospitality and hoped that some of them would come to Varanasi to wash off their sins!

The Assamese struck up their regimental song

Badlu Ram ka badan jameen ke niche hai--

It was a song sung in western style and some of the notes were beautifully whistled in perfection! Basically the song was about Sepoy Badlu Ram who had died in the War, but somewhere along the line the casualty regarding his death was not published. So the battalion kept getting his rations!

Colonel Rai finally extricated himself after almost four drinks—never again– he vowed!

SISTER VANDY AND THE JUMBOS

Surinder had a bad accident and suffered a minor back problem, due to which he had been posted as Administrative Commandant in Siliguri till he recovered and became Aye-One!

Surinder was careful about his spine.

Having read all about his ailment, Surinder knew all about his problem with the slipped disc. So, when he had pushed the staff car for some distance and tried to straighten up, he found that he had developed severe pain in his back somewhat akin to lumbago. After a restless night he warned Preeti that he was going to the Military Hospital to consult the doctor, because the problem appeared to be serious.

He drove down in his own car, with his luggage packed for a fortnight's stay. The RMO took one look at his face and knew that Surinder was in for a long spell because the disc would take time to stabilise. Surinder kept the car with him because it would be easier to go back home if he was discharged or allowed to go back home for a few hours.

The severity of the pain increased after the fourth day and Surinder began to feel really uncomfortable. The afternoons were easier because Sister Suzy would come over and she was a chatterbox. Suzy told them of all the local *gup shup* or news and kept a very strict tab on all of them. She was aware of Surinder's agony but then there was nothing she could do to alleviate the pain. So she made him laugh with her stories.

Suzy told them that the GSO3 (grade 3 officer of the General Staff Branch under the Brigade Major) of a forward brigade had landed in the hospital. He was on leave going to his sister's marriage
, but fate had other plans for him. He had gone to the toilet in the guest room reserved for him, but when he went to wash himself as most Indians do—with water– he used the bottle lying in the corner. It contained acid instead of water, normally used for cleaning the toilets and he had burnt his hand and his genitals. So he was being kept in a room under a mosquito net, to help his wounds to heal because he could not wear pyjamas.

Suzy called him *the officer with one ball*—the other one was slightly cooked said she!

Anyway one fine day Captain Shumsher hobbled in to meet us– wearing a lungi of sorts deliberately holding it away from his crotch. No one laughed for it was easy to figure his discomfort. Shumsher was a cavalry officer and told them of life at his brigade. Many of the posts had to be supplied by air, and in supplying a post of say 10 to 15 Sikh soldiers, a mistake had caused the package of cigarettes to be dropped to them instead of rum—one could only imagine the anger and frustration of these men surrounded by hostile environment and hostile neighbours. Yet many of the post commanders had developed excellent bonhomie with the locals who looked after them because in turn these posts kept them safe from hostile groups wandering in their areas. This was a land of spices and some grew abundantly in the wilderness especially *dalchini*. The locals were also expert weavers and wove their tribal patterns into their shawls.

The area had its surprises—you came suddenly face to face with a group of hunters clad in cod pieces and carrying sharp *daus* or machetes with bows and arrows to boot. Anything which moved or flew was game, albino buffaloes called *mithun* were local currency and the animals roamed freely with identification marks notched into their ears. These marks corresponded to similar markers made of bamboo and stuck along the roadside indicating each person's land jurisdiction in which he was king, jury and possibily executioner too! Yet life was simple and peaceful. The tribals did not drink the buffalo milk on the plea that if they drank the milk; the mithun became their mother, and which s.o.b killed his mother for food.

Shumsher healed slowly and was soon ready to leave. He had developed a liking for the beautiful Naga nursing officer who so devotedly looked after him. Both of them were madly in love and could not part with each other—Shumsher on his part had been a perfect gentleman.He promised to keep in touch and eventually as we learnt later, married the nurse. *It was the case of burning your balls to win a bride—any other takers?*

That began the joke session:

Cock and balls had a race
Cock fell down on his face
Balls the bastard won the race!

Pat came up with another one—Surinder warned him– Pat not another of your sardar jokes—(The Sikh community is the base for many jokes in India because the Sikhs are probably the only community which can laugh at themselves!)

It was difficult to laugh but even though it was paining—Surinder managed to laugh his guts out. It was the manner in which the joke was told and the Punjabi language which made lousy jokes sound really wonderful!

Frankie Babinall and Cynthia from the Oodlabarie Tea garden had come over to see Surinder, and Frankie could not help getting caught up in the joke session.

There was an old Colonel from the days of the Raj, who had gone back to England, married in his old age and fathered a beautiful daughter whom he called Annie. After a few years he had died and left his considerable property to her, but his solicitor told her that there was a letter which she could open only on the day of her marriage.

Time passed faster than she suspected and Annie fell in love with a handsome noble man called William, who would become an Earl after his father's demise. The couple got married and the solicitor came over to hand over her father's letter.

It was beautifully written and simply congratulated her on her wedding which he would have loved to attend. He advised her to open a safe deposit locker in which he had left her fifty thousand pounds as a honeymoon present. She was to proceed to India and from Delhi proceed to Jullunder where he had been posted in his younger days and recapitulate the wonderful days he had spent there as a young officer. He advised her to visit the market in particular.

So Annie and William went to Jullunder and found their way to the market.

As the couple were walking, they noticed the gentleman walking ahead of them in a very ungainly gait suddenly swerve and let go a stream of urine towards the wall. Annie was shocked and waited till the performance was over.

Then she hailed the offender, inspite of a tug from William, and said—

Excuse me, Sir, Doesn't the Police catch you?

The poor culprit turned to her and apologetically said—No Madam, there is a shortage of policemen—here we have to catch ourselves*!*

As he lay in bed for almost 25 days– evenings were best when his friends came over with Preeti and there was a flurry of the latest jokes.

But he missed his *chota* peg of whiskey! So he opened his heart to Major Sandhu one day!

Next day Sandhu came to see him with his wife Anita and she carried a thermos. Suzy's antenna was a-buzz and she was alert as if something wrong was about to be perpetuated; and so she asked Anita what was in the thermos.

Clear Soup– replied Anita and Suzy sauntered off for her rounds.

Sandhu could not control his laughter and said—Sir, you may have had many kinds of soup but you will love this one which was specially prepared by me!

As he poured the stuff, Surinder realised it was Peter Scot– his favourite poison.

Sandhu poured the stuff into a stainless steel tumbler and Surinder enjoyed his first drink after a long time!

Aaaaaaah great stuff! He liked the taste better than some brands of scotch!

The next day, Pat volunteered—it was his turn so he packed two large pegs into a half bottle of Bhutan rum and added some soda. As his scooter ride was fairly bumpy, the the Genie of the, soda became potent inside the bottle. As he parked his scooter, Suzy was standing with a quizzical look in her eye.

Pat smiled at her and then his smile froze as the pressure built up by the soda, broke the rum bottle in his parka pocket letting fumes of whiskey reach Suzy's nostrils!

It was sheer luck that Pat had put the bottle in a thick polythene bag which absorbed the flying shards, otherwise Pat would have been in thick trouble. But, bigger trouble stood in the shape of Suzy who gave him a dirty look– did not lose her temper, but just told Pat:

Sir, I think you need to go home and change your wet clothes!

As Pat drove off– Suzy sat on her chair and laughed her guts out! It was the guilty look on Pat's face—like a kid caught with his hand in the cookie jar!

Sister Vandita whom we all called Vandy came in to see Surinder. She was pregnant– with a prominent bulge, eight months or so we reckoned and blushed as she said—

Sir, I am pushing off on leave and just came to thank you for *all that you have done for me!*

Pat who could not let such a remark go waste, waited for Preeti to come and coolly admonished her:

Preeti, you of all the people I know, ought to be more careful about your husband—Vandy and he are upto some tricks--

Preeti was confused—What has happened--?

Pat looked at her aware that he now had a captive audience– continued—

Sister Vandy was here just a few minutes ago and she was going home on leave, so she came in to thank your husband.

What for? Asked Preeti.

For what Surinder had done to *her*—giving her that nice round bulge- said Pat without batting an eyelid.

Preeti began to cry.

Surinder gave Pat a dirty look and he apologised to Preeti. Surinder then explained that he has sent Vandy to his office in his staff car considering that she was eight months pregnant, to sort out some issues about filing her tax return through his Head Clerk; and she had come to thank him for his assistance.

Pin drop silence, and then it was fun to see Preeti chasing Pat in the lawn with her umbrella raised high!

The region was basically tea country and Tea Garden Managers lived their Brown Sahib existence with their snobbish noses in the air' as if they were God' gift to the region. Yet some were quite civil especially those who were from services families. You were invited at garden time, which was one hour ahead of IST. When you went to visit– no one would respond for some time, then an old timer would peer at you with rheumy eyes and ask you what you wanted. He would then reluctantly open the door and let you in, all the time keeping his eye on you lest you flick some artefact, and ask:

Pani layega?

Shall I get some water? If your answer was affirmative then the next question came in—*machine ka na matka ka----?* Would you like water from the fridge or the earthen pot?

Then another servant would come in with a trolley of home made eats—cakes and stuff called cookies.

Eventually memsahib would turn up in all her glory as if she had just emerged from a manicure and a pedicure!

Small talk comprised of the eatables that has been made for the New Year's dance, or preparation for the Annual Flower Show or how difficult it was to grow strawberries and tulips, the problems of keeping a goru or cow and the innovative shape the goru kamra or cowshed had been built in!

Most of the tea folk were a frugal lot and went into town on forays to buy their weekly supplies– their houses were so far away from civilisation.

But one envied the lovely and beautifully laid out bungalows, especially the ones on stilts!

The workers lived together in colonies and were paid wages by the contractor whose henchman coolly deducted whatever was owed to his boss for groceries or any other requirements taken by the worker on *udhar* or loan–who then went over to the old lady sitting outside her house with her pots of home made white coloured milky looking hooch; and took a long swig. The local elephants also loved the stuff and in the hot and humid nights would saunter over to the colony, lift the canopy of the hooch factory and drink the raw hooch to quench their thirst.

And then they walked the famous Hatari– Baby Elephant Walk!

Bums shaking across the road in wild abandon!

The local authorities had advised all the Army residents to desist from planting bananas and sugarcane because the elephants loved these—once Preeti, living on the first floor, opened a window to find one of these male pachyderms standing so close that she could have clambered on his back.

All she could do was to clamp her hand on her mouth to avoid letting off a scream!

The local Supply depot Commander complained that the elephants periodically rampaged his stock of sugar and rum. Someone suggested that they electrify the barbed wire fencing with a truck battery to enable a burst of current to sting their trunks. The elephants, it seemed had rudimentary knowledge of electric surges and had resorted to earthing the wire with one tusk dug into the ground and with the second breaking open the fencing to get at the rum and the sugar.

Basically the drill was that all the units were instructed to start up all their vehicles, switch on the lights and begin honking to frighten the elephants. Others were to start beating on empty tin drums in which oil or hydrogenated vegetable oil had been stored!

Another interesting unit which worked wonders for the soldiers was the cattle pound. As the time to go on leave came closer, the boys would go missing for an hour or so. They would scout for any cattle which had been let loose by the owners and capture them for handing over to the cattle pound which in turn gave them twenty rupees per head for the critters. So if an honest week's work was done the boys has enough cash to equip themselves with presents for their loved ones from Hong Kong Market in Siliguri!

Our Brigadier was a handsome man—six foot, fair with a cheerful glow on his face. As he walked into a party, he created a flutter amongst the ladies from the tea gardens. While being introduced, one very pretty, but *sozzled-on- gin and lime*; Bengali lady; he found that she would not let go of his hand after the introductions were over.

What do you do Brigadier?

The Brigadier was taken aback, but he recovered and said– well I command six districts which is a very large geographical area.

Without warning the lady took the Brigadier's hand and shoved it into her ample bosom and said—

Brigadier can you command these?

Not many people noticed, as the other officers had created a ring around the Brigadier, but his wife had noticed—*women always notice such things*!

As Surinder became better and rejoined the general stream of life in the station, he met the Brigadier during a party.

So Surinder, I missed you at a party I attended with these tea garden walas.

I heard about your incident with one of the Mem Sahibs—said Surinder with a slight hint of a grin.

The Brigadier liked Surinder; and said—Yup, it was so embarrassing—

Surinder continued to pull the Brigadier's leg—Sir– just curious--did you find *anything* there?

The Brigadier laughed—Actually, There was a lot in the blouse—but I was caught in a serious dilemma—on one end my manhood-*mardangi*- was exhorting me to keep my hand there till the lady pulled it out– but there was my wife giving me that look which only women can give to their spouses—my wife won and i had to take my hand out!

Come Surinder after this story we need another drink!

Surinder laughed so much that his drink spilled on his trouser bottoms– but no one could notice this because he was wearing a dark trouser.

The Area Commander was coming to inspect the Station—news came in that he was not only one of the senior most Major Generals in the Army but a very surly one to boot. The briefing had been arranged in Surinder's office and though adequate time had been allotted to the speakers, each of them cut down his briefing to the bare essentials and excused himself so that he would not have to go through any criticism from the old general. The General looked back and asked Surinder–

And how much time do you need Mr Administrative Commandant?

Surinder looked him in the eye and said– It depends on how much time you can spare and to to what depth you want me to explain the details of each case, Sir.

So, we are the *cheeky* sort are we?

No Sir, I was not being cheeky– merely stating the facts. said Surinder.

His Sub Area Commander gave him a look which just said—Easy does it!

But the die was cast—there was no going back—Surinder walked upto the podium with his notes, looked at them then and closed the file.

He realised that he was going to be with the General for three days– must he cower throughout? No, that was not going to be his style. If he did not close this chapter now, the General would brow beat him through out the three days.

He came out of the podium, stood to attention and addressed the General.

Sir, At the onset, I wish to apologise for my remarks which were not cheeky– I cannot dare to act in such a manner to a senior father figure, like yourself. Would you kindly forgive me if I gave the wrong impression?

The General was not prepared for this and said quickly—Forget the past and continue with your briefing, Colonel Surinder.

And so Surinder began the briefing, covering the geographical details of the Bagdogra and Siliguri sectors as well as the North Jalpaiguri area as well.Surinder went into the details of the many townships which the comrades had set up by encroaching on Army land, the illegal excavation of soil carried away by the poor to insulate their huts from the rainwater seeping in; the illegal felling of saal trees, portions of land occupied by some Gurkhas who were not aware of their mistake, the pylons erected by the electricity board on Army land and the next day they moved on to visit Siliguri sector. He also pointed out the boulders which were brought from the river bed and dumped on defence land.

At no stage did he feel the requirement to consult his notes, because he had a feeling that nothing could go wrong from now on; and in any case he had intimate knowledge of the subject. He went to the extent of suggesting to the General, that he could stop him at any stage of the briefing; if there was any issue where matters were not totally clear.

The Sub Area Commander explained to the General that Surinder had in actual fact, driven into a piece of land adjacent to the office of the Military Estates Officer, and given the encroachers ten minutes to clear out after which he would burn anything which remained standing on the land. In those ten minutes Surinder managed to close a case of encroachment which had been going on for more than ten years in a Communist environment.

The General nodded, impressed by his bravado and Surinder had won an instant admirer.

At the New Jalpaiguri Railway Station, The Sub Area Commander once again explained that the encroachments had been bull dozed by Surinder in one day.

The General looked at Surinder and asked,

I have some funds at my disposal which I would like to distribute. Can you suggest some deserving units to whom i can allot the funds?

I suggest you start with my Station Headquarter which has no source of funds.

The General asked—How much do you need?

Surinder looked at him and said—Fifty thousand rupees Sir.If I put this amount into a fixed deposit, i will be able to run my headquarter without having to request financial assistance from anyone.

The General agreed and so Surinder managed to get a television for three of his minor units and funds for the larger unit as well!

It was a good day—then why had everyone branded the General a prick?

Then Surinder learnt that the General had just lost his daughter and his wife in quick succession; leaving behind a six year old grand daughter, Shilpa, to look after. It was this loss which had made him a grumpy old coot, but essentially he was a good man.

It takes all kinds to make an Army!

As Surinder saluted the General at the airport, there was a small tear in his eye. He had taken a liking to Surinder and his forthright answers, his ability to maintain his goodwill amongst the local civilian authorities in spite of having a difficult job. He told the Sub Area Commander to recommend Surinder for a commendation.

Thank you Colonel– I have really enjoyed your company since the last three days.

Surinder's driver handed him a large parcel which he handed over to the General.

What is this?

A little gift for Shilpa, Sir, from Preeti and me!

The General took the parcel and hurried to his aircraft. At the top of the stairs he waved and went inside.

A few days later a letter arrived from him with a photo of a very pretty six year old clutching her huge Teddy bear and a scrawled note at the back which said–

THANK YOU UNCLE AND AUNTY!

The next day there was a call from the General, Shilpa wanted to talk to Auntie! So the two chatted animatedly for sometime till Shilpa cried—

I love you Aunty—promise me that you will come to see me when you come to Calcutta?

Preeti had no choice but to promise the little motherless child that she would.

Surinder was called for a temporary duty to Calcutta to explain the details of the encroachments on Army land and Preeti and he took Shilpa to shop for some shoes and leather bags with a trip to AC Market thrown in.

They also managed to meet Colonel and Mrs Jayant Chanda in Ballygunl Place. There was so much to catch up on. Bubli had got married and Paplu had joined Four Third Gurkha Rifles like his father. Mukri alias Mukherji was not traceable as he was not picking up the phone. Maybe the guy was not at home—anyway!

Many years later Preeti would receive an invitation from this little one for attending her marriage.

Such is life! Then Surinder told her of an anecdote doing the circles–probably the result of some mischievious mind.

It concerned General Menezies.

It was well known that he was a bullshitter and called a spade a spade So while on an inspection, he found a sepoy called Bhoop Singh, from the Jat regiment, detailed to be his sahayak or helper.

In spite of his cussing and his temper, it seems Bhoop Singh and he got along together very well. The general noted down the particulars of this humble soldier and during his next visit he was told that Bhoop Singh was earmarked for leave. As the formalities for leave were being finalised by the Company commander a message was flashed to him that Bhoop's leave was cancelled because General Menezies had sent for him.

So like old friends the General and he got along during this visit too. Bhoop was sanctioned leave and was finally at Jammu railway Station, getting ready to board the train when two Military Policemen asked him to follow them to the MCO, s office.

The MCO instructed him to report to a certain Headquarter, because General Menezies had asked for him. Without a murmur, Bhoop Singh returned for duty with the General.

After completing his duty, he was ordered to proceed on leave.

As he reached home, after the initial formalities, Bhoop decided to change " engine oil" as the soldiers joke, but his wife did not sound enthusiastic.

Now what is the problem– do you know how much i endured to be with you?—he whispered to her.

Arey ji, you know that I love you and you want it too, but she whispered back—Menses!

That blew the lid from Bhoop singh's cool—Arey Bhai– ye Menezies yahan bhi pahunch liya ke?

O brother! Don't tell me Menezies has reached here also.

This joke is not authenticated but a joke is a joke!

The Battalion in Assam and a Spot of Leave

The battalion was posted in the state of Assam and some of the militant Assamese students had gone underground. Essentially a very docile people, the state of Assam had been totally ignored. Never had any Prime Minister or the Centre taken any effort to improve communications, road rail or air in the state. While the rest of the country watched TV, this state continued with AIR the national Radio. It was small wonder that the community elders supported the militancy and even guided it. Essentially it was the case of the youth asserting itself, but with unbridled power grows corruption and arrogance.

Their outfit called ULFA had started off well and then the senior cadres had gone astray. They began by interfering in the tea gardens, had gone on to pillaging the country side and imposing some sort of taxes on the industrialists and the tea gardens, without realising that by stopping work in the gardens, a large number of workers were laid off with accompanying financial problems

Meanwhile the youth danced the *bihu.*

The local population in Assam were a very affectionate lot and while the women toiled in the factories, gardens and the fields the men folk preferred the manly sport of carrom board. Four bamboo stumps were dug, on which the carom board was placed while the players carried on playing the game while standing. There were Assamese, pale, mongoloid features and very simple in mannerism, the tribal workers—the *Adivasis* were dark and swarthy, whereas the Bengali population was a trifle sophisticated and wealthier because they ran the business centres, or worked as the babus in the tea factories. The Adivasis lived on a day to day basis—their children were either fishing in ponds, using catapults or bows and arrows to kill anything that moved. The land was fertile and the rain plentiful and so certain varieties of gourd grew abundantly. There was hardly any local fruit—any fruit which was available was the local pygmy banana, pineapple or oranges from the hills across the river. Probably no one had given a thought to the planting of orchards even for fruit like grapefruit and other citrus varieties. Jackfruit grew in abundance and huge piles of them were stacked on the roads waiting to be transported into the hinterland.

Crotons grew rapidly to the height of a small tree and it was said that the land was so fertile that if one kept his finger in the dirt for a few hours, it would sprout leaves! Leeches swarmed the country side and the greenery was so painful to the eye and the sight of a red blouse and *mekhla chadar* worn by the local women was a distraction. The women were attractive, and did not nurture the inhibition of the northern areas of the country.

They danced the bihu which was a beautiful ensemble created by clever gyrations of the pelvis—very sexy indeed. The simple notes created by a goat's horn were pure and appropriate. There was no inhibition in the interaction between boys and girls as in the Northern states and it was the local belief that the land on which the youth danced their folk dances, was blessed. The *bihu* on the face of it was a sort of a subdued *bhangra*; which was boisterous and much more colourful– nay livelier.

The language was difficult to comprehend initially–if Bengali sounded as though the speaker had one *rasagulla* in his mouth, then Assamese was as if the speaker had two *rasagullas* in his mouth while speaking. Rasagullas are the favourite sweets in the region.

People transited across Chabua, Lilabari, Jorhat, to Tezpur, Gauhati and Calcutta by the Indian Airlines flights, which criss crossed across the mighty Bhramaputra. Legend has it that the traveller who did not pay obeisance at the Kamakhya Devi Temple in Gauhati, would have to cross the river seven times, but a couple of flights from Chabua to Calcutta soon completed this requirement. As Surinder travelled to Tezpur in one of these flights, he was in uniform. A beautiful Assamese girl sitting in the middle seat across the aisle was keen to strike up a conversation with him, but she did not know English or Hindi, whereas Surinder did not know the local lingo. Another girl voluntarily acted as an interpreter and soon they reached Tezpur. At Tezpur this girl, a *Gogoi* from Lilabari, walked up to Surinder and held his hands affectionately and wished him best of luck. This gesture was very alien and had a very emotional effect on Surinder. This was the respect for the Army and for an outsider rolled into one and would haunt him for a long time– *a simple Assamese girl with the heart of gold!*

If you brushed someone by mistake the other person would apologise and your luggage was safe on the railway platform unlike in other stations. In those days. The cows probably had TB, and the grass was coarse and fibrous. In addition, the cattle were just about the size of donkeys. There were few means of commutation and in this part of the; country people travelled by and transported goods by *maar* boats, single and double boats or by steamers. The river was almost twenty kilometres across at places and shallow banks were numerous- - one crossed it in zig zag fashion following the long line of buoys installed by the Inland Water Transport.

The story went that someone wanted to know the origin of the word Babu, because he was an enigma and was found everywhere, and wherever he went he would soon carve a niche for himself—where did the title of BABU, originate?

Then a local Assamese youngster, who had just returned after completing his education in Darjeeling explained—

Mr Maxwell the newly appointed Superintendent of the Bengal Railway Board had remarked to his friend that the local males were quick to ape the English in their manner of dress and speech.—though they would not part with their dietary habit of maach and bhaat.

Said Maxwell to Jones his junior—We will make baboons of them yet!

The local clerk who heard him was delighted and said to his friends—The good news is that our new designation in terms of Maxwell Sahib's words is–that we will be known as Babus!

Everyone looked at him waiting to catch a hint of mirth in his eyes, but our youngster appeared dead serious!

Life moved in a very different stroke—on the villages adjacent to the road, one could see a set pattern—one or two houses, a pond with fish a couple or more coconut trees and a few beetel palms, which gave green fruit which ripened into saffron colour and inside was a nut called *Koi.* On a visit to a local's house it was customary to be offered slices of raw beetel nut on a half leaf of *paan* on which some lime had been spread. As one put the beetel leaf and nut in one's mouth, the juice caused the head to sweat and one felt a trifle hot and intoxicated. The regular consumption of this concoction blackened one's teeth.

Fish was abundant, almost everyone had a pond and the Bhramaputra had river porpoises too! The locals had coined names which sounded strange to us but were useful for them—for example a crossing of two roads was called *charali,* while the point where roads met in a T junction was *tenali!* One had to dry clothes whenever the sun shone otherwise fungus got in and caused damage beyond comprehension!

The language spoken by the locals and the tribal labour was harsh and singsong. It was a real twist of the language; just as the Mumbai walas had done to their Hindi vai *tapodi—only more refined.* A beautiful girl stepped on the road—she was carrying lichis—a very delicious fruit, a hot favourite of the Punjabis. She offered fifty pieces for as little as twenty rupees. The fruit was large in size, beautiful in colour and tasty as well. Preeti wished she could carry some more for her friends. The girl seemed to have some telepathic insight—she nodded to Preeti, disappeared and brought her a beautiful basket with a lid for her subsequent purchase.

They caught the train at Tinsukia, the Brigade Commander felt Surinder needed a deserved break— everyone jokingly said—the name as indicated by the railway signpost was Teen Sukhiya, spelt *Tinsukia– three comforts*, but actually there was none! The train was a jam packed metre gauge train which was converted to a broad gauge train after Gauhati at a station called New Bongaingaon. The meter gauge train would steam into the station and the coolies would cart your luggage onto the broad gauge train waiting on the platform. One was supposed to have corresponding seats confirmed in the broad gauge train, but the railwaymen were not gods, and sometimes your name did not appear on the charts—result—you fought tooth and nail with the TTE, because you had a wife and children to worry about, but the TTE just shrugged and sent you to travel in the second class bogey!

This was the East and there was no urgency of any kind and nor was there an emergency!

If you tried to yell at the TTE from close quarter, your clothes were sure to be spoilt by the spurts of beetle juice, from the paan he was chewing; with a ton of reddish fluid swirling in his mouth! Anyway, a few rupees later you were miraculously rehabilitated, when you had been drained out of all your energy, and not prepared for a move! Then one realised that this was a very long ride and it was better to be comfortable. Preeti always prepared parathas and chicken pickle for the journey because this lasted. Sometimes they would buy a bunch of the local pygmy bananas, called *Kol* by the locals–a variety which was delicious in taste-a slightly tangy flavour, and it had a very thin skin. The bananas ripened during their journey and lasted till Delhi.

Then there was the madness of Delhi—taxi drivers had agents scouring the platforms for passengers and they bargained you out of your wits! Eventually the coolies or porters haggled over the charges to be levied for the luggage and one moved on to the waiting taxi. It was a mammoth feat to exit from the Railway Station and they finally saw Connaught Place and were moving towards Pandara Road to Khan Market, Kotla Crossing and Defence Colony! At the crossing, a car driven by a driver, cut across their taxi, stopped briefly, the door opened and driver sahib let out a thick stream of beetle juice on the road!

Then without looking back, he took off!

After all the whole of Delhi was a large washroom and toilet rolled into one!

At their house the elders ran to pick up Jaskaran, The interest is always sweeter than the principal—an old saying in Punjabi maintained! Surinder joined the servants in lugging the luggage to their bedroom. Preeti went about meeting Beeji and Darji and at the same time clarifying certain thoughts which were troubling them.

After some rest, Surinder and Preeti went to visit CP—or Connaught Place. As Surinder stepped down from the pavement towards the main road, a bus came alongside and Preeti saw a funny fellow pouting his lips in an effort to spew a stream of beetel juice and saliva. Her promptness saved Surinder from ruining his new suit!

Whew!

Delhi had become a dangerous place– especially for new comers. The traffic was unruly, drivers who earlier were submissive and respectful, were now aggressive and prone to road rage—maybe this was the result of seeing too many movies, which had violence as the main theme—with a small to medium seasoning of sex!

The policemen were very organised and since most of them were Jats from the Haryana belts they refused to reason with you except for the colour of your money. The labour class seemed to come from all the surrounding states and slowly professions had become state based—like all the plumbers seemed to be from Orrissa, electricians were from UP, Nepalese and Garhwalis made up the fast food, and *Mo Mo, and fish, kebab, tandoori* joints!

In fact Kotla was inhabited by Kumaonese and Nepalese; Bhogal and Jangpura by Kashmiris and possibily Pathans and Iranis.There was a guy with a flowing beard supplying huge *naan rotis* on his scooter to several families in the area. One enterprising Kashmiri immigrant had opened a take away with some mouth watering menu on display. Shop keepers had begun displaying wares in Urdu sign posts!

Girls were wearing lesser garments and showing more skin—those working were busy trying to ward off stress by smoking and acting very urbane and grown up. The boys were having a great time notching up their kills, while porn ruled the day! It was a mad mad world—kids spent time drinking in the new fangled clubs, called discos and danced their heads off in them.

The Sikh and Punjabi communities could not lag behind—the youngsters preferred to avoid wearing turbans for as long as they could and their newly earned fortunes made them flaunt their good fortune—gold chains, flashy wrist watches and fancy clothes! Surinder called them Kukus, Biloos and Titoos. The girls had to be Goldie, Sweety, Pinky or Babli and they outshone boys in every way! The Billoos and company had to ride the latest bikes or cars with the maximum accessories and drive in the fast lane while the girls liked to splurge in the new country called the Malls! Papa would quaff scotch as though his life depended on the amount he drank; while Mumma would become a member in as many kitty parties as possible—

Oh gal suno---circle wadda hona chaida hai– it makes your circle wider!

One wondered-the way our people drank scotch– was there enough water to drink and bathe in Scotland or were the Scots drinking sea water?

Surinder sometimes pondered as to what would happen when his son grew up. This was evolution—he was not going to get judgemental—after all he had lived his youth in those times and now Jaskaran's time would come and mentally he must be prepared to see the worst—but if his parental guidance and companionship, coupled with Preeti's love; was going to be important for the children they would not land into a mess! Jaskaran was growing up—he was now in Class X.

Preeti broke the news to Surinder– she needed an operation and would not be able to have any more children. As she cried, Surinder felt sad, but he told Preeti not to cry– it was God's will. They would provide Jaskaran the best education possible. Their aim would be to become his best friends so that his need for a sibling would never emerge.

Preeti and Surinder visited their friends and relatives. His business friends threw lavish parties and scotch flowed all night. The ladies drank wines as though they were raised on the stuff– but not many knew what they were drinking or what to look for in a wine—or a cocktail! They simply drank to give the impression that they were very elite and cultured. They could recount the trips they had made to the US or UK and to the continent. Somehow few had been to the South Americas.

Culture could be bought! Bhangra needed no instructors and a little intake of booze was required to shed your inhibitions! Low cut blouses made– by *computerji* were the rage! And *Masterji* made the ladies wait longer than their dentists would—what a great generation!

Preeti would come home from these parties and laugh because Mamta Agarwal pronounced Crème de Menthe as *Cremey di Maa,* and Sushila Bhatia called Champagne– *Cham–pagne.* She confessed that it was difficult to keep up with these ladies who were literally globe trotting at the drop of a hat! Some were going courtesy their medical company, some were going thanks to their insurance company and others like lawyers had trips sponsored by clients—fully paid for with the proviso that you would get them adequate business on your return! Chartered Accountants went on company sponsored trips for saving tax money and politicians went abroad to study foreign village systems without wandering into one of ours!

Life was great– all this was only possible in a growing economy such as ours! Surinder realised that Army guys especially those who lived on their income and did not have access to money from home could not keep up with the Joneses! Not in this life time, because the kids were going to school in chauffer driven cars and little mem sahiba had her own car which she parked outrageously on the college pavement.

Truly this country would have languished in every walk of like if our myriad gods were not around to pick up the pieces!

He felt very much at ease at the Golf Club or the DSOI because one ran into so many friends, course mates and seniors. Everyone knew the other's budget and enjoyed his drink sagaciously without having to get high. Some ladies drank a shandy while some preferred a *chota or a burra* peg. There was an air of relaxation and the ambience was sober and friendly. Surinder ordered a large vodka and a tonic water for himself and a Bloody Mary for Preeti, with a *chota* peg of vodka Smirnoff. The waiter smiled and inquired about their health and their long absence from the club.

Groups were either regimental, course mate type, golf foursomes, bridge foursomes or had some other affiliation. If one of the ladies had lost her husband then the others escorted you to the club and left you home.

Preeti nudged Surinder, his old CO, General Katoch had walked in, and it was a great reunion with a lot of backslapping and bon homie. The General had grown grey and was now a Corps Commander—but he was at heart still Surinder's CO. He was keen to know all the intimate details of the unit– the officers and the men. Mrs Katoch held Preeti's hands and looked at her like a mother would. It was so nice to be together again. Surinder knew that his tenure with the battalion would be over soon, so he requested the General to plan a visit to the battalion. Mrs Katoch was also keen to meet everyone and so it was arranged that the General would come for the Raising day.

Their animated revellery would just not finish and soon it was time to leave. Surinder promised to meet the General within a couple of days before he departed for Chandi Mandir. He asked him where he was likely to be posted. Surinder explained that he had been posted to Bhatinda as the Col GS (SD)—not a very hot shot appointment, but one where he would learn a lot.

The General nodded and assured him that he would keep a tag on Surinder's reports because Surinder's board was due soon for his next rank. Surinder knew that the General would observe from a distance but would not try to influence anyone.

That was more than enough because he had confidence in himself.

At the Corps Headquarter Surinder found himself posted as the Colonel General Staff (Staff Duties) or the Col GS (SD)—or as the Cops Commander put it– the fountainhead of the HQ. All orders emanating from the General's office were issued to those concerned, by him. His other task was that he was the officer in charge of protocol and was responsible for arranging receptions of visitors to the headquarters, or the formation. He was also responsible for ensuring that everyone was correctly seated for conferences as per protocol and was responsible for the location of units as per their KLP. His boss was a brigadier who had six colonels under him—*kept the Sundays free* as someone aptly put it.

Brigadier Shanker Singh was from the ranks– a real go getter and very quick on the uptake as someone said. Since he was not convent or public school educated– he would listen carefully and if he liked a phrase or a word that some general had used, he would practice it till he had got it perfectly. He liked to work and did not mind being called a work-aholic! He was living alone and there was no attraction in leaving his office because his empty house reminded him of his family. He enjoyed slipping into his native guttural Haryanvi dialect and often threw phrases to his staff much in the manner that villagers used in the fields.

Surinder did not mind the Old Man—he took him as his father figure and they got along quite well. Surinder knew that his boss had not slept, there was a requirement from Command HQs which needed to be completed and put up to the Corps Commander next morning. Surinder also knew that his boss did not like a crowd and preferred to work with the Col GS (Ops) and possibily one more officer. So when the BGS turned up next morning, with blood shot eyes, Surinder knew that it was best to leave him alone—but there was an important visit scheduled and the draft programme needed to be approved at the earliest.

So he stood respectfully waiting for the BGS to speak to him.

Tun lath le ke mere sar par kyon khara hai re? Why are you standing at my head with a staff in your hands?

Sir, ek jaruri approval leni thi—There was an urgent approval i required from you sir!

He took the draft made a few changes and looked up—*Tene fixed wing aircraft allot karwa liya hai kya*? Have you got a confirmed allotment for a fixed wing aircraft?

Abhi nahin Sir—not yet Sir!

Arey– khoti teri bandhi hai Thane mein; aur tu laga kiraye pe dene— Your donkey is tied up in the police Station and here you are arranging to give it on rent—in other words when you do not have a firm allotment how are you planning for it?

Surinder grinned—Aap ke hote hue Air Force wale naa to nahin karenge—Sir with you here the Air Force guys will never refuse—

This would bring a smile to the BGS's lips and so Surinder would go to his office and wait—till he was called again—

The BGS would make a few changes again—

Surinder would wait again for the next call and take the original draft's fresh copy as well.

The BGS would make few more changes and then look up still not happy—at which point Surinder would put up a fresh copy of the draft. The BGS would change this one to his first annotation and hand it back.

Now Surinder would send for the concerned clerk and send out the final signal leaving one copy for the chief of Staff and Corps Commander's information.

This became a ritual. Plan A—the initial plan, would always win!

Bhatinda was a desert—but it had an oasis in the shape of a beautiful golf course. Imagine a course where huge beehives hung from the trees and greens where you had to shoo out the *neel gais* before *putting* on them! They loved grazing on the succulent grass. The Course had long fairways, and one could enjoy long drives– with the risk of losing your ball from a slight error.

But what the hell– where could you enjoy your game without worrying about the ball because the club sometimes gave you subsidised balls too!

The BGS did not play and when he was sitting in the office alone and needed some company he would send for Surinder, inspite of knowing that he was in the middle of a game. This love story carried on—and on--!

There was never a dull moment in Bhatinda for Surinder. Some senior general or the other would be visiting the Station and a visit programme had to be made for him and his spouse separately. While the VVIP was picking the Corp Commander's brains, the lady had to meet the Station ladies, visit the Asha Centre for children who were physically or mentally challenged. Also see the many welfare activities being conducted in the Station and visit any place of interest in the vicinity. If the VVIP was visiting forward areas of the Corps then a programme would be put in motion to take him to these places by road or by air depending on the availability of time. There would be a social function arranged for the couple to enable them to meet the officers in the Station.

Surinder often went down to the Dam Dama Sahib Gurudwara, one of the five Sikh Takhts, for here Guru Gobind Singh had rested during his battle with the armies of Aurangzeb. It signified a lull in the battle. It was also a pity that Panditji had given no serious thought to the valour of the Sikhs in his Discovery of India, nor to the fact that Guruji had sacrificed his sons for the faith. He had not given importance to the ninth Guru's ultimate sacrifice for the Kashmiri pundits. The land seemed to be seeped in the blood of so many brave warriors and invaders alike.

Most of the youth had left for Canada and other Western countries in search of a better future and the land was being cultivated by Bihari labour. Most of these labourers had found good pickings here and settled down in their own settlements bringing the habit of chewing khaini, to the Punjabis as well! Back home they were steeped in caste taboos and preferred not to work, but sell an acre of land to survive the year with the money it fetched. Other more enterprising jokers laid traps on the highway forcing the travelling busses and cars to pay for the Saraswati Puja, Durga Puja, or some other puja to extort money which was divided amongst the organisers of the loot!

Soon this land of the five rivers would become Bihar– laughed Laaloo!

Very few people travelled in Punjab by trains because the roads were so good and bus services efficient. Road side dhabas did a brisk business by making a deal with the drivers who were pampered by them if they stopped their busses at their locations. It was a dog eat dog case– a win win situation if you please. The bus driver was always considerate to the service men and stopped his bus to pick them up or drop them at the gates of the cantonment.

Bhatinda was cotton growing country– cotton was known as *narma*. The local college was the Government College and it never went on strike. The kids many of whom came from remote villages preferred the hustle and bustle of the college, to working in the fields. There was a notice board of sorts and warnings were written on it for eve teasers to beware or risk being beaten up by vigilante squads.

These were the keepers of the faith!

English classes were taught in Punjabi! During the interview of the students one went like this;

What is your name young lady?

Sir mainu samaj nahin aya—jara samjha deo ge? Sir i have not understood– can you explain—

Beeba– Main puchya hai– What is your name– *tuada naa ki hai?*

Sir main Punjabi wich naa das deyan—mainu English nahin aandi hai. Sir can i give my answer in Punjabi– I do not know English.

There was a time when Shakespeare was being taught by the professor.

Bacheyo—tusi ta jande ho ki Julius Caesar marno uprant jyada bhayanak ho gaya siga. O kiven hoya?

Children you are aware that Julius Caesar was more terrifying in death than in life. How is that possible?

Amrik Singh or Amrika put up his hand– Sir marnu uprant bhoot banuga te saryan nu darauga!

Amrik Singh or Amrika answered—Sir after his death he will turn into a ghost and spook everyone.

*Thik hai– Shahbash– lagda tusi pad ke aye ho!*This is indeed the right answer– looks like you have studied your lesson and come.

And Amrik twirled his moustache with pleasure!

It was in such circumstances that the children from the Cantonment learnt their P-english as they called it! And they laughed their way home.

A Time To Reflect

Life at the Corps Headquarters began to mellow down. As usual there was a bonhomie at the senior level but at the junior level there was a healthy rivalry, which translated into fierce loyalty when it came to other formations whether they were higher or lower ones. It was a very real relationship which kept every one tuned on!

The BGS was working furiously and soon Surinder learnt that there was to be a very major exercise without troops where many generals were to attend– some from other formations. Since these senior officers were to be received, Surinder briefed his team of LOs (Liaison Officers), Liasion JCOs and vehicle drivers in detail and issued the coordinating instructions well in advance so that every unit could act on them.

Similar conferences were being held in the other branches as well. Eventually the BGS also had his conference which included Brigadiers, colonels and a medley of junior officers too. The BGS welcomed all those who had come to participate and briefed them about their duties. Since he had a soft corner for Surinder, and wanted the audience to know this, he said probably in jest—

Now Surinder– I want all these instructions issued by this evening and if this is not completed in the time frame that I have laid out I am going to chew your balls.

Surinder jumped to his feet and said– Excuse me Sir! I take strong exception to your unveiled threat to my spherical jewels!

The BGS had not anticipated this and was flustered—Surinder my boy have i hurt your feelings? If so let me put on record that I am sorry!

Surinder did not relent—Sir! We have worked together for two years and this is a long time. During this period you have chewed my balls several times and you are aware that very little of them is left. May I request you to leave the remainder alone because my next Boss may also have similar ideas and I do not want to disappoint him!

For a flick of a second there was pindrop silence and then the BGS let out a full throated laugh and the audience followed suit!

Come here Surinder– I want to give you a big hug!

The exercise kept the BGS very busy and Surinder realised that the constant sitting in his chair, chain smoking and lack of exercising was taking its toll.

After a few days, Surinder found his Boss in agony—doubled in pain. When he inquired from him it turned out to be a case of piles. Surinder rang up the Military Hospital, asked for the Surgeon, a young Major and fixed an appointment. He had arranged a scooter tube from one of the younger officer and he took the BGS to the MH. After the examination, the Surgeon decided to operate immediately due to the condition. Without informing anyone Surinder had the BGS operated and admitted to the ICU. Soon after he regained consciousness, the Lady Doctor in charge of the ICU rang Surinder up and told him to come quickly. The BGS was smoking away-- something taboo in the ICU where serious patients were admitted. Surinder had the BGS shifted to a single room. But the BGS was not happy and requested to be sent home. The Surgeon agreed on the proviso that dressings would be done at home

Slowly the wound healed and the BGS was back in his chair and everyone heaved a sigh of relief! Not many people knew that it was almost impossible to keep the BGS away from the office—they had to literally tie him to his bed.

Life in the headquarter revolved for Surinder between weekly conferences issuing instructions for VIP visits and receiving or seeing off guests. During one party at the Officer's Mess, Surinder took a scotch for the VIP. It was dark and just as the waiter poured out the soda, a black insect floated upwards—bugger had been drinking the scotch on the sly!

The visiting General had a sense of humour—he said:

Colonel—Can you replace this whiskey? I would have thrown the blighter out with my finger but he is one of the stinkey types. Shame to throw away scotch but- -!

Surinder said—Got to grant him fine sense Sir! He decided to carry out kamikaze in your Scotch and not in any other indigenous brand!

The General nodded—Yes! Give him that! and Surinder changed his glass.

The Brigadier looking after the guests was overhearing the conversation:

Surinder please be careful next time—

Sir! I hope you are not implying that I put the black monster in the glass deliberately—said Surinder and walked off with a chuckle!

The General's train was past midnight—and after the party he went off to sleep. As Surinder came to take him to the Station, he was looked tired and his clothes were looking crumpled. Surinder was in his uniform, because of which the simple Railway personnel mistook him for the General. The train was waiting and soon a second train steamed in.The train in which the General was to leave was being disinfected—it had come from Gujrat where an epidemic of major proportion in the shape of plague had broken out.

While the General was having some coffee, Surinder managed to inter change his reservation from the train from Gujrat; to the other train, shifted his luggage and the TT came to give him the tickets and to inform him that it was time for them to depart. Surinder casually took the TTE aside and thanked him profusely for his assistance.

The General was about to board his earlier train when Surinder requested him to alight and board the second train.

Why did you change my train Colonel? asked the General.

Then he was hit by a sudden smell of the disinfectant; and it dawned on him that Surinder had done him a favour for he would not have been able to sleep because of the smell!

As the train left the station the General thanked Surinder and waved!

It was during one stint of leave from Bhatinda that Surinder noticed the book on the pavement at Darya Gunj, just opposite the Moti Mahal restaurant. He had glanced casually at it and gone past when the pictures of officers and men on the cover beckoned him to take a second look. The book contained details of Indian prisoners of war in Pakistan. It was published by Trishul Publications, NOIDA India. The cost was about Rs 195/-and it was a volume of 464 pages with detailed accounts and photographs about the plight of our prisoners in Pakistan. Apparently the Indian Government had no use for them and probably closed the case because they were an embarrassment!

However the authors Brigadier Man Mohan Sharma and Lt Col Rajkumar Pattu claim that the apathy towards the PWs was essentially because Mrs Indira Gandhi, the erstwhile Prime Minister of India had ordered the repatriation of the Pakistani PWs without securing the release of the Indian PWs! She took this arbitrary and dictatorial stand by snubbing Babu Jagjivan Ram Shri YB Chauhan, Generals Prem Bhagat and Inder Gill. The authors feel that these gallant servicemen were decorated with fictitious awards posthumously, even though they were alive; this made one's hackles rise with horror. The authors had been brutally frank!

There was an account of Major Sandhu, of 15 Punjab Regiment. He became a POW on 04 December 1971 and his name was announced by Pakistan Radio on 05 Dec 71.He had lost an arm and to add insult to injury a statue of his was installed at Wagah despite protests from his wife Jasbir. They had been married for a very brief period and had been blessed with a daughter, one who knew her father only from photographs.

Surinder returned to go to the Base Hospital and there on a chair sat a lady resembling Mrs Kanwal Jit Sandhu! He wished her and sat with her. She was staying quite close by– near Niti Bagh and he promised to look her up. It was a heart rending story of privations, hardships in bring up her daughter, getting her educated and then arranging her marriage. Her repeated requests to everyone for support in locating her husband and the assistance from Colonel Pattu. But the Government refused to budge neither did the Army!

In Army parlance, these valiant soldiers *had been written off*!

That night Surinder could not sleep. He woke up shuddering in a sweat thinking of the shoddy treatment these poor guys would be receiving at the hands of the Pakis. If some were dead– were they thrown into an unmarked grave forgotten for posterity except to their loved ones?

Why was the Government of India sleeping over this issue—the Americans would not have got into this mess and if they had they would have bombed their way out of it. Gives the common citizen some solace, otherwise why would a soldier fight if no one wanted to recover him from the clutches of the enemy or at least reclaim his body and cremate or bury him with due respect.

This was a point for reflection.

The trip to Delhi had been very illuminating. They could not get a direct train to Delhi and got off at Ambala took a deluxe bus and were on the road to Delhi. In front of them sat a small mousey guy who was leaning his head precariously on the ample bosom of an attractive young lady—she appeared six months pregnant and was obviously uncomfortable because she had slid a buttock off the seat to get away from the belligerent advances of our friend. Surinder told Preeti to ask her to exchange seats with him and took her seat himself. Now he pushed our friend into the corner and stuck his shoulder into is armpit and began squeezing. At Delhi our friend was last seen massaging his arms and shoulder while grimacing in pain!

The other thing which he noticed in almost all the new buildings was the framed pictures hung on the walls of every landing to dissuade beetel munchers not to spit on the walls. Across the street there were two fellows trying to break down a wall by urinating on it together. Scrawled on the wall was a sign which said—*those who piss here are dogs!* Our people have not learnt anything after so many years despite their claim to be the dawn of civilisation!

Why the local administration could not provide these basic amenities, was beyond him! Men who have the right to vote also have the right to urinate in a proper place!

It was a time to reflect—was all the money in Swiss banks that of the political parties? Was that the reason why no serious attempt was being made to recover it? Why was the judiciary not cleaning up their act– why had a tainted Judge been appointed the Chief Justice of a State. Why were jail birds having a great time– thanks to their political connections—why was the Stock Market in the hands of unscrupulous elements, what was happening– now every government official wanted money for their office club and blatantly fixed the rates to be paid which were being shared on some basis between the staff!---was he descending into melancholy!

As Preeti and he walked in Connaught place, a group of blonds in see thru kurtas walked towards them accompanied by a guide. Suddenly there was a cloud burst and the girls got wet, their kurtas outlining their beautiful perky busts. As Surinder's eyes followed them ' Preet's commanding voice ordered

Eyes to the Front! *Samney dekh!*

These Army wives were terrible!

The trip to Bathinda was ordinary– they went back by chair car and slept most of the way except when the pantry crew came up to offer refreshments.

Next morning Surinder wore his uniform and was back in the office.

The BGS suddenly called him and gave him a big shout. The reason he claimed was the shabby state of affairs in the Conference Room. Surinder was quite sure that the Conference Room was perfect There was more behind the anger displayed by the BGS.

Then the BGS told him to follow him to the Conference Room. As he opened the Conference Room, the lights came on and someone had arranged for the song CONGRATULATIONS to be played in the background.

The BGS smiled and congratulated him—Well done, Son! The Board results have just come in and you are through!

And then there was a deluge of congratulations as he cut the huge cake brought for the ceremony! It was a quantum jump inside the pyramidical ascent upwards. Life was changing for him and time was flying—Jaskaran was in the NDA and was chafing at the bit—he wanted to join Six Third–in his father's footsteps.

It made him smile—it would be a very proud occasion for Preeti and him!

Surinder threw a bash for his friends and everyone had a great time. The Jazz band was in attendance and his friends laughed, drank ate and enjoyed themselves.

DUSHERA

Come September----the rains had long gone and so had the humidity. It was the smell of fresh fragrance which filled the air, the birds appeared chirpier than ever and the trees looked full with their new plumes while a sense of joy filled the atmosphere before the winter set in. October was approaching and many began the tedious effort of opening their boxes to bring out their woollens which had been so painstakingly mothballed after the winter.

Since Army officers carried their whole households with them on postings it was always better to insure one's luggage before handing it over to a mover because it was all you had accumulated over the years. Sometimes if you got a bigger truck– your car went in it too! So after one loaded the truck. it was pointless to worry about its safe arrival at your next destination—one left it to GOD Almighty!

In fact, most Army officers, their wives and children began to think of their impending moves as soon as they had completed two years at any military station—their think tanks wondering where they would be posted, because India was a huge sub continent—would it be a peace or a field posting and which sector they would be posted to—West, North or East! Their priorities were accommodation, education, admission and finally what the job was about. The Army had been considerate; in that families were allowed to retain accommodation at their present place of posting, in case their children were appearing in the Board Exams. Since Jaskaran was in the IMA, this was least of their worries.

Preeti and Surinder awaited their move patiently. Frankly, Surinder was enjoying himself a lot because; his status had improved now that he had been cleared for brigadier. It meant that he would have to take over a Brigade with its three integral infantry battalions and any other sub units which were grouped under command. The BGS invited him to a walk so that he could advise Surinder on some of the important points to keep in mind when taking over a brigade headquarter.

The suspense was soon over because he was posted to Chutmalpur.

It was a feeling of nostalgia as he stepped into the familiar palace which served as the Brigade Headquarter, where he had once visited as a Captain; to meet his uncle Brigadir Charanjit Singh MC. The KLP or the designated building for the headquarters was to be constructed soon, but with his clout the Rajah of Chutmalpur always managed to have the project delayed and received inflated rent for his palace. As he walked in, the outgoing Brigade Commander Brigadier R Mahalingam VSM, came to receive him. A tall handsome officer from the Madras Regiment, he shook hands with him and gave him a big hug. They had done their Junior Command course together and had been good friends. He waved off his staff officers and took Surinder by the arm to the Mess and ordered some beer to be served.

There is plenty of time to take over, so let me hear from you what you have been doing since we last met.

So the two carried on till both of them had filled in the gaps. After lunch, during the walk Mahalingam briefed Surinder about the brigade and its components as well as the principal personalities. He would prefer the rest of the briefing to be conducted under the aegis of his Deputy Brigade Commander because he could then interpret anomalies correctly for Surinder's benefit!

It was a peace station and children playing in the garden shouted a loud– Good evening Uncle!--- as they saw them. The ladies nodded and the troops saluted the pair as they sauntered by.

So how do you like your first day in the Brigade? asked Brigadier Mahalingam.

Can't complain so far thanks to your hospitality! Said Surinder.

Well I have ordered the BM and the DQ to brief you about the programme for tomorrow. If you want any changes, feel free to make them—you are amongst friends!

Surinder laughed and agreed.

The next day the BM and the DQ gave out their detailed briefings while the Deputy Commander– Colonel Shamsher Singh moderated their briefings wherever the facts were not represented correctly or there was a deviation. Brigadier Mahalingam interspersed his views only to elaborate on issues which required deliberation or were anomalies. Surinder asked clarifications where required and by evening they were done.

Soon Surinder signed the relevant documents and took over his duties.

Surinder did not want to accompany Brig Mahalingam on his farewells because the battalions would be inhibited in their style of farewells for the outgoing commander. After taking over he went over to meet the GOC at Chanderpur for his formal interview. It would also give him a chance to meet the staff at the division headquarters. Back home he attended his dining in at the Brigade Mess and then he called up Preeti as usual to give her a feedback on what to expect when she joined him. Soon it was time for Brigadier Mahalingam to proceed on his posting to a staff appointment, he was leaving for Sohanpur to take over as the Brig Adm or Brigadier in Charge Administration.

The invitation card from the paltan reached him while he was returning from the Div HQs. The CO was keen that Surinder and Preeti join the battalion in celebrating Dushera, one of the most important festivals for the Gorkhas. It would also give them some time with Jaskaran who was due to pass out and was an Under Officer. Preeti reached Chutmalpur and Surinder applied for leave for three days which was sanctioned.

They drove to Dehra Dun in their car and reached 6/3 Gorkha Rifles at eleven in the morning. Everyone was happy to see them and the CO had deliberately arranged lunch in the JCO's Mess where he would get a chance to meet old friends and adversaries alike! The older JCOs took the liberty of pulling his leg and the younger ones were simply overawed. In spite of Surinder's appeal that he was getting on in age and needed a respite from drinking beer which gave him a pot belly– his protests fell on deaf ears and he wound up on wobbly legs. The Junior Commissioned Officers (JCOs) seemed to vie with each other in offering Surinder a drink. If popularity was to be measured in terms of drinks offered, then he was a winner by a mile!

A trip to the toilet became necessary to offload the distilled beer he was carrying in his bladder and he went to his room and slept. Preeti knew that her husband was not a heavy drinker but during trips to his beloved battalion, he could never be firm in saying no—because the drinks offered were a sort of bonding with old friends!

At night Surinder called up Tony:

Tony, may i request you to the dinner an informal one and please invite all the children as well—Preeti and I want to meet the future generation!

Preeti arranged for suitable gifts for them all.

Their sahayak had become a Subedar now and when he came to visit them in the evening, with his wife and children he was proud of his brood.

Ram Ram Sahib said he and gave him a stiff salute—he wore a Dhaka topi and regimental mufti.

Yo mero family cha- he said pointing proudly to his wife and the kids– a girl and two boys!

Preeti gave his wife five hundred rupees to treat the kids. Surinder and his old sahayak chatted as though they were friends and his children wondered how their father who was a very stern man had doffed his serious face and was laughing away with gay abandon. There was a strange bon homie between officers and their sahayaks which transcended all frontiers—it was more of a kinship! There was a knock on the door and Jaskaran stood in the doorway in his regulation worsted suit. While he met his mother and Subedar Dal Bahadur with a hug, he formally shook hands with his father.

Good evening Sir!

Surinder was proud of him, , for he knew that Jaskaran would remain formal with him as long as he was in the paltan and he knew deep down that he would make a fine officer.

The evening in the Officer's Mess was a lively affair with the pipe and the jazz bands competing with each other for Surinder's attention. After he had danced with Preeti, he handed her to Jaskaran and walked over to both bands for small talk. He recognised some of the boys but the others were all new. General Katoch was due to reach the unit the next day, both Surinder and Preeti were very excited. Colonel Rai had become a Brigadier too and would also be coming over. Raj, Shukla and Muthu had sent regrets, while Randy who was now a Colonel GS, in a division headquarter promised to come if leave was granted and no serious militant activity persisted. It promised to be a very happy reunion. Saikiya's daughter Bul Bul, had married a youngster called Amit Gohain. Preeti gave her a small cash gift in an envelope and also kissed her on the forehead. Brigadier Rai's son Birendra came up and saluted Surinder. He was married and introduced his wife Anju and baby daughter to Preeti. Preeti followed the same drill with Anju as well. Surinder knew that she had planned all this in advance after speaking to Tony's wife Angela. Tony was now the CO and Preeti could not help telling Angela about her reception in the battalion, as a young bride; at Tony's mercy.

Everyone was having a great time– after all it was one big family; all on the basis of the famous quote– *birth gave me relatives, thank God I can choose my own friends.* This was a unique feature of the Indian Army, that such friendship overcame caste, creed or any other obstacles and stood the test of time. *It was secular spirit in its finest form.*

Dinner was over and Surinder presented both bands their rum bottles and the evening ended. The next night was the Variety Entertainment Programme, designed to keep the spectators awake till the time of *Kalratri* when the sacrificial buffalo would be sacrificed to the Goddess Kali or Durga. The variety show was a lively affair which commenced with a prayer to the Goddess invoking her blessings for the occasion. It was followed by many item where dancers dressed in the costumes of the particular region of Nepal displayed their culture in its finest glory. The last item was generally the *khukri* dance and all this was interspersed by skits—some on the favourite personalities of the unit, others on the personalities they did not approve, of and of course some depicted life back home or any funny incident in the battalion which could make the crowd laugh their guts especially if it was accompanied by excellent mimicry.!

The idea was to keep the guests everyone awake with sing song, drinks and snacks so that they could witness the *Kaal Ratri.*

All the officers and JCOs wore Nepalese caps and regimental ties with a white shirt.

It was time for the Bara Khana, or the grand Dinner.

Since this was a function of the Subedar Major, there was a Bara Khana or grand feast arranged by him for the guests. The guests included pensioners and their coming was interesting; because they got nostalgic meeting their friends in their companies, battalion the officers and JCOs. And did they have stories to tell– everyone gave them a very patient hearing because they were soldiers of yester years. The years had not dimmed their feelings for the *paltan*, the smartness in their salutes or their ability to quaff a couple of drinks down the hatch! They wore their garlands around their necks with pride and took part in all the events savouring the honour bestowed on them. Some had brought their spouses along– some had brought their children or grand children along to show off their paltan. The battalion had made administrative arrangements for all of them.

One of the designated boys, who would be instrumental in sacrificing the buffalo during *Kaal Ratri,* was on fast for almost nine days, praying that the sacrificial animal be felled in one blow of his *khukri*—the traditional curved short sword of the Gorkhas. The maula, or the sacrificial post, had been prepared and there was a very heavy sense of religious fervour in the air. The time for the *Kaal Ratri* was approaching and the *Panditji, Pujari*, helpers as well as the firing party took their place. Panditji spoke his religious *shlokas* and sprinkled water on the forehead of the sacrificial buffalo. The idea was to make it shake its head which signified that it was willing to be sacrificed. At times the priest had to pour a few drops into the ears of the animal in order to coerce it into shaking its head. As soon as this was done, the rope around the neck of the animal was thrust through the hole in the *maula* and the animal's forehead was pulled towards the *maula* to enable the pujari to get a good swing on the neck. At the appointed time as the crowd of spectators began inching forward to get a better view of the proceedings, the *Panditji* checked the right time for the sacrifice and gave the final nod to the *Pujari* who swung the heavy sacrificial khukri and severed the animal's head, simultaneously, the guard commander signalled and a volley of blanks was fired. The helpers dragged the animal's torso around the maula in jubilation while the Commanding Officer and Subedar Major were congratulated for the kill.

The Commanding Officer—Colonel Tony Fernandes, tied a white turban on the *Pujari's* head to honour him for his feat and presented a cash award as well.

Then there was a riot of laughter and everyone cheered the CO because he had cleared a major hurdle– had the animal's head not been severed in one swing of the *Pujari's khukri* it would have signified a year of bad luck for the battalion– something which the men, JCOs and officers believed stoically. Bad luck could come in any form—commanding a unit was fraught with problems and it was good to have all the Gods on your side.

The sacrifice signalled an end of the festivities for the evening

The CO and Subedar Major stood apart congratulating each other—*We have done it*!

Come on boys you deserve a drink! shouted Tony—and while some officer escorted the families to their homes, the officers piled onto the Commanding Officers jonga for a trip to the Mess. Drinks were served and the whole lot of officers began to unwind from the tension. Some did a jig others broke into song and some just sat with a smile and surveyed the boisterous scene.

There was a party next evening and everyone could afford to relax in the morning. So after another round it was time to wind up.

The next morning, the unit *Panditji* or the religious teacher was ready to bless the battalion weapons which had been laid out appropriately. Suddenly the champions—one of the boys of each company herded in about six goats each. This was the ceremony known as *Maha Balidan*—literally meaning Giant Sacrifice. They would pull the string tied around the neck of each animal and hold it under their foot and at the opportune moment cut off the animal's head with one swing of his khukri. If any of them failed to do so in one swipe, then his face was covered in blood and he was disqualified from the competition. The winner was presented a cash prize by the CO and a white turban was tied on his head. The meat of the goats slaughtered was declared as sacred, then distributed to the companies, families and the Officer's Mess and the JCO's Mess.

Sometimes newly commissioned officers were also initiated, and this time it was the turn of Lieutenant Govind Singh Bhist. Govind was a short stocky and well built officer but as he took his swing, his foot slipped in the blood and the razor sharp khukri slit his shoe and cut through the centre of his foot between his toes, four inches into his foot. Bhisht was oblivious to this fact– he was quite happy that he had severed the goat's head in a single swipe. People saw the gash only when blood spewed out of his foot.

The doctor was called, the shoe removed and foot tied up and his foot stitched in the MI Room.

Devi le rakta mange hola—The Goddess must have required human blood—said the Subedar Major shaking his head solemnly.

The matter was closed– no further discussion.

The functions had been planned meticulously and all the officers serving and retired partiscipated with gusto. Next morning was the *Tika* ceremony– wherin all ranks were blessed by the *Panditji,* the officers and the JCOs. As the General blessed Brigadier Rai and Surinder, they took turns to bless the CO and the Officers and the Officers in turn went down to their companies to bless their men. The blessing comprised of putting fresh sprouts of wheat stalk behind the ears, pasting rice soaked in yoghurt on the forehead and shaking hands with the traditional invocation :that the Goddess bless them and their families, with prosperity and promotions and fulfilment of all their desires. May the Goddess also bring peace and happiness to them and their families.

Then came the singing and dancing– everyone was on a high, and those who did not drink looked on without getting into the prevailing mood. A slight intoxication removed many of the inhibitions in anyone and tended to make them boisterous and happy; with that devil may care attitude—after all it was celebration time wasn't it? The dancers slowed down as the hot sun increased the effect of their drink and made them drowsy. Slowly everyone sat down and the officers wound up to go home.

It made a very pretty picture.

It was the same with the officers and the JCOs who had travelled considerable distances to celebrate *Dushera* with their *paltan.* The JCOs invariably wore their regimental mufti—regimental bottle green blazers with regimental crests and regimental ties, white shirts with grey worsted trousers and black shoes. Some wore their Dhaka topis and others wore the regimental black caps with the regimental badges atop.

The Mess Secretary was Major Chaturvedi. When he was summoned to meet the Second in Command and told to discuss the menu for the dinner for *Dushera,* He summoned his Mess Committee members and decided to pick their brains first—brain storming– he called it.

Ok, Mr Food Member what do you have to recommend?

Chaudhary looked at him and said– Very simple Sir! We go by standard plan and standard calculations.

Chaturvedi eyed him suspiciously– it isn't that simple young man– there is a lot to plan.

Chaudhary opened his file and began to rattle off data– making Major Chaturvedi's head spin because he did not believe in figures and statistics—he simply believed in his motto– just do it!

Any way Chou—let us hear what you have to say—slowly. Said Chaturvedi.

Choudhary began—

We have the guests from the Dogras—CO, CO's wife and one officer--total three, similarly the Garhwalis and the Sikhs are going to have three each making nine. Add to this seven from Brigade Headquarters making it a total of sixteen. The DC and his wife will come along with the SDM making it nineteen. Also add four civilian guests making it twenty and we have to cater for another four guests who turn up unexpectedly, which makes it twenty four and with our strength of fourteen including the ladies, I have catered for the total of thirty eight.

Kapoor chipped in:

Now we have twelve ladies and twenty six gents. We will assume that only two third of the gents will drink which gives us eighteen. Of these, four will drink beer at the most while the rest will drink whiskey, and rum. The requirement of beer at max three per head or a dozen bottles have been segregated in the tub which will be filled with ice. The requirement of the ladies at two soft drinks each assorted has been added with emphasis on the cola drinks and for the soda drinkers we have placed an order for sixty bottles of soda. Glasses are available with silver tankards for the beer drinkers. Bitters are available for those who want a pink gin and lime. All the popular whiskeys are available and so are three brands of beer. There is a bottle of white wine and a bottle of red in case someone wants.

Choudhary continued:

The menu is based on four major factors, common to all, only for non vegetarians and then for vegetarians and finally dessert. Common to all comprises Salad, *rice, tandoori roti* and *naan,* as also *rajmah, raita and papad.* For non vegetarians we have chicken roasted and mutton do piazza while there is matar paneer and mushroom curry for the vegetarians and finally there is hot gulab jamun with ice cream. *gulab jamun* has been catered at one and a half per head while ice cream at two slices per head. Each brick of ice cream gives us eight slices of ice cream.

Chaturvedi nodded– the boys had done a good job in planning the meal now they would have to take care of the execution if he sold this idea to the 2IC.

What about snacks?

Without a word Choudhary handed a list to Major Chaturvedi, who grinned because it was exactly what was required by the 2IC.

Excellent chaps– would you like to go and discuss this with the 2IC?

Choudhary smiled—our job is over Sir—now you have to bell the cat—we will be near the Mess phone in case you need us!

Major Chaturvedi did not realise that Chou's maths was a trifle faulty!

TANVEER

She was the daughter of nobility---her father came from an aristocratic family from the Punjab of undivided India and the family, aware that partition was looming on the distant horizon had in fact substantially disposed off their land holding for the best local offers at that time and quietly sent all the family members to Delhi, where they had bought a palatial mansion on Tuglak Road.

Darji, as the old patriarch was reverently addressed, had bought a sprawling business from a Muslim family which had opted to move to Pakistan. The old men had sat together, sipped tea and discussed the handing and taking over, of the remaining properties at the Delhi and Rawalpindi end, in a very honorable manner, embraced and decided that—both families would be paid in cash at their final destinations by their respective banks, ensuring that both families emerged stronger financially. They vowed that their friendship would continue for ever!

She was not even born when all this happened and would never know the terrible holocaust which would engulf so many other families from both the countries after partition For her life was about partying and visiting so many countries during her vacations with Papa and Mamma and also her little brother Amrik.

As the years passed in quick succession, and many a leaf fell during the fall or autumn, Tanveer turned from a skinny girl into a tall, full bosomed graceful, cultured and lovely princess– someone you wanted to continue looking at and admire, for she never had a bad word for anyone and was always ready to help in the myriad chores at home. She was the life of the party and her mother was so afraid of bad omens that she insisted that her daughter place a small black dot or *bindi* discreetly behind her ear!

At college she had many friends and her best friends, Jasmine and Dimple were both charming girls like her in almost all fields. The girls were very close and though they were polite to every one they understood that their relationship was a trifle different from the others. They had designed codes to be used in their conversation which allowed them privacy and caution and thus they kept each other well versed of happenings in college. They kept teachers happy because their grades never fell and they always prepared for their classes well in advance!

Sunday was a day for getting together on the swing, eating mangoes or, tamarind from the old tree—which the old gardener would break with a long bamboo on which he had attached a sickle! As seasons changed, the Indian climate brought forth amazing delicacies for them in the shape of papaya, *chikoo, falsa*, pomegranate kiwi, cherries, water melon– *tarbuz*, musk melon, banana, oranges, pears, custard apples, peaches, grapes, and many type of fruit, actually you could have anything you wanted if you had money!

Time was passing and soon our lovely girls found that their parents were looking at photographs of handsome young men! The girls were aware that the time to part company was approaching and so they clung to each other—lest they lose sight of each other—separation was an unbearable and ugly thought!

Then time struck the first blow!

The first to succumb to the sound of wedding bells was Jasmine—her friends called her Jazz. An offer had materialized in the form of Sonny Aggarwal—his family had huge land holdings in Bareilly and were contractors, deeply enmeshed in politics– not the local type but with aspirations at the state level. It was a good offer and Jasmine's parents were satisfied. Since both families were well to do the financial arrangements went off without a hitch and wedding cards were decided upon as soon as Punditji confirmed the dates. Dimple Khanna and Tanweer Sethi liked their brother in law to be– at least he had an honest looking face and handsome to boot! Jazz better watch out– he was the type to put on weight as soon as his marriage settled down!

Jazz knew that her friends would come to her wedding and she did not need any kind of assurances from her friends. The three friends quietly went over to Lajpat Nagar's Central Market looking for bargains in artificial jewellery– not that they did not have enough of the genuine stuff– but they wanted harmony in fashion with their college mates-no use in flaunting their assets and inviting jealousy—besides it was unsafe to wear genuine stuff—imagine a small time thief on a motor cycle slapping a respectable lady, throwing her artificial jewellery in her face and shouting—wear genuine jewellery next time and make it worth my effort—you silly woman– it was the case of the pot calling the kettle black!

Each party thought that they had got the better of the shopkeeper, but how would Roshan Lal make so much money that he could buy his wife a thick gold bangle every month? Life is unfair in general—don't you think! Anyway the girls had a great time and after all a tiring day of shopping calls for some chaat! So they gorged on, *pani poori tikki and dahi papri chat*. They had come in Jazz's car and she dropped them home. The phone rang and her fiancé wanted her to tell him, where she had been galavanting around– and when she told him about the *chaat*– she could almost hear him drool!

Poor baby!

The marriage drew nearer and Tanweer and Dimple went shopping for their clothes. Tanweer paid her Masterji– tailor—200 INR, so that he could go for a late movie and see the design that a leading lady was wearing, in order to replicate it. Masterji was not thrilled– his wife would not be pleased– so Tanweer paid him for two tickets so that Begum could go too Ah—the joys of youth! Dimple decided that she would visit a boutique and pick up something ready. They had to look glamorous too- -!

As they tried out her outfits—Tanveer said jokingly– listen Dimpy you better watch where your bust is going—and received a quick rebuttal—you just watch your butt, Missie! They were changing from young girls to beautiful ladies, so butts and busts just had to change with the times!

It was decided that the marriage would take place at the Chemsford Club and the arrangements for the catering went to Kwality, the drinks were arranged through a cousin of Jazz's father– a pompous looking Army officer– moustaches and all! Other volunteers chipped in and promised to arrange a *punditji*, cars flowers, music and much more Jazz intended to enjoy herself– you get married only once in this country—so why not live it up! She wanted her friends to stick to her– it made her feel secure even though her future mother in law and her father in law were kind old people and wanted her as a daughter not a daughter in law! She had only one sister in law Nupur, who was married to the editor of a popular magazine and who was equally smitten with her! Nupur had made the arrangements for their honeymoon– much secret secret!

Tanveer and Dimple slept for two days in Jazz's place but decided to revert to their own homes as guests started pouring in– besides it was difficult to find one's clothes in all that chaos– but they promised to come early on the evening of the marriage and be with Jazz during the *jaimala*– garland ceremony where the bride and groom to be-- exchange garlands.

As the groom's family arrived– the girls watched the procession from the terrace—the groom sitting on a bleached charger with a *sarbala*, a sort of best man who also rode on the charger, if you please—probably a nephew sitting at the back, clinging on for dear life and wailing that he be taken off the horse! Someone walked upto the groom and said—

Hey you know something– you can still escape this misery– just swing the horse around and GO-before it is too late!

But our groom was like a zombie– hooked line and sinker—for life—a dodo. He was determined to be her slave for life!

The guests kept trickling in– some coming in late deliberately to get noticed—some coming with excuses—*aap ko toh pata hi hai– kitne busy hote hain*—you know how busy he is! It was the Punjabi way– you had to say a sentence in Punjabi or Hindi and then repeat it in English—not so with the Southerners, Bengalis, Gujus or the Oriyas who felt secure in numbers and chatted deliberately in their mother tongues even if someone from a different community was around! Punjabis were like potatoes—you could put them safely into any vegetarian or non vegetarian dish! They had to try out every dish– so that they could talk about it later– otherwise who could imagine pasta and *momos* selling like hot cakes in Delhi—although, initially the Punjabis preferred their *momos* fried! Then came the awareness that steamed *momos* were too good– *no oil shoil yaar*! Very good for the tummy you know! The *dosa* had already conquered the North-along with its cousins– *the idli* and the *utappam!* But the Northeners had not yet understood the genuine taste of *sambhar* as made in the South—what they served at best could be called Punjabi Sambhar; just as those in the South could not replicate *channa bhatura, rajma, makhni dal or tandoori chicken*– but the trade off was great!

Why I am laying out these details is because stalls at an Indian wedding take the shape of Indian Mughlai, Chinese, and sometimes Italian cusines.No food stall was complete without a fruit or a *chaat* stall– no use describing a *chaat* stall to you– you gotta eat the stuff man—feel the chilli and sweat and fall ill the next day possibily but it is difficult to resist going past this stall without trying out something sez you! It is just like going to Kathmandu and falling ill with some sort of tummy problem– at which the locals laughed and shrugged—*huncha*—it happens!

There was nothing like hot *gulab jamun* atop a slab of ice cream! Here, it went like this—

I scream
U scream
But we all scream for ice cream---

and all these homo sapiens young and old made a bee line for the stuff even if soufflé or pastry was around!

Some kind souls also placed *meetha or saada paan* at the exits which made the evening complete! Sometimes you found a spouse running around to find his better or bitter half and show her the delights he had discovered for him or her! Most people believed that they should recover in full– the cost of the present or the cash they had presented to the bride's family irrespective of whether it added to their *waste* lines or increased their sugar intake or gave them a severe case of indigestion!

Grosse!

So while people were in the mood for gorging, the groom sat on his throne awaiting the arrival of his bride to be; surrounded by his trusted lieutenants! Some were armed with a spare set of shoes or *juttis* or traditional handmade footwear; to enable the groom to retain his pride after his footwear was stolen by the *salees* of the bridegroom– sister in laws yaar, and for the return of this footwear–he would have to pay suitable dole or compensation! It was a tradition and no one seemed to mind really.

Tanweer and Dimple watched all this and wondered whether they too would have to suffer this. Tanweer decided that she would convince her fiancé to rise above all this and go for a smaller wedding with the closest of both families—any savings would be deposited in her bank account—no point in wasting money or feeding overfed people! Dimple laughed---Women proposeth and God disposeth! It was a male dominated world– MCP—so any plan like this would succeed only if the bridegroom suggested it.

We shall overcome---!

And it was time to escort the bride to the podium so that she could exchange garlands with the groom! The excitement in Sonny's eyes was evident, but Jazz was expected to resemble the true epitome of an Indian bride—coy, demure and shy with eyes on the ground for it was bad manners to look directly into the crowd or at the groom—the guests expected this from her and loved her for this! The women from both sides were comparing the match and passing comments– some complimentary and some not so nice as if Jazz was an object to be commented upon.

She could not care less about comments– the evening belonged to her—

As they completed their formalities, Tanweer looked up and her eyes locked with a very handsome Sikh in a black suit; looking bemused– at her--?She tried to look away, but could not and a shiver ran down her spine! Is this love at first sight, she asked herself—no it does not happen this way—then he was gone. Dimple was too busy chatting so Tanweer took her elbow and took her aside—

Did you see that handsome *serd*?(--a common word in the dictionary of the so called elite for Sardarji)

Dimple pretended that she had not—which one– the guy in the black suit?

You naughty little—yes that one! Will you just find out some details about him please? Just a *leetle* intro---

Dimple grinned– it was not like Tanweer to show interest in males– so this must be serious—lets see where he disappeared—then she spotted him at the bar– someone was forcing a beer on him and this guy was politely declining it– maybe he had a role to complete just like them! So Dimple decided to play the savior and pull out our hero from his current predicament. At least he is not a boozer---especially when liquor is close at hand.

She walked up to him, placed her hand on his elbow in a familiar gesture and said—

Kuku, I require you for some work—Kuku was let off the hook and he smiled gratefully!

Incidentally, I am not Kuku, I am Noni!

Does it matter– I saved your backside– did I or did I not--?

They say a lady needs to be escorted to a seat, especially if she wishes to engage Noni in conversation!

Sorry, mumbled Noni, and escorted her to a seat away from prying eyes—now what—

Incidentally, I am Dimple Khanna!

I am Major Jaskaran Singh Sahni—I am from the Third Gurkhas! The unit is in Almora!I am Sonny's classmate and Sonny requested me to be his Best Man! I do not know what my role is– I suppose I have to remain vigilant enough to ensure that his footwear is not stolen! Is that it?

What about you– why did you drag me here—I do not think we have ever met—have we?

Dimple smiled—no have not, but I was keen that you meet a dear friend of mine—

Matchmaker are you? Very young– and pretty too---

No but if I can introduce two nice people to each other– what's the problem? Where are you from—Delhi?

Right this time– Defence Colony to be precise—F block! Want to know the number too? Small family– one younger cousin sister– married and living in Australia with her family—me-- I am a happy bachelor with no intentions of getting hooked in the near future! My father is a retired Brigadier– I joined his battalion!

Fauji brat!!

Yup—you can call me that—I am actually taking it as a compliment! So Messenger of Introductions—like a MC—how do we arrange the formal intro?

Do not pull my leg please—maybe some time later you might want to thank me—maybe buy me a gift too—so keep those fingers crossed buster! Anyway you just hang around here and I will tell her to come over. And listen—offer her a juice or something– she definitely does not drink! Just hang around-----

Jaskaran did not panic! Such a scenario was straight out of Bollywood! What if she was pulling my leg– too good to be true—but his luck might just change—so he hung on, waiting for the miracle—so far he had been a busy bee—professionally on top and he was the apple of his CO's eye! He had no time for girlfriends or dating girls only to waste good money—he would rather wait for his next course to Mhow, go over to the patent tailor he swore by, and get a new suit or a tuxedo stitched—if he could spare the cash– a tweed coat with horn buttons would do fine!

Anyway, as these confusing thoughts hurtled through his mind, he saw a beautiful creature approaching him—Wow!

She smiled gracefully and offered her hand towards him—Hi, I am Tanveer!

3

BOLLYWOOD SCENE

Jaskaran was in a quandary—to bolt or stay– that was the question!

Definite scene from Bollywood—and the girl was so cool—shit! Forgot to ask her name too---funny guy you are my dear—anyway– need to consolidate your resources—remain cool—and be as polite as ever—give her five minutes--after which walk off without looking back—right! Too late here she comes--

Hello– I am Jaskaran Singh Sahni!

I am Tanweer Sethi!

Both of us are *Khukrains*—Crooks Klan as some used to joke! Khukrains are from the warrior clan.

Do you always send out a patrol before you reach the objective? Sorry for the fauji parlance but only this could aptly summarise the events so far! Anyway what's on your mind?

Sorry– I did not mean to offend you– just wanted to make sure you were available—I mean not already married—you know the famous line—*the good ones are already in the bag*!

I could say that about you too!

What are you doing these days?

I just completed my graduation and am planning to do some kind of course in fashion designing or jewellery designing abroad. That is-----only if Mr Right fails to ask for my hand.

I am glad you are focused—!

Look Tanveer—I like your direct style—please convey my thanks to Dimple for the intro– I like you and would like to know you better– can I call you?

Please?

Tanveer looked at him and said– my aunt seems to be headed this way—Dimple will give you my number and you can give her yours or your address if you don't mind—you know security and all—

Jaskaran laughed—it had been so easy to talk to Tanveer---Okey!

Hello– her voice seemed musical, effortless and divine—and she was a beauty—maybe it was not the right word to describe her! She could not be called voluptuous or ravishing– words which made her appear vulgar. Angelic was a more appropriate word—she was cultured, beautiful and the girl of his dreams. Worth waiting for anyway!

Tuglak Road is where we live—it is an old mansion! I have a younger brother Amrik– we call him Billoo! My father is a business man.

OK--I am from Def Col—F Block-just behind the bus stop.

What is this cloak and dagger stuff– who is your friend?

She is Dimple Khanna– a very close friend of mine, my buddy actually– Jazz the bride;was the third! We are thick as thieves as they say and it was on my request that she spoke to you!

Not upset are you?

No no– said a very confused Jaskaran—there was no question of control—things were going too fast! Was he being victimized by Tanweer and Dimple? One thing was clear—Tanweer was worth courting! And he had Dimple to thank! Where was this leading to–

Tanweer looked very composed---can we meet whenever you are in town?

I would like that Tanweer—blurted Jaskaran.

Here is my card—write soon Ok! And give me an address where I can call you or write to you. I have a couple of days more in Delhi—why don't we meet? If you like you could bring Dimple too– I like her style! You know the DSOI, at Dhaulakuan? Meet you at seven thirty in the lobby; Monday—right?

Tanveer nodded– it had a nice ambience about it and you had privacy if you wanted to—Fine! We can fix that up later.

Ok said Tanweer—they would be there- --Dimple has her own car! Amrik can drive us down.

There were many questions Jaskaran wanted to ask this siren– but proverbially– the cat got his tongue and all he could do was to keep on gaping at her—taking in all of her face her mannerism, her heaving bust and the twinkle in her eye---probably she was doing the same—but she appeared more confident and relaxed!

Some movement caught her eye and she started to move off– my aunt's coming—see you later alligator!

Our hero was confused—it was not proper to discuss such events with buddies or relatives---better ask Mom, she would know how to proceed! So he chartered a course to his mother's location. He caught her eye with a troubled glance. He signaled her to come over.

Hello Beta(Son)—something troubling you?

Look Mom—You know I generally have no time for girls, but I just met someone interesting—she is over at the pool side talking to her aunt probably---turn around slowly---don't stare Mom!

His mother saw Tanweer and her aunt—I know her Aunt—she is Jasbir– she was in my college but her subjects were different.

That made things easier—what luck!

Mom—Can you go over—it is important—but I am not going bonkers– so relax—OK!

Mom sauntered over and Jasbir recognized her—hello Pritiji---*Ki haal hai*—long time no see?

Mom pretended to be caught unaware and was introduced to Tanweer—

Oh! You know her mother too—yaar—*Maninder di gal kar rahi haan*---I am talking of Maninder--She was a year junior to us but she was popular because she was the only one who could mimic most of our teachers and get away with it! Remember the time when she was mimicking the Princi—and she walked in and sat down quietly waiting for the performance to end!

The only difference was that she liked the performance and gave a pat to Mani and requested her to give a small item on Teacher's Day—for which she would give her some more ideas—what a lady!

Tanweer– I remember your mother—a very lively person and she always had time for everyone else—how is she? And who is your father?

Auntieji—my father is Rajeshwar Singh Sethi– he looks after my father's interests in imports and exports.

Are you talking about Raj? The one who went to Harvard and came back with his beard intact and without an American in tow?

Tanweer was confused—her Aunt Jasbir explained—Tanweer, those days it was common to find that some of the Sikh boys who went abroad promptly shaved off and then got married to an American, never to return to their motherland—rarely did we come across some one like your Dad!

My husband also knows Raj ji—they have some business connections too—small world!

Pritiji—where are your children?

.I have a son Jaskaran who is a Major now and is posted at Almora. They are known as *barsati* majors— barsati means monsoon, because they are not substantive—if someone senior to them gets posted in then they have to shed rank.

So this was Jaskaran's Mom—everything is fair in love and war—if I could deploy Dimple, why cant he send his Mom to do the same—But I like her!

And she knows my parents too!

Why don't you and Maninder drop in at our place– we live close to South Ex—F Block, Defence Colony, my husband Surinder, took premature retirement and went into business when his father fell ill. I will give you one of his cards.

And so the ladies chatted till Jaskaran's mom had learnt everything about Tanvi as she was called at home from what she wore to what she did not and what were her favourite culinary delights and what the name of her tailor was! Gathering intelligence was of prime importance—her husband insisted and she agreed---!

The Army taught you so many useful things- -----she could have easily written a flawless Annual Confidential Report on her prospective daughter in law to be—giving her all niners—and convinced her husband that she had made a good choice—after all it was going to be her job to groom her in the social graces which are the backbone of the Army---!

That is if Tanvi wanted Jaskaran to rise to the top---the view changed as you rose higher!

Tanvi– please remember me to your mother– please tell her to bring you over to our place sometimes especially before Jaskaran finishes his leave—otherwise you will have listen to college or Army gup shup—Bye then---

Preeti was an accomplished artiste– her lines were rehearsed and she put feelings into every word she spoke—after all she had helped her husband organize so many functions and feted so many senior ladies so graciously that they all remembered her even though she had left the Army social circuit long ago!

But you could not ignore the course get togethers where the husbands became boys again and the Gorkha Brigade get togethers where you met dear old friend closer than relatives still willing to give their life for you, and catch up with the news of the children! And what about your invitations from the paltans for Dushera and Battle Honour Day!

It was also good to meet her son who had made his father proud by joining his regiment and battalion—but in the paltan this boy would become a soldier and address his father as Brig Sahni, and her as Mrs Sahni, in public- --something his father liked and in turn he always addressed Jaskaran, as Major Sahni—

Preeti decided to take her husband's assistance in arranging a good match for their son, because getting a good girl with a sensible head on her shoulders was as important as getting a good boy especially if they came from good families, the families knew each other and the lineage was known!

Gal suno—listen—have you realized that Jaskaran has grown up—his unit has just arrived in Almora and we could plan his wedding which may give him almost three years with his family!

Hello– where is the bride—asked her husband looking up from the newspaper---

I have found the right girl for him—you know her complete family–nice people—we have do some stage management darling—

Since you have done all the legwork– I will chip in and do my best—when do we start?

Now! said Preeti—before Surinder went back to his paper!

Rajeshwar's number is with you– call him over with Maninder and their children for dinner on Wednesday, and I will sound Papaji and Beeji about this—do not take NO for an answer! Jaskaran seems to have made up her mind—so lets help him out and give the needed push.

With that she walked over to her father in law, s bedroom so that she could sound him out, also he would be able to fill her in with so many more details—he had such a memory for people that it amazed her and Beeji knew everyone in the baradary—clan!

As she told Papaji about Rajeshwar– he nodded– you are talking about Sardar Bishen Singh's son—he should be a little younger than Surinder. Your Beeji and I had attended his birthday celebrations in Pindi! His great grandfather had lived for 90 years which was rare during those days and so when he died they had made a special bier for his cremation– decked up with mirrors all around, with sandalwood garlands laid over the corpse and decorated the sides with beautiful silk cloth.

All those who attended were invited for a meal and served saffron rice with sweets. This was done to honour the soul of a grand old man who had lived long enough to see his great grand children and fulfilled all his obligations to his family!

Preeti nodded—so the family was a respected one—the first hurdle was cleared!

On Wednesday, Preeti was happy to find that Maninder and Rajesh were at their place for dinner with Tanweer and Amrik. Amrik held a bouquet of flowers which he handed to his mother and Maninder presented them to Preeti. Surinder greeted the children and took Rajeshwar's arm and whisked him away to the bar.

What is your poison Raj?

Raj smiled and settled on Black Label while Preeti and the children had some mocktails. Maninder agreed to have a Bloody Mary later. Jaskaran escorted Tanweer outside along with Amrik and they started to chat. Amrik settled for a beer while Jaskaran sipped a sprite. He wanted a clear head tonight because it was a very important evening for him.

A question of a life time!—as he explained to his mother.

Preeti had smiled—her son was finally growing up and reminded her of Surinder when he had become her betrothed. So correct and so formal in his behavior like his father and yet, Jaskaran was much more at ease and confident of himself. This was the new generation– very different and keen to have direct dealings instead of being shown photographs to choose from. A big difference from Darji and Beeji who had been engaged, when they were seven or eight and married when he was sixteen and she was twelve.

Darji and Beeji walked in a little later and were introduced. Raj touched Darji's feet as per the prevailing custom and Darji explained to him how well their families knew each other. Raj marvelled at the old man's knowledge of people, personalities, places, relationship and events. These old timers were a veritable encyclopaedia and since most of them hardly learned to read and write, they developed their memory banks to encompass everything they needed to know.

Everyone knew everyone!

Life was easy when you had money, time was not at a premium and one could venture out to be with friends or relatives. these old geezers had seen all, and lived a full life, drawing their monetary requirements from the family *Munshi* or Head Clerk. In joint families even the clots survived while those who had brains made a killing. Friends gathered together drank, swore and continued a debauch life till they settled down. The ladies of the house had their own circle and had their own fun and frolic while playing their catty games as women all over the world will! The senior lot preferred to drink upstairs away from prying eyes and allowed only the most trusted servants around because the subjects covered in their conversation covered every scandal that they knew or any shady deal they could think of, hence the requirement for discretion. Chicken and mutton dishes were sent up to keep their gourmet desires satiated while whiskey was supplied in abundance. Many of them led debauch lives with a mistress or two tucked away in some hideout.

Personality was inherent if you either had abundance of money, lands or were a senior public figure. Many were also employed in senior government posts and had a status of their own, but these people knew that their actions were watched by the police and indiscretions– social or monetary were conveyed to the administration.

A little later the children were summoned and introduced to the elders. Since Sikh girls were not expected to touch their elders feet they merely approached them and bowed their heads and were rewarded by a benevolent hand caressing the top of their heads as a blessing. Darji, Beeji and Surinder liked Tanweer instantly just as Maninder and Raj felt the same way about Jaskaran. This was a perfect example of the saying that marriages are made in heaven.

Darji looked at Beeji and nodded and Beeji walked over to Maninder and placed a gold necklace in her hands, her eyes said the rest. Maninder looked her husband's way and he nodded and she hugged Beeji. Maninder was happy and she guided Beeji towards her daughter, opened the box and offered the necklace to her. Beeji took the necklace and put it around Tanweer's neck to signify that Tanweer was now officially engaged to Jaskaran. Raj called Jaskaran and gave him a big hug as acceptance that he had gained a son. Both Tanweer and Jaskaran went to seek the blessings from Darji who was shedding tears of joy unabashedly. He was happy to see his grandson engaged during his lifetime—a major achievement– if only the Almighty could allow him to see Jaskaran's children.

Amrik turned photographer and began taking charge. He was on the top of the world.

Surinder suggested that an *Ardas* or prayer solemnize the event and this task was undertaken by Darji. After the *Ardas,* both families moved to the dining room where Preeti had set a beautifully thought of cusine. Maninder was very happy too and she gave a warm hug to Preeti only to be captured in Amrik's camera!

So over dinner, Surinder and Raj realized the importance of an arranged alliance and how important it was to belong to illustrious lineage. The same event would have taken much longer if one's antecedents were not known.

Surinder took Raj's hands and gave him a file.

Raj, I created this file to simplify my marriage with Preeti and it was worth it even if people thought it was a crazy thing to do. Please feel free to adopt this or any other measure to ensure that the marriage is performed comfortably—I am available for suggestions at any time. You also have

Darji's backing on this. Maninderji, thank you for your beautiful gift today—Preeti and I always wanted a daughter—you have filled in this void and we promise to keep Tanweer as happy as she is in your house!

As Manninder, Raj, Tanweer and Amrik left, Preeti realized that her life had come to a full circle and now they would see the children follow their own path. She hugged Beeji tightly and did not say a word– the hug said it all. Surinder put an arm around his father and his son and reflected on the same issue—your children grew through you!

THE DSOI

Jaskaran fixed up a meeting on a Monday with Tanvi and Dimple---with Amrik of course! He took them to the bar and ordered their snacks. Carefully, he posed them a question---would you like some beer, shandy or a Bloody Mary?—because only some girls from liberated families were used to having an odd drink once in a while.

A Kingfisher for me please—said Amrik

I would prefer something soft said Tanvi—and settled for a tonic water.

Dimple was curious about the Bloody Mary.

Jaskaran told her it contained some tomato juice, a small or large vodka, some tobasco sauce, a sliver of lime and all this in a glass which had the rim neatly swiped with lime and thrust gently into table salt which clung to the rim like a border. A leaf of mint was sometimes welcome!

Dimple said she would like to try it out and so it came to pass---Jaskaran advised caution and told her to sip with decent intervals and everything would be fine---

Jaskaran ordered a Peter Scot.

So with the drinks ordered and snacks on the way—it was time for *gup shup---chit chat!*

The waiter, Ram Prasad, his fathers's favourite waiter gave him a *salaam* and hovered around waiting for the snacks to be ordered and recommended the *chicken tikka* and the *shammi kebab.*

Amrik, what are you planning to do—asked Jaskaran

I am going to become a pilot, Sir—been preparing for my commercial pilot's license and plan to fly an Airbus. I don't live here– I am in the USA and hope to be absorbed as an instructor in my Academy, which will help me to accumulate my flying hours. I have to leave within the next few months I am a natural they tell me! I hope to do well despite the gloomy future being forecast for the Aviation industry!

Dimple was impressed with the set up at the DSOI, and the camaraderie these Army guys had with each other and of course the appropriate courtesy they showed to each other—there was a very decent atmosphere– the ladies and children receiving a lot of attention and respect!

There were groups of all kinds—some were course mates– old men some with wives and some without; some were younger age groups while in some cases it was just one or two families—old friends she presumed. Some groups even had single old ladies—widows who had lost their husbands but continued regimental or course friendship till the very end. There were interruptions as young officers met them touched their feet with respect, and exchanged pleasantries—probably children of friends.

The DSOI had become home for some of the old timers—hubby came back from a game of golf and joined his wife at the DSOI, where she waited for him with a glass of beer diluted with a soda or a tonic and vodka after collecting the monthly requirement of groceries and the monthly quota of liquor. Sometimes their fauji children joined them if they were posted in Delhi or they were on leave. It was touching to see old friends helping out each other– clinging to each other for support and swaying with the gait which comes with process of aging! Relatives could never be as close as this---*for birth gave me relatives– thank God, I have the ability to choose my own friends.*

Regimental camaraderie went so deep that many officers from the same battalion settled down together, irrespective of caste or religion simply because they wanted to be together!

Dimple was impressed!

Can I cut in—stranger?

Dimple looked up to find a tall smart guy looking down at Jaskaran.

Jaskaran literally jumped into his arms–

Hi Sir– what a surprise?

Major Anil Kapoor made himself comfortable and ordered a beer too.

What brings you here, Sir?---asked Jaskaran.

Actually, I am on temporary duty. Some documents had to be delivered to AHQ and I was sent—no one expected me, so everyone has pushed off to Shimla—we have a *kothi* there.

So I decided to come to the club and have my dinner here alone if I did not meet anyone interesting!---and I hit the jackpot this time!

Jaskaran—are you going to do the honours or do I have to introduce myself?

Jaskaran apologized and quickly explained that Major Kapoor was also from his battalion and was a Delhi wala to boot! Having done a quick mental assessment of the prevailing situation, the pros and the cons– the terms of reference to be kept in mind, Major Anil volunteered to take Dimple and Amrik for a guided tour, leaving a grateful Jaskaran and a bemused Tanveer behind! After all what are battalion officers for—comrades in love and war—and this was a win win situation—he had the lovely Dimple beside him---!

Jaskaran took Tanveer's hand which was exquisite and– Hey, I love you sweetheart!

Tanveer thought to herself- -she had seen this coming but she was not prepared for the forthright manner in which Jaskaran had confessed his love for her!

Proper protocol of course—trust me– said Jaskaran—just take care of your people!

I will keep you happy and I promise you won't regret your decision. Somehow Fate brought us together and she could use some help from us---what say you dear?

I agree—but keep it under wraps for the time being—I am a little superstitious—next time we meet– lets keep the others out—here's my address and phone number---!

And here's mine said Jaskaran and passed her a paper with the details.

I like Anil—he seems to be a nice guy—have you noticed the twinkle in Dimple's eye--?

Jaskaran could not care—he had won the Queen of Hearts and was going to let Anil look after himself—he was no baby and Dimple was a good looker too—

He concentrated on admiring Tanveer now that they were spoken for and realized that he had really been lucky– she was a great catch and he had to pinch himself a couple of times to convince himself that it was true!

Just in time– Anil, Dimple and Amrik sauntered in and sat down as if they were exhausted!

Jaskaran excused himself ordered a drink for Anil, a refill for Amrik and Dimple shook her head to say NO! As he went over to the Men's Room, he smiled in the mirror, clicked his heels and showed himself the Thumbs Up sign and decided to grin!

Someone watching him realized that this guy was happy and smiled as he locked eyes with Jaskaran—

Good Luck—Man!

As he returned, everyone was laughing at Anil's jokes—he had plenty of them and he could mimic the boys in the battalion very well too!

It was time to close the bar and the waiter rang a little bell to indicate that the Bar was closing—making sure that there was enough time for one or two die hards to grab another drink!

Shall we---asked Jaskaran standing behind Tanveer's chair waiting to pull it back.

These courtesies which came so naturally to these officers– simply appealed to Dimple and she was happy.

Anil was constantly at her side and she was flattered!

Would you like to have dinner?

No, it is late and I had promised Mom that we would be home for dinner—as Jaskaran pleaded with his eyes she said– I also have to discuss an important matter with her!

And so the evening came to an end– both girls felt a light tingling because of the events which had influenced their lives and Amrik was happy with his beer!

I say Amrik, are you OK with driving or do you need some help asked Jaskaran.

No problem– I will drive said Dimple and that closed the chapter!

Beware the Bloody Mary– Maam! Anil grinned wickedly– do phone when you reach home safe and sound---

Jaskaran— interested in a drink at my place?

Sir– you know me—I am not much of a boozer—besides you know Mom will hound poor Dad till he has me in his sights! How long do you have here before you leave for Almora?

I have to take the documents back to Bareilly and was told that this may take a couple of more days——I have decided to educate myself, so tomorrow I will pay a visit to the University and fill up my forms for completing my BA.

No no---don't get the wrong idea, I am not about to resign or something—just trying to get an education I would recommend you do the same! I thought– it would be great to complete my law course after I finish my BA.

But I am free in the evening and we can go for a movie if you like.

Jaskaran said he would call and ended things there—Mom might have something worked out—besides they had not discussed Tanweer—

Hey Jaskaran—I like Dimple– all right if I go full throttle with her--? Promise you– very honourable intentions up here and here---pointing to his head and heart!

Praise be to The Almighty—the mighty tree teeters at last!

Of Love, Life and Death

Raj was pleasantly surprised when he read Surinder's file– it was very decent of him to have given it to him with the assurance that Darji had also given his full backing. Normally, in Indian marriages lavish decorations and contentious display of wealth signified one's status in society. Here was a groom's father requesting that the nuptials be planned as simply as possible. He was very touched and spoke to Maninder before putting his annotations on Surinder's file, for discussions with Surinder; before he finalised the arrangements. The entire idea made sense because no one except the closest of relatives and the best of friends were actually interested in the marriage ceremony– they would be more interested in the drinking session, meeting old friends and partaking of the delicious cuisine.

Surinder's opening remark– *Our samdhis, or our in laws, are our strongest arm in the hour of need!*--took Raj by surprise and bowled him over and converted his mind thinking in consonance with Surinder's thoughts.

He would take some assistance from Tanweer and her friends because they knew the current thoughts of the younger generation. Tanweer would be a trifle disappointed with not having some of the current rages like the Qawalli nite and so and so forth—but Surinder had wisely deleted such ceremonies. He agreed that they should stick to the essential rites laid down by Shiromani Gurudwara Prabhandak Committee, the rest was infructuous.

Having made his first draft, he took out a hard copy and drove over to Surinderji's house. Surinder was waiting for Rajeshwar and met him warmly. They went over to the little office Surinder had created for himself and began to go over the details point by point till both of them were satisfied that every detail was covered. From Rajeshwar and Surinder's lists they consolidated three lists—His, Hers and Ours. These covered guests from Jaskaran's family, Tanweer's family and common friends of both families. Hard core guests were marked with an asterix to ensure that these were to be invited for the marriage ceremony.

Chalo– lets have a beer. Said Surinder

Why did Maninder not come with you? We could have chatted and made some shopping plans while you were working.

Raj shrugged his shoulders—I did ask her but she plans to visit you when she can spend some prime time with you.

After a chilled glass of beer, Rajeshwar bade goodbye to Preeti and Surinder.

The decision was that they should solemnise the wedding soon so that Jaskaran and Tanweer could complete at least two years of married life together before the paltan moved to field area. If Jaskaran was lucky, he would be posted on staff and this would help him to start a family.

While these thoughts echoed in Preeti's mind and reminded her of her own rendezvous with her husband's paltan, Jaskaran had fixed up a movie with Tanvi, after which they would have dinner with Dimple. Jazz and Sonny were also coming and so was Major Kapoor. The evening looked promising. Dimple's family were happy that Anil came over to meet them and approved of his cultured manners. Dimple shone in his company and they liked the match—the only problem was that Dimple had not indicated interest in marriage yet, she diligently pursued her course in jewellery designing. One day, Dimple's mother took Tanvi aside and asked her to find out what the game plan was.

So Tanwi gave her a big hug,

Auntieji just invite Major Kapoor's parents over, then see what happens!—both Anil and Dimple were feeling shy of talking to their parents.

Sonny invited them over to visit his farm house in Chatarpur and they all agreed to meet there next day.

Please come early– we have a miniature golf course and a swimming pool. Feel free to swim or play golf—we have a damn good cook and the bar is well stocked! There will be music too-said Jazz.

So Jaskaran Tanweer, Dimple and Anil went to the farm house in Dimple's car.

Hey guys why don't we get married in a staggered manner so that we can attend each other's weddings? Said Anil.

Since I am senior, i will make the sacrifice first!

What sacrifice is that? asked Dimple

My bachelorhood– end of days!

Everyone laughed—you call that a sacrifice?

The idea is good– how many days gap do we need? Asked Jaskaran.

Anil was thoughtful. CO is not going to let two of his best officers languish in Delhi for a month each—right? So I will request him for two weeks permission to get married and three days to attend yours; the battalion's rep, and you can do the reverse—ask for three days permission to attend my marriage as the battalion rep and two weeks permission to get married. Of course you will plan to get married; as soon as Dimple and I get married so that we can attend and then you hang around in Delhi while we go to Almora to make preparations for your reception! Right!

The evening was really great—the pool was excellent and all the men folk swam till their eyes turned blurry! The snacks were excellent and Sonny had managed to obtain quails which were roasted and served to all those who were not vegetarians. The girls enjoyed the scene and talked about their college days, laughing to their heart's content. Sonny was a likeable guy and a genial host who quickly broke down all communication barriers between Anil and himself.

I say Sonny– aren't your people strict veggies? asked Anil?

Look Anil- hey, that was when we banias(a caste signifying the merchant families) did not know what we were missing. Now we are marrying three friends and that makes us some sort of soul mates. So relax and enjoy yourself because such moments are rare in one's lifetime. Come on i am going to show you a live show that I saw in Denmark and let me tell you it was fabulous.

If Jazz hears about it then she will kill me.

They moved to Sonny's office where he had arranged to show them the movie he had filmed in Denmark. It was beautifully made and the show was exotic—almost making the entire show seem pure—the women were exquisite, the males looked like Greek gods, well endowed and-- well the show was entirely about unique ways of making love. All of them agreed that the factors of lust and vulgarity were conspicuously absent. The director had done an excellent job with the story line too.

As they walked back to the bar—Jazz came up and asked Sonny for the keys to his office.

What is the matter? Asked Sonny.

Nothing serious darling– just wanted to show the girls what we saw in Denmark! Any probs with that?

While Sonny sputtered, Jas went in to pour a beer as if he had heard nothing, while Anil could not hold back his laughter as Sonny sheepishly handed over the keys.

It was a lovely evening—everyone had realised that their relationship was unique and they must nurture this special relationship. Anil bonded easily with Sonny and Jazz, a fact Jazz had conveyed to Dimple too.

They headed home and dropped Tanvi first– Jas followed her with his eyes and at the door kissed her quickly before her Mom came out, then they dropped Jas off and Anil proceeded to Dimple's house where he had left his own car. They were reluctant to part, so Dimple suggested that they sit on the steps leading to the fountain. Time flew as they held hands and kissed tenderly as all love birds are wont to do.

Anil and Jas had confirmed berths in the train to Kathgodam and they were leaving in the evening.Tanvi and Dimple had to really use their wits and ensure that the parents did not decide to see off their prospective sons in laws, but left this to their daughters and Amrik was declared the Knight Defender-who would escort the girls to the station, and bring them back.

Anil Sir—looks like we will have to pool in and gift Amrik a suit for looking after our investments.

Amrik felt happy that he had accumulated such excellent brothers in law for he had decided to treat Anil also as a brother in law—Dimple had been a sister for him. In fact they had all played with him and looked after him since he was a toddler. Why not– it would be a privilege to look after Anil and Jas as well as Tanvi Didi and Dimple Didi. (Didi was the word used for elder sister.)

As they headed for home, Tanvi began to sob—she was missing Jas already.

Come on Tanvi—take it easy, at this rate you are going to have me in tears too! said Dimple.

She dropped Tanvi and Amrik and drove off to her house which was not far off.

As they entered the house there was an eerie silence which greeted them. Nonplussed they went to Maninder's room and found Raj and her sitting quietly as if deep thought.

What is the matter Mom? asked Tanvi.

Maninder hugged her and told her that Darji, Jas's grandfather had suffered a massive stroke and the doctors had given him very little time. Surinderji had been informed and he would reach late in the night by taxi.

Surinder reached home very late– there had been an accident on the road and many people were injured. Like a good Samaritan, Surinder had taken charge of the situation after the local SDM had requested him to help out. Between the two of them and the local DSP of the Police they had managed to send the wounded to the hospital, identify those killed and protect their belongings in the local jailhouse. The SDM, a youngster from Delhi had been grateful and thanked Surinder for teaching him the tricks of the trade. The entire process was completed in an exemplary manner including the documentation supported by photographs.

He promised to pay Surinder a visit in Delhi soon.

Thank you Sir for your guidance! said Rajesh as he shook hands.

Surinder spoke to the doctor and learnt that things were not looking good. In the morning Darji opened his eyes and beckoned Surinder.

Betaji—come over with my Munshiji and let me brief you about the business because then you will not be able to sort it out.It is worth a lot of money and took me a number of years to set up– so do not let it go waste.

Darji—tusi aram karo-. you must rest!

It was all Surinder could mumble as he looked at the frail frame of his father—a friend of so many years. Munshiji came over and showed the accounts and transactions to Surinder as Darji oversaw the entire proceedings. It reminded Surinder of the many occasions during which he had handed or taken over.

When it was over, Darji took Surinder's hands in his own and said—*Betaji*, I know you will become a General in your own right. My humble request to you is that you should consider leaving the Army and taking over the family business, for there is too much at stake and our family honour is also involved. I am sure that you will be able to double the assets in a short span of time. A large number of families are surviving because we have employed them.

Surinder took his leave and walked out after the old man slept.

Betaji—Your father is right. You cannot abandon a profit making business, especially where you do not offer any bribes or indulge in unfair practices. said Munshiji.

Surinder was close to Munshiji and overcome by emotion and tired from his journey as well as the accident, he wept on his shoulders.

Preti and he held hands on the metal bench in the lawn and having made up his mind—Surinder decided to visit his friend Brigadier Ramesh Gandhi who was the Deputy Military Secretary. As Surinder poured out his story, Ramesh asked his Staff Officer to bring his file to him. Ramesh looked at the file and said:

Surinder you have been earmarked for a posting to France—as the MA. You lucky bum.

Hey Ramesh—I would have been delighted, but considering the prevailing circumstances, I am here to tender my resignation.

Are you sure?

There is not an iota of doubt in my mind—I must quit and take over my family business before something happens to Darji—it is his final wish. He even told me I would become a general, but he wants me to let go.

Ok, let me see if the MS is in his office—I will fix an appointment for you.

The MS or Military Secretary was Lieutenant General PPS Dhillon, who knew Surinder well. He appreciated Surinder's requirement and promised his full support, but told him categorically that the Chief would not accept the resignation considering Surinder's track record and he would not be happy to overlook the endorsement in Surinder's dossier about his being tipped as the MA to France.

And then MOD Babudom, had to be convinced too.

Anyway General Dhillon promised to take things one at a time– Que sera sera!

As advised, Surinder bunged in his resignation in the prescribed manner through proper channel and left an advance copy with Brigadir Ramesh and said his silent prayer. In the evening, Darji was a little relaxed and gathered his family around him. He met them all and gave his gold pocket watch to Jas, while he gave the keys of his safe to Surinder. The house keys went to Preeti and he told them all that Beeji was now their responsibility. He even joked a little and asked Surinder and Jas to share a drink with him. He called Tanvi across, kissed her forehead and signalled to Beeji who came to Tanvi and draped her neck with a *Nau lakha* gold necklace. A very exquisite and rare necklace worth a lot of money..

The doctor shooed them out and Nurse requested Darji to rest a little.

The next morning, Darji woke up with a smile and expressed his thanks to the Almighty that Surinder had listened to his request and tendered his resignation.

Then he folded his hands, requested permission from Beeji and his children and slumped silently- --his journey to the next world had begun.

Surinder spoke to his Uncles and decided to organise a befitting farewell for Darji. As usual he laid stress on the requirement of the bare necessities and at the end of the prayers, he would request all those present to partake of the ritual of langar or a community meal. At the culmination of the ceremony and in the midst of his closest family members, he donned the white turban signifying his succession as the head of the family.

He was now responsible for his family's welfare!

THE COMMANDER'S ANNUAL INSPECTION

Brigadier Sukdev Singh was the Brigade Commander, and was otherwise addressed as the Commander. He was from the Sikh Regiment and as usual his yardstick for efficiency was the one with which he was familiar in his own regiment and with his own troops. In Sikh regiments, there was no need for detailed orders– the officers and the JCOs knew what they were expected to do if their officers gave them a broad outline.

Not so with the Gurkhas, because they had to be told exactly in clear terms as to what was expected of them. The thumb rule was that if something was not done as expected then it was the fault of the officer who was supposed to brief them. A system evolved whereby all those being briefed were asked to repeat their orders till they had got them down correctly. Thus officers from Gorkha Rifles were prone to repetitions and this amused others when they were posted to staff and to top this up they would depute others to ensure a double check to ensure that the required work was completed efficiently.

At times they even tried this on their families till their wives and children rebelled on the plea that—you are briefing us as if we are your johnnies!

Another peculiarity was that they reported every problem to their superiors whereas others carried out corrective measures on their own unless the problem was too big to hide! So when the Commander issued his dates for his annual inspection—the officers of 6/3 GR were busy making a foolproof plan for their inspection whereas the officers of the other regiments issued broad outlines and relaxed.

Colonel AB Deshpande got his officers and JCOs for a pre inspection conference to ensure that everyone was on the same grid for the count down to the inspection.

He addressed his officers and JCOs.

All of you are aware that the Brigade Commander is carrying out his Annual Inspection. All of you know what needs to be done, yet many of the younger riflemen have not been through an inspection, so it is imperative that all ranks of the paltan are aware of the conduct and made wary of the pitfalls so that we do not have to cut a sorry figure on some trivial issue. We have no skeletons to hide nor any ghosts we want to lock up, so please work hard and ensure that this inspection gets over with a big pat-on– the back for us as always!

Orders were issued for each part of the inspection—documentation of the Adjutant, Quarter Master, 2IC and the MT would be meticulously completed and in case of doubt the Staff at Brigade Headquarters could be consulted. All the Company commanders would practice drill, range practice or BPET so that they could toughen the boys for the inspection–everyone was to plan and come in GOOD timing and no one should be found in the enclosure for SATISFACTORY time. Training charts were to be complete and Company officers should be able to account for each soldier's role in the training cycle for the year and his leave plan be indicated as expected. Mobilisation stores were to be repaired and bundled up separately by platoons including the specialist platoons. Planning for mobilisation based on transport was to be finalised and all ranks were to be prepared. All Company Commanders should be able to brief the visiting officer about his planning for each of his men according to the chart and reasons as to why leave had been planned in the manner shown on the chart.

The briefing lasted for the complete day and it was worth it because gears had begun turning and everyone had mentally begun to think of the inadequacies in his command.

In the evening, as Colonel Deshpande was walking with the Subedar Major, he asked him—Sahib, i was thinking of issuing instructions that all ranks except the officers should speak in Nepali. What do you think?

The Subedar Major could not hold back his laughter and he felt it was a good idea.

Next morning as antiscipated, the Brigade Commander rang up the CO and said– *Kala Murga*—which was the code word for mobilisation.

The CO rang up the Adjutant and the Subedar Major and gave them the code word and the time for mobilisation. The Adjutant alerted the Company Commanders and the Quarter Master so that all those concerned could execute the plan.

Working parties from the allocated companies reached the ammunition dump, the *kote or armoury,* ration barracks and without a sound the transport moved into place with flags indicating their allotment. After each vehicle was loaded, it moved to its designated place in the convoy ground, which was swiftly filling up. As soon as the last vehicle trooped in the reports were handed over to the JA, who promptly handed them over to the Adjutant after a check.

The Adjutant reported to the 2IC who saluted the CO and the Adjutant marched up to the CO and gave him the report. In a typical manner the Adjutant took a step forward to hand over his report and then a step backward to return to his designated place.

The Commanding Officer was alerted by the Regimental police by a whistle and he braced the battalion shouting the word of command for attention. Unlike standard battalions rifle battalions had dispensed with the formal and time consuming words of command. All that Col Deshpande shouted was:

SIX- -----THUD! And lo and behold the battalion came to attention.

He marched up to the Commander, saluted and in a crisp tone gave him the report.

He then sought permission to carry on with the drill of mobilisation.

Once again the first vehicle crossed the Start point on time and Six Third Gorkha Rifles moved like a well oiled machine.

As the battalion reached their destination, the transport under the company commanders moved to pre designated locations under respective guides.

Swiftly dismounting, the men offloaded their transport which was marshalled and marched off to the rear leaving the F echelon vehicles which was to remain with them.

The Commander was impressed and went over to the Pioneer Platoon and spoke to the senior JCO:

Subedar Sahib aap ka kya kaam hai, jab aap lambay samay ke liye halt karenge?

What is your task if you were to stay for a longer period?

Without batting an eyelid Subedar Mohan Singh Gurung– a giant of a man, spoke in Nepali:

Sahib, yesto halat ma defence jasto bandobast hola. Tesko matlab cha ki Adjutant Sahib ko hukum paune biti ki hamro pioneer platoon le Ops room, khanne ko taiyari garnu parne ho Hazur!

A prolonged stay would be akin to a defensive situation and my platoon should be ready to dig and set up the Battalion Operations Room.

The commander smiled.

Very Good, carry on!

As he proceeded to visit the battalion he was satisfied that the battalion was well trained and would do well in operations.

Late in the evening, he called off the exercise!

The next day the staff officers came over to check the documents and give their reports regarding the paper work generated in the battalion. A few minor issues came up, but there was no serious problem.

The Commander and his staff went happy from the battalion.

As he was about to get into the jonga, Brigadier Sukhdev Singh said-

I say Deshpande hats off to you guys for learning the language and teaching the boys the skills they have mastered!

Colonel Deshpande could not resist a grin as the commander's entourage drove off. He congratulated the 2IC and the Subedar Major on a job well done.

Shall we beer up boys?

There was a big grin all around—as Jaskaran and the youngsters took the cue, kicked their bikes into action and roared to the mess to ensure that the arrangements were OK.

It was a well deserved rest and the youngsters who had been under intense pressure rocked!

By the time the CO entered the Mess, all the families were sipping their drinks and the children were playing in the lawns. Music was playing and the waiter turned up to offer a silver goblet of beer to the CO.

A POSTING WITH THE RR

Jaskaran received his posting to a RR battalion. The term RR stood for Rashtriya Rifles and these battalions comprised men and officers from all the rest of the Army– so you had amongst the officers– infantry, artillery or even officers from the Armoured Corps. This was akin to a posting in the Assam Rifles, but the composition of the troops in RR battalions was fantastic and the officers were interacting with troops from the entire gamut of arms and services. The motivation was so good that the men bonded with their task beautifully and gave excellent results.

The Commanding Officer was Colonel A Sreenivasan, and he was originally from the Punjab Regiment. Having been initiated into life in the Army with the Punjabis, Sree wore a thick *kara*—steel bracelet as his Sikh troops wore and he sported a gigantic moustache which had encompassed his whiskers and a portion of his beard into it as well. He spoke excellent Punjabi and could out-abuse anyone if required.

Everyone joked with him that he should apply for the *Upkeep of Moustache* allowance. Sree smiled his shy smile and laughed. He liked the very dedicated, well brought up Jaskaran from 6/3 GR. When his wife, Lakshmi came to visit, she liked him too; and in private; he would touch her feet because she had adopted him as her son; in place of the one, she lost in Chennai in a motorcycle accident. Sree had a lot of faith in Jaskaran and knew that his reports would be authentic, accurate and would contain sensible recommendations too. The other officers suspected the special relationship Jaskaran enjoyed with the CO and his wife but no one bothered, because this was a personal thing and neither Sree nor Jaskaran would take any advantage from it.

Jaskaran now had a two year old son and called him Inderjit. Tanveer was coming to join him soon and Lakshmi quickly brought her and little Inderjit into her extended family.They made an interesting group. Sree was not tall but at five foot eight inches he was all right. Lakshmi on the other hand was just five feet three inches as against Preeti's five foot seven inch frame. But they were a happy lot and Preeti gave Lakshmi a mother's status which was reciprocated by Lakshmi as well—by treating Tanvi as her daughter.

On her anniversary, Lakshmi presented her a beautiful kancheepuram saree.

Whenever Jaskaran went on patrol, Tanveer and inderjit slept in the guest room of the Commanding officer. Young inderjit, like all toddlers his age understood the love only grandparents could offer, and soon he began calling Colonel Sree—Thatha and Laksmi– Paatti. Many a time–especially on a Sunday, Tanveer and the other ladies would be surprised to see him sleeping on Sree's tummy with hands clasped around him. When Colonel Sreenivasan went for a walk– Inderjit would race for him, catch his little finger and walk away with him. On the return trip, he would be fast asleep on Thatha's shoulder.

One day Jaskaran came in very excited and told Preeti that Colonel Anil Kapoor and Dimple were coming to stay with them for a night. Anil had taken over 2/3 GR which was across the Poonch River. Tanveer could not control her tears—she had not met Dimple since their marriage and this was really a great occasion. They had a three year old girl Sasha.

Colonel Sree and Anil had done their Staff College course together and Laksmi knew Dimple too. There was a surreal excitement in the air when the Kapoors arrived. After a bath, Tanveer and Jaskaran walked to the Guest Room and both the girls cried because out of a variety of reasons—joy at the unexpected reunion, the requirement to catch up on news of each other and of course meeting the children.

Since Sree and Laksmi had requested them to come to the Mess for dinner, everyone got ready and went. The Mess was situated facing East, and was virtually an orchard with every Commanding officer adding to the variety of fruit available. Sree had planted excellent variety of plums from saplings procured from Srinagar and these were growing well.He now planned to plant pears and apricots. The upper foliage came from the wanut trees which gave a lot of fruit—nowhere could one imagine eating fresh fleshy walnut, white in colour.

Colonel and Mrs Sreenivasan were perfect hosts and all the present officers chipped in to make the evening a pleasant one. The actual fun was privy only to the children who were undisturbed and totally pampered.

After dinner the Kapoors went over to the Guest Room, and soon Tanveer and Jaskaran joined them. The girls lay in each other's arms and held hands, while Anil and Jaskaran chatted about several subjects of common interest. The children had gone to sleep and the talking continued interspersed with bouts of coffee.

Anil and Dimple had spent a week end with Sonny and Jazz. They had one son– Sandy, who was almost four years old. It was great and Sonny had taken them for a helicopter ride which was fun. That night they had not slept either.

Next day Anil had to go, so Dimple and he bid a tearful goodbye to Jaskaran and Tanveer.

Incidently, Jas—I have to go to Delhi and buy a flat from the AWHO because my younger brother had been busy, and has taken over the ownership of the ancestral house in Green Park. Since my father had passed away, Mummy had become involved with a prayer group and moved into their Ashram in Mount Abu. Young Master and his wife decided to go for the *coup de grace!*

This was another pitfall of serving in the Army, one's siblings got busy gnawing at your roots like rodents and parents could act as guardians till their age, mental and physical health allowed. Greed was a dirty word and such situations were very detrimental to families with joint properties. Imagine each brother locking up a room in the family house!

After Colonel Anil Kapoor and Dimple left, Jas held Tanvi's hand and tried to take her mind away from the memories cluttering her mind and the facts leading to Anil's ouster from his family property. Maybe this is good for them—Anil, s brother was always envious of his popularity and Anil would have never been happy in the family house anyway.

There was a conference in the sand model room at 1500 hrs where the 2IC would brief the patrols–CO would be attending the briefing.

As a precaution, sentries were placed outside the Briefing Room.

The 2IC, Lt Col Kripal Singh, reported to the CO who nodded. Colonel Kripal Singh briefed the first patrol under Major Jang Bahadur Singh and sent it off to make the necessary arrangements and preparations.

There was to be no discussion with any one else.

Jaskaran and his Senior JCO Subedar Parduman Singh were summoned later and in a hushed tone the 2IC briefed them about their operation. A message had been received from higher headquarters that a group of militants– almost a dozen of them had crossed over and were hiding in a cave in Sector 3.Headquarters were of the opinion that this was the advance party– the main group would enter under cover of Pak artillery fire later, and it appeared that this force was planning an attack on the canal headworks to inundate the entire area Northern region and make it unfit for armour to manoeuvre towards Bhimbarwala. This would be a critical disadvantage for our forces if the enemy planned to take this important border town. The Advance party would uncover their ammunition and food caches– who knows they may even have some RPG or shoulder missile launchers with them.

Jaskaran– you can take a platoon with suitable weapons with you. Make sure none of these blighters escapes. The mission is very important.

The CO spoke softly.– Jaskaran, I will be accompanying you, but you will be the Commander of the ambush party. I have a different role altogether.

Jaskaran nodded—he knew the cave and knew that it was not an easy task, because the top of the cave was a ledge from where a clear view of the surrounding area was available. A couple of snipers with night vision devices could keep anyone from coming within two hundred meters of the cave—and the route of escape was very well defiladed. A couple of his boys would have to sneak up from a narrow route to dislodge the sentry or sentries quietly, and cut off the routes of escape to the stream; while his RPG teams got a good view of the cave for a direct hit. The rest of his patrol would be distributed so that escape was impossible and the ingress route through the stream could be covered, just in case one or two of the militants were lucky enough to reach there.

Jaskaran got his group together and briefed them thoroughly. He made them repeat timings, routes and procedures till they had memorised every detail. Photographs, documents and any items likely to make any sound were left behind while all the items to be carried were secured, blackened and tied to ensure that there was no sound. Ammunition was collected and cleaned to ensure that there would be no misfires. Amrit Bahadur and Damar Bahadur who had been instructors at the High Altitude Warfare School were earmarked to block the escape route and quietly dispose off the sentries on the top of the cave. There was no need to worry—if surprise was lost the sentries were to be shot.

Colonel Sree and the Intelligence JCO were ready.

Jaskaran gave the signal to move and the party vanished into the night without a sound. There was thick foliage and hence one had to avoid making any sound.

It was a tough march and soon all of them were glistening with a fine layer of sweat despite the cold air. At the earmarked base Jas ordered them to shed all their unwanted stuff so that they could give chase if required. The Pak border was just fifteen hundred meters away and they had to kill the militants within this area—they did not have permission to cross the LOC.

Almost a few hundred yards from the cave, the pointsman stopped and gestured.

There on top of the cave, Jas made out the silhouette of a sentry–stretching his arms and walking about. As they watched, the sentry abused the insects biting him and lay down. Jas signalled to Amrit and Damar Badur and they broke off without a word. As they watched they both emerged a little later and one of them slashed the head off the sentry whose headless body twitched for a couple of minutes. A small pencil light beam signalled all clear and Jas ordered the RPG teams to move to their locations. Simultaneously, he signalled for the cut off group to move. A few minutes later both teams had indicated their progress by pressing their pressel switches. Jas, Colonel Sree and their group waited till there was no movement from the cave. There was no way out of the cave, except the entrance.

Then Jas ordered the RPGs to fire into the cave.

There was a roar and then absolute silence.

A little later a militant staggered out but was shot dead. These were hard core guys for whom life did not have meaning—they simply looked at death as a means of obtaining the reward of the celestial virgins, waiting for them in *jannat* or paradise.

Heaven must have an endless supply of them!

On Jas's command a search party went into the cave—bodies were littered in smithereens and blood was spattered all over the walls. Near the cave entrance one militant who was presumed to be killed suddenly sprang up to attack Jas, who sidestepped and gave him a reassuring kick in his groin. The militant fell on a bayonet and secured his own death warrant.

There was a shout from the stream—one militant who had gone to defecate was trying to make a break for the escape route. The cut off group shot him down when he refused to surrender and lay his weapon down. These were deadly men—worse than snakes and there was no point in taking prisoners.

Colonel Sree quickly went into the cave and with his torch light began to identify the dead militants from the list he had. As soon as he identified the man he was looking for, he began searching his clothes and pulled out some documents in a dirty cloth bag, enclosed in a plastic shopping bag with the name of the shop in *Urdu*. Inside was a map leading to the arms and ammunition as well as the food cache. The writing was in *Urdu* which the Int JCO was conversant with.

Sentries in position, Sree called for another platoon to assist in laying out the dead militants and segregating the ammunition, arms and the foodstuff found in the cache several meters away in a hole dug near the roots of a dead pine tree. They found radio sets, Kalashnikov rifles, grenades with Pakistan Ordnance Factory markings and several pistols, dynamite, ammunition of assorted type, foodstuff to last for a fortnight, machine guns and ammunition and some special equipment as well as woollen clothing.

Not a bad haul, considering all twelve militant dead were accounted for.

Sree shook Jas's hand hard and told him he was proud of him. Then, he shook off his emotions and told Jas to get the men together—the sentries were to remain vigilant. The men were to blast the cave so that it could never be used again.

Jas did as he was ordered and shook hands with his senior JCO. Both men looked at each other as soldiers will do and nodded to indicate a job well done. It was enough because no more was required to be said.

Sahib, Vapis jane ki taiyari kijiye aur larkon ko ikatha kariye--

Sahib, get the men organised for the return trip quickly!

The rest of the battalion was elated—the unit had done well and the ambush had been executed like a surgical operation without speaking a word. The dead bodies were hauled in and then began the photo session and the identification parade. Ten of the twelve dead were identified as hardcore militants with detailed records, while the other two were either new recruits or merely porters. Mugs of hot tea did the rounds while the *langar* sent across *puris* with vegetables.

The Sector Commander came over along with the Brigade Major and looked over the dead and examined the captured equipment. As he turned to Sree, he grinned.

Well done Sree—he said.

Dont look at me Sir! It was all Jaskaran's effort from start to finish! He did a great job—*nale ik lafaz vi kisi ne nahin bolya!* Not one word was spoken by anyone!

The Sector Commander shook hands with Jas and told Sree to write a strong commendation for him—

Your English is good- - i hope—a well written citation gets results!—he laughed.

Jaskaran, please congratulate the men for a job well done and break them off for some rest and a bath—you deserve one too son!

Jaskaran went home and his jubilant mood was so contagious that he got his little family involved too. Tanvi tried to wrest out the details from

Jas, but he was just too evasive. Eventually he told her what had happened in a broad outline. Tanvi went and brought his regimental cane—

Should I spank you for dereliction of duty? You still have not told me the complete details—she fumed.

Before you do that– our son needs to sleep or he is going to drop where he is tottering—

Don't change the subject-- putting Inderjit to sleep.

And risk the entire lot of ladies learning about every little detail—you know what the CO will do?

And you think I am itching to tell the world how much I know--? Tanvi mimicked Jaskaran.

No, but please admit you do like to shoot your mouth off don't you!

Tanvi ran after him with the cane, but Jas was too nimble for her and caught her from behind. And then the inevitable happened—Jas's hand got entangled in her *kameez* front, the buttons became undone providing him greater leverage and he realised that he had fruit in his hands. A kiss on the neck yielded results and the other hand with a life of its own found greener pastures to explore and suddenly the enemy gave up all resistance and turned around to smother his lips with her own. Since the little one was fast asleep on the bed, they found solace on the carpet and gave vent to the arousal within them. It wasn't a wrestling match, but a beautifully orchestrated effort which left them both satisfied.

Jas kissed Tanvi and asked– encore?

Tanvi nodded and the second stage began slowly with small kisses, and gradually graduating to the French kissing stage and then gaining momentum till it all reached a crescendo, and then burst like a balloon!

That signalled a cease fire for the evening.

They slept there entwined in each other's arms till it was time for their morning tea.

If there was a heaven on earth then they had almost reached there—but then all lovers do--!

What is a French kiss asked Tanvi innocently?– with a mischievous smile.

What do you think you have been indulging in though out the night, you silly girl. said Jas.

Then why call it a French kiss?

Maybe they were the first ones to get it patented! retorted Jas.

Thank God they stopped at the kiss—they could have patented love making and we would have paid tax every time we made love! Imagine how much money they would have made merely by taxing our countrymen alone!

A Fatal Foray

It was training and then followed by training—because this was the only way to save lives. The stress was on field signals by day and other assorted methods by night. Anyone caught making a sound or violating training norms was hauled up and had to provide all those present with sweets or some other delicacy. It was in the midst of this training that a summon came for Jas to report to the sand model room.

A patrol was to be organised, because Noora, the local informer had told the 2IC that a dreaded Afghani militant Fazlul, had entered the area, with a Pakistani Major who was known as Major Babur. There was tension in the region because Fazlul, with a height of six feet four inches had a strong appetite for women—the more the merrier, and the younger the better. Babur on the other hand, a mere five foot eight inches tall, man with beady eyes and a hooked nose like that of a carrion eating bird, was a religious fanatic who believed that he was an avenging angel sent by God.

Drawing the blood of his victims and the subsequent torture, were his forte.

The combination was a Jekyl and Hyde affair and when Fazlul lay waste to the women—Babur enjoined them to atone in prayer, because it was God's will that they suffer—why had they not joined the Mujahideen movement? And to close the issue Fazlul carried away the boys of the families. They shuddered because it was rumoured that he was bi sexual too. Noora was therefore a representative of the locals who were tired of losing their women and boys to this incorrigible pair of regular bastards.

Noora's message was therefore an appeal from the locals, who had been terrified of being subjected to the horrors perpetuated by this pair and were eager to get rid of them. The whereabouts of this *zalim* or cruel pair would be relayed to Noora who would lead the security forces to them.

Jas studied the terrain and went over the weapons and ammunition he would like to carry with him. He deliberately requested for additional men, because he felt that it was necessary to train them-you could shed some; if they were not required, but you could not train the new comers in a jiffy. He requested that Noora and he be allowed to know each other so that synchronisation in mind and body could be achieved. He also wanted to find out if Noora was exaggerating or he was actually telling the truth.

Sat Sri Akaal, Sahibji

Salaam Noora.

Aur kya khabar hai? Itne pareshaan kyon ho, mere bhai? Why are you so depressed?

*Sahibji, baat hi kuch aisi hai—woh dono phir agaye hain– is samay dono panch admion ke sath ghusne ki taiyari kar rahe hain.*That pair is coming back and are trying to infiltrate with five others.

Yeh Khabar kahan se ayi hai. Where has this news come from?

*Sahibji—mera rishtedar us paar hain aur kal raat in dono ne unke ghar mein bahut bat tamizi kari—hamari bahu betiyon ke sath bahut zulum kiye aur unko bahut mara bhi.*Sir these two were in my relative's place last night where they misbehaved and beat up the women too.

Noora began to weep silently and looked at Jas—*meri apni beti bhi to wahan byahi hai. Suna hai uske sath bhi badsalooki kari hai– main kaise bardash kar sakya hoon? Maine to use phool ki tarah bada kiya hai. Uski Maa to do din tak behosh rahi.*My daughter is also married there and I understand they misbehaved with her too—how can I as a Father, tolerate this?My wife is unconscious since the last two days!

*Baki gaon wale bhi dar rahe hain.*The other villagers are afraid too.

Kuch karo sahibji—and he caught Jas's feet.Please do something Sir!

Jas picked him up gave him some water and tea, and something to eat. Noora could not eat– he threw up.Jas got him to wash and then lie down.

Essentially Noora felt that the duo were hellbent on terrorising the countryside and Noora had got some disturbing news that his daughter married across the border had also been molested. He was visibly very upset.

After an hour Noora and he discussed the likely routes of ingress which Fazlul and Babur would take and where they would head once they had crossed over. They also tried to fathom the motives behind the infiltration– one reason was to cause *daishat* or terror and the second could be to target a military installation.

The only military installation was the engineer park or the ammunition dump which was a little isolated.

The plan was to proceed to a junction from where the devils could take any of the routes across. There was an isolated log cabin used by the cow herders to rest when they went out to graze their cattle. There was a ravine on one end where thick foliage cut out any line of sight and visibility was a few meters only, the other side was a gradual slope and one could pick off the militants by fire.

Jas planned to move with twenty hand picked men. He would take one group to the hut and ensure that no one escaped from that side.

The lower area was to be guarded by Subedar Shaitan Singh while the area above the hut was to be covered by Subedar Krishna Rao. The group left quietly and soon melted into the shadows. There was an eerie silence and not a single leaf fluttered– it was as though the weather gods had come to watch the fight.

Suddenly one of the leading scouts pressed his radio pressel switch thrice, which meant enemy close by.

He had seen a flicker of light in one of the windows of the hut.

Jas alerted his groups who began to slowly converge on the hut. Aware that sentries could have been posted, Jas had instructed his JCOs to be cautious. Soon they spied a lone sentry leaning against the wall of the hut. Subedar Shaitan Singh sent a pair of his men who crawled within feet of the unsuspecting sentry, slit his throat, and picked up his Kalashnikov. As Subedar Rao's group charged the hut, then shot two of the terrorists. Fazulul's bulky figure ran out and he swung into Jas who shot him point blank. Babur lay concealed in the bushes and as Jas crossed him, he let loose a burst of fire from his automatic into Jas. The burst caught Jas in his chest towards his right shoulder and threw him into the ravine. No one saw Jas fall, but Havildar Puran Singh killed Babur with one burst from his sten gun.

It was still dark when the groups gathered together.

Then came the realisation that something was amiss– Jas was nowhere to be seen. The thought that he could have been hit by fire never occurred to them because they always thought he was their lucky charm and therefore like Achilles– invincible. The fact now dawned on them that he was missing. If he was missing then where was he—no one thought of looking for him in the ravine. They kept shouting his name and looking for him on the slopes.

When the dead militants were laid out– they realised that two were not accounted for—could these two have abducted Jas across to POK? It was not easy to abduct Jas, he was a tough guy!

The matter was reported to the CO who sent the 2IC with a platoon to comb the area. This group also missed the ravine totally and no one ventured beyond a few meters. Another day passed without trace of Jas. In the late afternoon, a *bakerwal* or a *gujar* (nomadic muslim cattlemen or goat herders), who was trying to locate a lost calf; came across Jas hanging from a branch by the skin of his teeth—one little shake would have sent him hurtling to the ribbon of a river gushing thousands of feet below. Javed gingerly extricated Jas from the branch and laid him on the track. A whistle blown by him brought a few of his friends to come running to his aid and a litter was organised. They transported Jas to a clearing where a group of huts was located. Jas was still unconscious and when the Old *Gaon Bura,* Headman, looked at his condition and the state of his wounds, he could not hold back his emotions—

Take him to the last hut in the corner and arrange hot water, -he gasped. I will collect the herbs and come.

The torn clothes were cut away and burnt, the wounds were washed with medicated hot water and after a detailed inspection, it was pronounced that Jas had no bullets in his body, the wounds were not septic and except for this leg which probably broke in his free fall everything was all right. There seemed to be severe lacerations on his head indicating that his head had struck somewhere. His turban was missing, and a search party was sent to look above the spot where he was found.

Burn it there itself so that no one knows what religion he belongs to.

Munshi– circumcise him quickly– we do not want the terrorists to suspect anything—put on some local clothes and cut his beard like ours and arrange a *Gujar topee.* When he gets better teach him the *Namaaz and the Kalam* from the *Quran Sharif* so that he can pass off as one of us.

Our friend will be with us for a long to come. he said scratching his red beard. The red colour had come from using raw henna on his beard.

And listen—tell Naila Bi to take care of him

Naila was his brother's daughter who was widowed when her husband was shot by the terrorists for resisting their orders to join their group.

Naila was washing clothes when she was summoned to the village. She lived alone and was the ideal choice for the task because Jas could pass off as her ailing husband. The first thing she saw was Jas's hand on which he was wearing a *kara* or steel bracelet– a must for a Sikh. She removed it and hid it in her little trunk away from prying eyes.

As far as the village was concerned the matter was closed and Jas became Bashir Ahmed. Bashir opened his eyes after nine days and found no familiar faces. His attempt to stand up, were met with extreme pain in his leg; above the ankle where it had broken both the bones. He gave a yell of pain which brought Naila running to him. She was relieved to find him awake after his long slumber–

Wecome to the land of the living Bashir! she said and sat on her knees to give thanks for his recovery. Then she gave him some water to drink and ran to tell the Gaon Bura the news. He took her inside his hut and forbade her breaking the news to anyone and in future also she would only report to him.

As the Gaon Bura went to see Bashir, he found him looking very weak and ordered that a diet rich in butter and clarified butter be given to him so that recovery would be speeded up. His attempts at conversation were met with a stare– Bashir had amnesia. He had lost his memory due to the injuries on his head during his fall.

We will see what happens! said the old man. *Inshallah*—something good must happen soon.

Bashir began to walk a few steps and a little more each day as he picked up strength. Naila fed him bone soup with roti and some vegetables cooked in butter. She began to see the fire in his eyes which was so essential in a man– to recover completely without becoming a burden on anyone. Sometimes he simply put his head in her lap and slept like a baby. Slowly she took him outdoors and one day she took him to the waterfall where he had his first real bath. His raw red wounds has assumed a lighter colour and the wounds had closed considerably. As he sat on a large flat stone, she scrubbed his back clean and put his fresh clothes back on him.

As she turned to go, Bashir caught her hand, pulled her to him and kissed her—more out of gratitude—the manner in which, a patient would to his selfless nurse. Naila was taken by surprise and caressed her patient's face in affection. But this affection grew and one day- not against her will– Naila became Bashir's lover. It had to happen– she concluded, but she had expected to be the one to initiate the union. Secretly she was pleased, not only was Bashir a very good lover, but very caring as well. Naila also had not been with a man since the time the terrorists had killed her husband— she was lucky that they had not gang raped her that day.

She had become accustomed to sleeping on the ground next to Bashir's bed. Bashir invited her to join him on his bed and the two slept enjoined as one. She was not beautiful. but she was attractive in a handsome sort of way and her assets were her big boned body, wide hips, with breasts any western photographer would call– magnifique! She was built for bearing children and for hard work. Soon she initiated Bashir to the intricate method of milking the cows and how to be careful of some of the cows; who could land a nasty kick. *After all no lady liked her tits pulled or squeezed without her consent!* Bashir laughed at her very innovative pun!

Bashir married Naila with the consent of the village and Naila's parents. They felt relieved because they realised that Naila would not get married without a desire able mate—someone she could honour and respect. The *nikah* was supervised by the village *maulvi* who gave them his blessings.

The village got together to present a new hut to the newly weds and Naila stepped in to find that her father had contributed some utensils, a few plates of the enamelled type a few spoons and a beautiful bed with mirrors at one end. The Old *Gaon Bura* had presented them his beautiful bedcover and her brother in law-her dead husband's younger brother had gifted the two cows. He was very happy to see his sister in law married, because the grief of his brother's death would now dissipate.

Bashir was surprised to see the spirited Naila become a domesticated and meek housewife. This Naila he did not like and one day as they lay spent after a hectic bout of love making, he told her that he wanted his old Naila back. She could not stop laughing and told him in equivocal terms:

Bashir I hope you do not regret your decision of today!

After a year, Naila gave Bashir a little baby girl and made his happiness complete. Bashir had worked hard and had within a year collected sixteen calves and a dozen goats. Most of the calves were cows and would soon provide adequate milk for various uses! It would also bring in much needed cash from the sale of milk, butter and clarified butter called *ghee.*

Bashir was contended with his fortune and loved his lttle family. One day he had gone to the village fair or mela and Naila was holding Neelu by the hand. The din was nerve shattering and Naila was confused. A large truck speeded towards them and the poor thing became mesmerised– she froze in her tracks and the driver rammed into her.

Baseeer she screamed and as Bashir tried to push her, he was hit too, but he fell to one side with Neelu safe in his arms.

Amma! cried Neelu and ran to her but the life force had left from Naila's body.

The crowd had got hold of the driver—let me go—he pleaded. They dragged him to Bashir so that he could seek his revenge.

I have a daughter just like yours cried the wretch– I could not stop the bus because the brakes failed– Allah have mercy!

Bashir signalled to the villagers who arranged for a charpoy—and they carried Naila back to the village. Bashir buried her in finery and said a prayer for her. Suddenly he fainted, and had to be carried back to his hut. Neelu was being taken looked after by his sister in law.

During the night the flashes began and by morning, Bashir could remember that he was Jas and not Bashir. His father Tanvi and Inderjit flashed back and he longed to be with them. He dressed and went to the Gaon Bura's house where he prostrated himself before his feet.

Chacha! (Uncle) please tell me what happened? he cried.

So his story thus far was unfolded before him.A food of feelings for his friends and relatives from the village overtook him and he realised that he owed everyone a thanks for assisting in saving his life. They all had taken a grave risk to have provided him shelter—the terrorists would have killed them all if they had found them sheltering an officer from the Indian Army.

He presented all of them a calf each and left the pair of cows for the Gaon Bura.He gave the goats to the village for religious occasions.

With folded hands, he took leave of his foster family crying all the way till he caught the bus to Jammu. At the Railway Station, he brought some *alu puri* and fed Neelu. The Jammu Tawi departed in time and they reached New Delhi safely. They proceeded to the waiting room to wash and then he saw a full length mirror for the first time after so many years. As he looked into the mirror, he saw someone he did not recognise—he had grown grey and lean. Happy that this disguise would do till his mission was accomplished, Jas took his daughter's hand, deposited his luggage at the Baggage Counter and got his receipt.

Lament Your Loss My Lady

Colonel Sree was in a quandary, what would he tell Tanvi? His first thought was to call Laksmi and as she learnt of the tragedy– she began getting hysterical and began wailing– for Jas was her son too. How could fate take two of her sons away from her—it was just not fair! As she cooled down, Sree told her that they had to gently break the news to Tanvi and then to her father in law. Laksmi was a wise lady– she understood her duty as the Commanding Officer's wife and geared herself for it but she was not sure whether she could keep a straight face too long; for she was only a human.

As Sree and Laksmi neared Tanvi's cottage, she held her husband's arm for strength—for she really needed it. They made Tanvi sit and Laksmi held her shoulders as Sree narrated the encounter to her. Tanvi listened and then she froze—no tears in her eyes—just a hard look. It was a little frightening for both of them because crying was essential. Crying released the dangerous emotions inside an a person which had to be let out. Perplexed– they did not know what to do. Then Inderjit came into the room– saw the sad faces and rushed to *Paatti* and began to cry.

Tanvi picked him up hugged him tight and then this opened the flood gates. It was difficult to see Tanvi's grief. Sree looked away while Lakshmi held on to her. Later after a glass of water, Tanvi calmed down. She did not respond to any questions, nor did she nod her head. She just sat running her hand through Inderjit's hair.

Sree left them and proceeded to his office; from where a call took him to the CO of the Signal regiment. As soon as the circumstances were explained, he was patched to Brigadier Surinder Singh's residence. The Brigadier listened carefully and quietly explained the encounter to Preeti who wrung her hands and began to sob softly. He then called Tanvi's parents and told them to come over. Rajesh and his wife sat stunned when they learnt the news. Surinder told them that he would be leaving by train at night and a jeep would pick him up the next day at Jammu. He would bring Tanvi and inderjit back home.

The next day Surinder reached Jas's unit late in the evening. Sree was waiting for him in the office and together they left for Tanvi's cottage. Tanvi had packed and as she cried on Surinder's shoulder, he consoled her and carried little Inderjit. Next morning they left the unit for Jammu– Sree and Lakshmi found it difficult to part with inderjit.

Time is a great healer! Slowly normalcy returned to the house despite a shroud of despair.

Tanvi decided to reorganise her life and live only for Inderjit's sake. She took charge of the household and felt it was her duty to look after her family. She took Surinder to the DSOI and rang up his cronies too, so that he was never alone.

Preeti preferred to be at home and look after Inderjit. Preeti refused to be consoled. She retreated to her bedroom and refused to meet anyone. Her time was spent in prayer because she refused to believe that Jas was dead. Since his body had not been found, she lived on hope, ate very little and often put her head in Tanvi's lap and cried bitterly.

Republic Day was approaching and Surinder found that Army Headquarters had sent an invitation for Tanvi to accept receipt of the Asoka Chakra for valour during peace time which had been awarded to Jas. The State of Uttar Pradesh had given her a monetary award of ten lakh and gifted her ten acres of land in Landor village. Delhi State gifted her a petrol pump on the road leading towards the Agra Expressway.

As Tanvi, escorted by an officer from her husband's battalion, climbed the podium to receive Jas's award, she looked at the President who looked away because he could not look into the grief that her eyes contained.

During the tea, she discovered that she had been given someone else's parchment and her escort had a tough time locating the one for Jas. The Ministers were so busy filling their mouths with potato chips and *ladoos* that Tanvi could not bear to look at them.

Hello Mrs Sahni- said a kind voice and she found the Minister for Law standing next to her.

What are your plans– have you given a thought to what you would like to do?

No frankly– No.

Remember grief grows and gnaws you from inside—have you thought of becoming a lawyer? No No I don't mean a criminal layer but say a specialist in say Aviation or Corporate Law.If you do decide give me call. This is my card and I will have someone to guide you through the process of applying fot the next course.

Goodbye and best of luck.

Surinder and Tanvi went to see the village Sarpanch to claim their land. The Sarpanch and the Tehsildar looked at them as if they were mad.

Sardarji—yeh Sarkar majak karti hai. Aap ko jo jamin diya hai woh gyarah tukde mein bati hai aur sabhi tukde land maphiya ke kabje mein hain. Jaan pyari hai to jameen ka vichar chod do!

Sir, your ten acres of land is distributed in eleven parts, each has a land mafia member sitting on it. Better to leave if you value your lives.

Tanvi looked at her father in law—Papa, can you imagine me a farmer? Lets go quickly! Their visit to the District Commissioner's office led them to a thoroughly corrupt organisation bent on extorting money even from her!

Surinder felt miserable—is this the nation one fought for? Suffered privations for? Sacrificed prime time for and even died for?

This was a nation recreated from possibly; the remnant survivors from Sodom and Gomorrah. There was no reason why a tidal wave as big as the one from the Bible should not sweep these dirty corrupt and shitty people into the sea to perish. They sat praying before stone gods and goddesses doing exactly what their stone gods forbade them to do. It was the opportune time for the Lord of the Underworld to move his headquarters to the surface because very few honest people were left. If there was a God, then let him appear and throw some fear into the populace and make an example of some of these rascals; because Man only understood strength and fear. Why should God be merciful– why should he not crack a whip and get everyone in line? Only then would the weak and honest ride horses till they too succumbed to temptation and desire.

He drove back home seething with anger to the office of the Army Wives Welfare Association. The Secretary, a retired distinguished looking Colonel with silver hair, sat smugly behind a lovely table.

Hello Sir and Madam, I am Colonel Sher Bahudur Singh Panwar. Please, I am at your service.

He leaned forward as if he was listening attentively to whatever was being said.

I am sorry, this is a state matter, we cannot do anything for you.

What can you do Colonel? Besides twiddling tour thumb of course?

Sir, I expect some respect for my chair!

Yes, so start earning it! Your chair, Sir, is as wooden and heartless as you are– may we see Mrs Sant Ram, the President of the AWWA, or are you going to prevent us in that requirement too.

Sir, Mrs Sant Ram will be available in her office on the next Monday– I will fix your appointment for ten thirty.

Surinder was sure nothing would come from meeting her except some lip service—but he was going to shake her up a little if he had to. A visit to the Petrol Pump site was even more appalling. The road was completely in a ramshackle state and not many vehicles frequented it, except a couple of tractors belonging to the local farmers.

An old timer brought them some water.

So they have allotted you this pump? They have reserved this for our martyrs. You are the fifth allotee.

It helps them get headlines in the papers and that is the end of the story.

Go home Beta—this is no place for a lady– the insides are used as a toilet. Just go and don't look back.

So this was what the noble Government of Delhi had to offer. A visit led them to the man who allotted these pumps—he would not let them go to the Big Boss, unless adequate money was paid—only the would a pump be allotted in the city.

So Tanvi have you seen the rot in this country? And then to hear of them talking of becoming a global power!

Papa– I am going to study Criminal Law and train my guns on these rascals-said Tanvi tears streaming out of her eyes—tears of hurt—tears of determination and tears of disgust.

3

GOD RESIDES IN THE HEAVENS

Preeti was stunned to hear about her son-and like all mothers she refused to believe that her son was dead.

Her logic was that his body had not been found and there was no trail of blood. He was a six foot soldier and it was not easy to whisk him away across two kilometres or so even if three people were holding him and it was impossible to carry him easily.

The point she was making was that he was still in our territory, probably wounded and desperately in need of medical attention. Then why was no one taking her seriously. She wept and cried when she was not praying and begged Surinder to leave her at the Gurudwara twice a week with her maid.

The Granthi or priest came over to talk to her, provide solace and comfort, but she would not respond as if she did not care. The pain was hers to bear and soft words of advice were not welcome. But she was too polite to tell people to mind their own business and leave her alone with her demons.

At night she never slept, but stared at the blank ceiling or at a large photograph of Jaskaran which she had installed in her room. She looked forward to visits from Inderjit who understood her sorrow and ran to her room as soon as he came from school. He was a good child and would sit in her lap holding her hand and caressing it.

Tanvi had become a good lawyer. It kept her busy and she worked very hard..pushing herself so that she could retain her sanity. Her defences broke down when she visited her mother in law, for she could not bear to see her suffer. She would put her head in her mother in law's lap and Preeti would stroke her head gently and tell Preeti anecdotes from Jaskaran's younger days.

She refused to eat and only Tanvir could make her swallow some toast with milk. Her pretty face had become sallow and there were dark hollows beneath her eyes making her look gaunt and sick. Tanvi also believed what her mother in law felt deep inside—Jas was alive and kicking—they were not looking hard enough for him.

Her father in law was a pillar of strength and held his family and business together through sheer will power. His attitude was different– he felt that his family members had been loaned to him by destiny– and probably the Almighty—only in this birth and each had a defined role to play for a definite time. There was no need to cry over relationships over which one had no control.

The *Geeta Saar* was the key—man came alone, naked and crying– why keep crying for someone who did nor belong to you– maybe his son was in a better place—only the void of his presence remained. He looked after each member of his family individually and comforted them. Preeti and he had already accepted Tanvi as the daughter they did not have, and he often wondered if he should breach the topic of her remarriage—she was still young and he would give her away as if she was his own daughter.

He was afraid of her reaction to this and was scared of hurting her sentiments. Let me wait a little more, he consoled himself. He was proud of her success as a lawyer, because she was not greedy and went out of her way to research her cases so that she always won and since she knew the situation at home she took only a few cases so that she had time for Inderjit.

Their life became a routine—Muthu and his wife came over and so did some of the other officers who were in Delhi for a marriage or were just passing through. Surinder did not go for any functions except the Gorkha Brigade lunch. It was a meeting place for his friends. And he could meet them all together. Preeti had become a total recluse and now tied her hair in a pigtail. She had left everything to Tanvi and did not bother about the running of the house.

It was a strange combination of personalities.

It was Inderjit who changed drastically– he became a very mature child and gave the impression of having become a wise boy– beyond his years.

REUNION

The counter clerk called out to him—*Oye Mian*! You are a long way from home!

Yes—I am a long way from home, yet i am close by! retorted Jas.

They took an auto and as they reached Jas's home they found Inderjit going to school.

A little while later, Tanvi came out took her car and drove off.

His Father came out last– looking old, but walking ramrod straight as he always did. Resisting the urge to run to him as his father stumbled and then controlled himself, Jas sat outside the bus stop and watched.

In the evening, Dimple dropped in to meet Tanvi, and they were joined by Jazz later.

Lets all go to the club tonight and we will take the kids with us too. Tanvi did not want to go.

Stop brooding yaar! said Jazz

No you guys go– I want to be at home with Papa.

As you wish and Inderjit was bundled into the car and they left.

Papa, would you like a drink?

Ok, I will have a Vat 69 said Surinder.

Tanvi made him a drink and added a little water to soften the soda. Normally he used a stirrer at parties.

What are you having Tanvi, *Beta*?

Papa– I will settle for some red wine.

Would you like to go to the club? I can take you if you are keen– we can have dinner at the club itself. If you like i can ring up Muthu Uncle.

I think It is a good idea.

Muthu agreed and he said Meenu and he would be ready to leave for the club in fifteen minutes.

As they left the house, they noticed this man in gujar attire sitting with a little girl, but did not think about it.

Jas picked up Neelu playfully and carried her till they came to an auto which dropped them to Nizammudin Railway station. There he gave Neelu some hot tea and a large bun to eat. He settled for a tea and a samosa—a triangulated spicy delicacy. He was not really hungry, but his mind tried to recap the day's events and figure out his plan of action..

Tanvi was living alone.

She was taking care of his father

Her friends were looking after her.

Tanvi was not seeing anyone else.

He had not seen his mother. Was she alive– was she ill?

With this input to go on Jas decided to change his attire. He tied a turban, rolled his beard, and bought a trouser, shirt and shoes for himself. He went to the mirror and surveyed himself—not bad, he thought to himself. Not the original Jas, but he resembled a distant cousin. He also bought an ensemble for Neelu and the by ten in the morning, they reached home.

As Jas rang the bell, the maid answered and invited them inside to sit.

Surinder walked in to find an unfamiliar face and there was this little girl with a cherubic smile on her face.Jas folded his hands in a *Sat Sri Akal*, but words would not come– he stood trembling, till he prostrated himself in front of his father. All he blurted out was one word:

Papajee!

The bells rang in Surinder's head and he hugged Jas close to his chest lest, the mirage fade away. Could it be possible after so many years—was it possible that *Sache Patshah, the True God,* had answered his prayers and returned his son to him?

Surinder gradually pushed Jas away from his shoulder to look at him—it was Jas alright, but a Jas who had suffered a tremendous ordeal.

This is my daughter Neelu—actually Nilofer. Her mother was my wife Naila, when I had amnesia. I am here because of Naila who nursed me back to life and her fellow villagers who looked after me as their own.

Inderjit, who was standing in the doorway, quietly came to Neelu and took her hand. He led her to his room and gave her some toys– then he went and brought her a Pepsi and a sandwich.

Then he ran to his father who hugged him tightly.

As the news broke, Preeti came in supported by her maid. She held Jas and wept silently. Surinder was sure that she would recover soon– her days of grief were over. She had to be coaxed to drink some milk and have some toast—in fact she was just surviving on this. He wondered how Tanvi would react when she returned from the Court. She had become a very good lawyer, as if she understood the profession naturally– as though she was always destined to become a lawyer. Her time was precious and she had to let some cases go because she prepared well for the ones she took, because she wanted to win them.

Surinder rang up Dimple and broke the news to her gradually and requested her to break the news gently to Tanvi so that the shock would not be so great. As Dimple broke the news to her, Tanvi folded her hands and prayed silently to God Almighty for creating this miracle. Preeti waited for Tanvi to come.

Just then the sound of Tanvi's car came and Tanvi ran inside– saw Jas and ran into his arms and then fainted. She was carried to the bed by Jas who held her hand till she recovered. Surinder slowly learnt the complete story and opened his son's shirt. As he looked at the wounds which were still an angry red, but fully healed, he thanked the good Samaritans who had saved his son and given him back to the family.

The news spread like wild fire and Preeti insisted that they all go quickly to the Defence Colony Gurudwara as a family to thank the Almighty for sending Jas back to them

Muthu and all the regimental officers came over each carrying bouquets and wine or scotch bottles. Glasses were brought and they drank a toast to Tanvi and Jas. The bell rang and Brigadier Sree and Lakshmi walked in. Happiness was complete when CO and the Subedar Major of 6/3 GR, turned up with all the officers and their families driving in from Meerut.

With great amount of difficulty, the children were put to bed and makeshift beds arranged for the ladies. The rest wanted to hear Jas's story. They gasped when they saw and touched his wound and then wondered how he had survived the ordeal. His leg hurt a little and needed attention– probably the union had not taken place correctly.

The next day the CO informed the Adjutant General's Branch that Jas had returned and a team from the Intelligence Directorate came in to interrogate him, and to verify his story. Then Jas was shifted to the Military Hospital for a detailed check up. He was found fit as a horse, except for his leg where the crude splints had not correctly united his bones.

With Tanvi's permission, they operated and reset Jas's leg fracture. He was put in a plaster and then this was an ordeal of six weeks only. Jas began to look his normal self and a tailor in Gopi Nath Bazaar outfitted him for his uniforms. CDA was instructed to reinstate Jas with his pay and Jas received his arrears too. A new car came in and Brigadier Sree had bunged in another recommendation for his raid in which Fazlul and Babur had been killed. This had been accepted and Jas was due to receive another award on the next Republic Day.

Jas was posted back to his battalion and as he stepped into the battalion there was an eerie silence– then someone shouted—

Hamro Jaskaran Sahib Ho Ki hoina?

Ho ho! they shouted and he was carried on their shoulders– happily though he felt he would break another leg if they dropped him.

The CO and the officers watched this chaos and when Jas was gently put down, he saluted the CO and sat in his office. Panditji appeared from nowhere and applied him a tikka and blessed him.

Today on special request lunch is in the JCO's Mess.

At the JCO's Mess, there was a great amount of hand shaking till Jas thought his hand would fall off.

Sahib we have a surprise for you!

There was a beautiful cow waiting for him—The Subedar Major could not suppress a laugh

We thought you would miss your old friends– but kindly do not try and milk this one– it is a bull!

And everyone laughed!

Go on get me a beer, said Jas- and let us drink to the finest paltan in the whole world.--6/3 GR- *ho ki hoi na?*

Ho Ho Ho!

Everyone chorused.

Later in the evening, Jas lay besides Tanvi and caressed her hair.

Jas– Can we go to see your village? I want to present them a generator and a TV.

Is that the reason you want to go there?

No

Then what?

I want to pray at Naila's grave and meet the people who looked after you and eventually returned you to me.

Ok! That is a good reason– we will plan as soon as my plaster comes off!

I love you, bloody Gurkha Johnny!

Why? Because, deep inside you are one hell of a kancha!

Tell me Tanvi—when you got the news that I was missing--- did someone cry for me?

Yes, I did and all your friends and your family.

Anyone else?

I don't think any body in our country really understand your sacrifices, especially for soljers, because soljers die and fade away- only their widows, parents or children weep for them—no one else has time to cry for you!

And our country cares nothing for you or they would have raised hell for our prisoners of war languishing in Paki jails, or for the soldiers who were mutilated by the Pakis or that matter those who fell in many Kargils.

After all a politician can give ten times the compensation to the victim of a hooch tragedy, but fail to acknowledge the sacrifices of the country's soldiers!—it does not provide him political mileage!

Listen Jas, relax– as she held his head on her bosom.

Someday, they will all be shaken from their slumber to account for their misdeeds!

Lightning Source UK Ltd.
Milton Keynes UK
UKOW051123180612

194620UK00002B/70/P

9 781467 067393